"Has it ever ___ ___ ___ I might not ___ ___"

Oh, yeah, Jake thought. He just didn't want to believe it. Clare had haunted too many nights—too many days, for that matter. He couldn't go anywhere, do anything, without thinking of her.

Oh, he'd told himself he wanted to comfort her. How easily he'd convinced himself he could offer her that much without guilt, that Don would want him to.

But with time he had come to realize that his comfort was the trail of seeds used to lure a bird, to lull it and tempt it and tame it. Witness his shock now: He couldn't believe she wouldn't instantly fly to his hand.

ABOUT THE AUTHOR

Janice Kay Johnson is the bestselling author of over twenty books, and her deeply emotional and involving stories have enthralled readers around the world. It will come as no surprise to her many fans that Janice is an enthusiastic gardener with a definite preference for "old" roses, or that she's an experienced "basketball and soccer mom." Janice lives in Washington State with her two daughters, two dogs and (at last count) nine cats.

Books by Janice Kay Johnson

HARLEQUIN SUPERROMANCE
483—SEIZE THE DAY
561—HOME AGAIN
627—HER SISTER'S BABY
648—IN THE DARK OF THE NIGHT

Janice Kay Johnson

HIS FRIEND'S WIFE

Harlequin Books

TORONTO • NEW YORK • LONDON
AMSTERDAM • PARIS • SYDNEY • HAMBURG
STOCKHOLM • ATHENS • TOKYO • MILAN
MADRID • WARSAW • BUDAPEST • AUCKLAND

ISBN 0-373-70677-4

HIS FRIEND'S WIFE

Copyright © 1996 by Janice Kay Johnson.

This edition published by arrangement with Harlequin Books S.A.

® and TM are trademarks of the publisher. Trademarks indicated with ® are registered in the United States Patent and Trademark Office, the Canadian Trade Marks Office and in other countries.

Printed in U.S.A.

HIS FRIEND'S
WIFE

CHAPTER ONE

CLARE TALBOT had been a widow for more than a year. In her waking hours she seldom thought anymore about the fire that had taken her husband's life, although in dreams the horror replayed itself. But the night after Jacob Radovich walked back into her life, her nightmares became reality again.

She'd begun that morning by showing a house on the south end of the island, so she didn't arrive at the real-estate office until nearly eleven. The low, gray-shingled building was at the end of the picturesque main street, which sloped down toward the ferry landing and Puget Sound. Today the blue water glittered with dancing shards of light, and the sun was warm, promising another unusual Indian-summer day. Glancing in the rearview mirror of the car, Clare took a moment to brush her thick chestnut hair and carelessly braid it. At least this way it was off her neck. She'd grabbed her briefcase from the front seat and was hurrying across the wooden sidewalk when a woman's voice called from behind, "Clare!"

She turned to see Sharon Rogers, the high-school librarian, advancing on her with another woman.

"Clare, are you planning to come to the Parent Association potluck? I didn't see your name on the list."

Clare smiled. Sharon, petite with a frizz of dark curls, was the closest thing to a friend she'd made in this isolated community where she would be forever regarded as an outsider. "Yes, of course I'm coming. I hadn't decided what to bring."

"We're loaded with salads," Sharon said frankly. "Oh, Clare, do you know Alison Pierce? I'm sorry, I wasn't thinking..."

Clare had been very conscious of the tall woman with the sleek auburn hair and cool brown eyes who'd been standing a step back. "Yes, we've met," she said.

Alison inclined her head. "How could we fail? After all, we have something in common."

Obviously puzzled by the sardonic note in Alison's voice, Sharon glanced at Clare for help. "In common? I'm afraid—"

"My husband." Clare managed to sound nearly amused. "Alison and he went together in high school."

"Oh, dear," Sharon began, but Alison shook her head.

"Don't be silly. It's ancient history. Clare and I run into each other about once a week."

"True," Clare said, smiling for Sharon's benefit. And it *was* true, so why did she always feel so uncomfortable around Alison? The other woman had been pleasant enough, but there was something about her eyes. Something too cool, detached, as though she didn't feel anything. But she must, because she'd apparently been madly in love with Don at one time.

Clare was almost relieved to see her stepson approaching. Mike slid to a stop on his mountain bike, spurting gravel, which rattled against the wooden sidewalk. Ignoring the others, he looking at Clare accusingly. "I tried to call. Where've you been?"

"Showing a house," she said, giving the other women an apologetic glance. "What's the problem?"

"I'm going over to Geoff's. Grandma wasn't home, either. You said to let you know."

"I said to *ask* me."

They stared at each other, tension locking their eyes. Aware of their audience, Clare made her gaze soften. "Yes, you may go to Geoff's. But if you're going anywhere else, leave a message. And be home by five. Okay?"

The dark-haired boy's shrug indicated grudging acceptance. "Yeah, all right," he muttered. Without a goodbye, he shoved off, gaining speed as he pedaled up the narrow main street away from the harbor. Frowning, Clare watched him go.

It was a moment before she realized that she wasn't the only one staring after Mike. He'd disappeared around a corner before Alison Pierce wrenched her gaze back to Clare. She was so pale Clare took an involuntary step forward.

"Is he Don's..." Alison's voice trailed off.

Clare suddenly understood. "Yes. I'm sorry. You haven't met him? He doesn't look anything like Don, does he?"

Alison gave her head a shake. "Mike? Is that what you said his name is?"

"Yes."

An awkward silence fell. Sharon hurried to fill it. "We shouldn't keep you, Clare. Anyway, here comes the ferry. If we don't want to be caught in the traffic, we'd better get a move on. Shall I put you down for the potluck?"

"Sure. For anything. A casserole maybe? I can bring it over hot."

"Fine. I'll talk to you later."

Clare nodded. One last time, before the two women turned away, her eyes met Alison's. The detachment was back, and Clare had to repress a shiver. What a strange woman. Or maybe *she* was the one who was reacting strangely. Good Lord, did it bother her, after all this time, to think of Don with another woman? Was she subconsciously blaming Alison for her own unresolved feelings?

Well, Don was dead. It wasn't as though Clare had to worry about competition. The past was the past.

Still, once inside the real-estate office, Clare didn't go to work right away. She sat looking out the window at the Sound, not really focusing on the vivid blue water or the stream of cars unloading from the huge green-and-white ferry that in the summer brought tourists from British Columbia or Seattle and year-round provided the only highway to the outside world for the islanders. Clare's mood had nothing to do with Alison Pierce, except that the other woman had made her think about her marriage.

But not for long. She wouldn't let herself. The anniversary of Don's death had come and gone, and her life had changed. Clare turned away from the window and clicked open her briefcase. She should be celebrating the sale she'd made this morning, rejoicing in the sunshine that had brought a last trickle of tourists to this small island in the San Juans in October. Not remembering fire and madness.

The ring of the telephone banished the past. With relief Clare picked it up. "Yes?"

"There's a gentleman here who's interested in property," the receptionist said. "Can you see him?"

"You bet. I'll be right out."

Her briefcase stashed in a drawer, Clare left her office. The man who stood in the waiting room had his back to her as he looked at pictures of available property posted on the wall. All Clare had was an impression of dark hair, faded jeans and a black shirt that covered broad shoulders before she said pleasantly, "Hi, I'm Clare Talbot. Do you see anything that interests you?"

For one curious instant, she thought he hadn't heard her. Then, in what seemed like slow motion, he turned. Or perhaps she had only slowed the moment down in her mind, to cushion her from the shock.

His straight dark hair still brushed his collar, his lean face with the prominent cheekbones hadn't changed at all. His mouth was still intolerably sexy, his gray eyes just as wary and watchful. He simply stood, hands shoved in the pockets of his jeans, and waited.

Clare fought the swirls of darkness, the nightmare and the guilt his presence made her remember. Almost as stunning was the sharp stab of joy and physical awareness. Only when the silence had become so intense it was painful did she say, in a voice just above a whisper, "Jake. I can't believe it's you."

He didn't smile. "Is it such a shock?"

She swallowed. "No. Oh, no! Of course I'm glad to see you! It's just..."

"You wonder what I'm doing here."

"Yes, I suppose I do."

He didn't answer for a moment, but at last he shrugged. "I'm moving back to the island." Even his voice was the same, low and rock steady, unflinching. She used to long for something to shake him.

"But..." Clare closed her eyes, opened them. "Did you know we'd moved here?"

He hesitated for no longer than a heartbeat, but she noticed. "Yes, I knew."

She felt raw suddenly, a year's healing ripped away to expose the fragility of what lay beneath. Didn't he understand what his presence did to her? Once he had been everything to her, her salvation, her sanity... her temptation. The last time she'd seen Jake Radovich, he'd held her as the fire destroyed the fragments of her life. Did he now expect her to be mildly pleased to see him, as if he was any old acquaintance?

When the silence had gone on too long, he said, "Why do I get the feeling there are people you would rather had dropped in?"

"It's not that. Of course it's not. I... think about you sometimes, Jake." It was a lie. She had tried so hard *not* to think about him. "But seeing you made me remember. Just for a minute, anyway."

Frown lines showed between his dark brows. "Damn it, Clare, I didn't have anything to do with Don's problems. Our friendship had nothing to do with Don."

A gray fog of despair closed in on her and she half turned away, her hands curling into fists as she laughed bitterly. "Oh, come on, Jake. It had everything to do with him. You know that."

"Do I?"

His tone surprised her and she turned back. His mouth had tightened into a grim line and he looked angry. His words were clipped. "Wouldn't you rather talk about this in your office?"

Clare didn't know how she'd react to being closeted with him in such a tiny room. But he was right of course. Hadn't he always been? She didn't want the receptionist to hear the story of her life. In such a small community, everybody knew the bare facts. What nobody had guessed was how deeply wounded she'd been—and still was. Even Mike, who was closest, who'd been there, didn't know. For him, she'd been strong.

But Jake Radovich had seen everything, heard everything. It horrified her to remember the secret feelings she'd confessed to him, the tears she'd shed on his shoulder. He'd known her most hidden anguish. Sometimes at night, she'd faced the fact that he knew her soul, and she wondered if he cared. Or had he been kind to her only for Don's sake? She'd never had the courage to ask.

"All right," she said abruptly, striding toward her office without looking to see if he was following. But she knew he was, with a prickling certainty she hadn't felt in a long time. She'd always been able to sense his presence. At the beach she would turn her head, and there he'd be on the deck of his house, watching her with that cool expressionless gaze that hid his emotions. Did he feel anything but pity for her? Had he ever guessed the one shameful secret she scarcely even let herself know?

Clare waited just inside her office until Jake walked past, closing the door after him. As he crossed to the window and stood looking out, she stayed beside the door, wanting to keep the width of the room between them. She'd never understood the effect he had on her. At maybe six feet, he wasn't unusually large, nor was he bulky with muscle. And yet he overwhelmed her, made her feel things she had no right to feel.

"Why, Jake?" she said to his back. "Why would you want to return to Dorset Island? Don said you hadn't even visited here in years."

He sighed and faced her. "Are you assuming that my reasons have to do with you?"

"Of course not! I wasn't accusing you of... of haunting me or anything like that. But seeing you like this, so suddenly, brings back memories I'd rather forget. Can't you understand that?"

His mouth twisted. "All too well."

"Then?"

"Maybe it's time you come to terms with those memories."

"I have!" She bit her lip, then lifted her chin defiantly. "Of course I have. I talk to Mike about his father. And I've gotten on with my own life. But that's easier to do without someone around who's seen you at your lowest."

"Lowest? What do you mean?"

"Sometimes I think I did nothing but cry."

The sudden compassion in his eyes undermined her defenses, but it was what he said that threw her completely. "You were never weak, Clare. Never. Did you feel like you were?"

Anguish tightened in her stomach. "Oh, God, of course I did. It could have been different. It didn't have to end the way it did—if only I'd acted faster."

He came toward her, shrinking the office. It was as though a shadow had fallen between her and the bright window, making Clare feel as if she was suffocating. She pressed back against the door and he stopped suddenly, frowning. "Are you afraid of me?"

If only it was that simple!

"Don't be ridiculous!" she denied, making herself relax rigid muscles. "It's just—" she hesitated "—you've always had this effect on me. Damn it, if you didn't always wear black, and if you'd smile sometimes, you wouldn't be so...intimidating! You make me nervous, that's all."

He raised his brows and smiled, unnerving Clare even more than he had with a dark frown. His voice was deceptively gentle. "And you don't know *why* I make you nervous?"

Of course she knew, although she would never admit it. She said fiercely, "Don't play games with me, Jake Radovich. Tell me what you want."

For an instant she thought she saw a rueful flicker in his deep-set gray eyes. "Ah, but I don't think you're ready to hear that."

She was just reckless enough to say, "Try me."

A muscle flexed in his jaw and any humor on his face vanished. "You tempt me, Clare."

The air was thick, hard to breathe. She felt the crackle of danger she'd somehow evaded for so long. Perhaps it was the safety, and loneliness, of this past year that drove her to taunt him.

"Obviously not enough," she said.

Jake moved then, in that disquietingly quick graceful way he had. One second he was several strides away, the next he was in front of her, his fingers gripping her chin. His eyes had darkened to something near black, and he stared down at her for a shattering instant. "I'll regret it if I do this," he muttered.

For one second Clare was paralyzed by astonishment and longing so intense it almost brought a cry to her lips. And then she came to her senses and wrenched herself away. Shaking, panting for breath, she stared at him.

"Someday," Jake said so softly she barely heard him. "Someday it won't be like this."

"No?" Guilt washed over her like acid rain, stilling her inner tremors. "Don't count on it, Jake. If that's why you're here..."

"Believe it or not, kissing you isn't what I had in mind for today. I've never pushed, Clare." His face was shuttered, his eyes remote. "So. Are you going to show me houses? Or do I need to find another agent?"

Hating herself, still Clare hesitated. If he was going to stir up memories and pain and unwanted longings, didn't she deserve some recompense? Shouldn't she profit from his arrival, at least in this small way? Or was she kidding herself about her motives?

He was waiting, and she made herself stare stonily at him. "Very well. I'll sell you a house. Why not? That's my job."

"Good." Jake shoved his hands in his pockets again. "But not today, I think. Maybe by tomorrow you'll have gotten used to the idea."

"Never." Clare wasn't sure if she'd said it aloud or to herself until his face hardened.

"I couldn't have done anything, Clare. You know that. You know how Don felt about me."

Her husband had been violently suspicious of the whole world, but perhaps especially of Jake Radovich, who'd once been his closest friend.

"I never blamed you."

"No?" He raised one brow, subtly mocking her.

It freed her to be unreasonable. "You could have tried. You were his friend! You could have—"

"What?" He sounded angry again. "Confirmed his belief that I wanted his wife?"

"Of course not!" Her fingers twisted together. "That was ridiculous! You could've convinced him—"

"Ah, but it was true." Jake's smile wasn't pleasant. "And you knew it. Didn't you?"

"No!" The darkness was swirling about her again, threatening to suck her in. She'd trusted him, if not herself. "No! If I'd known, I'd have never..." Her voice failed her. "Never..."

"Sought me out?" he said cynically. "Cried on my shoulder? Come on, Clare. You needed someone. But the feelings between us scared you, didn't they."

Between us? She shook her head dumbly. "You never said . . . never touched me like that. No. It's not true."

"It *is* true." But then his voice changed, became low and rough as he took a step closer. "Ah, damn. It doesn't matter, Clare. I'm not being fair, am I? You couldn't do anything but deny it. But Don is gone now."

She couldn't look at him. "So I should just close the door? Is it that easy?"

"No," he said quietly. "Not easy. I know better than that."

Clare couldn't seem to think of anything to say. She felt a little dizzy, even disoriented, battered by the intensity of his personality. In the year since Don's fiery death, Clare had almost succeeded in forgetting Jake—except in her dreams. She'd never expected to see him again, never *wanted* to. He was part of a nightmare she hadn't quite escaped. And yet, now that he was here in her office, nothing about him was exactly as she remembered. It was weird, as though she'd double-exposed a photograph, and the two images weren't quite aligned. She'd forgotten his smile, for example, and yet she must have seen it often. And somehow she dreamed of him always dressed in black, like a shadow on the edge of remembrance. He *was* wearing a black shirt, but it was soft and worn, faded comfortably and tucked into perfectly ordinary well-washed jeans. If he chose, he could pass in a crowd without a second glance. That astonished her.

The touch of his knuckles on her cheek was feather light, and yet it jolted her like an electric shock. When her startled gaze met his, Jake smiled. His eyes were warm and tender, his mouth gentle.

"I'll see you tomorrow," he said softly. "It can't help but get easier, you know."

Before she could move, he was gone, his footsteps as silent as always. Clare stood stock-still, frozen with memories and a panicky awareness of her reaction to him—her husband's best friend.

STIRRING THE SPAGHETTI sauce that simmered fragrantly on the stove, Clare glanced up at the clock. It was five past five, and no Mike. He wasn't overdue enough yet to make an issue about it, but tonight she felt on edge. She needed to tell him about Jake, to warn him. And yet she had no idea how he would react. But of course tonight of all nights he chose to be late.

Not that it should surprise her. Mike pushed every rule, every curfew, every small request to the limit of her patience. Seldom beyond; he was smart enough for that. But just far enough to test her authority. It was as though he wanted silently, constantly, to remind her she had no real power over him. He wasn't hers and never would be.

The strange part was that he'd accepted her as a stepmother. As things had gone wrong and their tight little world had rocked out of control, they'd been allies. Only after his father's death, when Mike understood that his grandmother couldn't take him, that Clare was all he had, did the thirteen-year-old begin his tiny jabs. She'd been patient—maybe too patient—but a year had passed now. Surely he realized that she wasn't going to desert him, that for better or worse they would see out his growing-up years together. Or did he? Did he still fear she would discard him when he became inconvenient?

By five-thirty her impatience had tightened into frustration, and she snatched the telephone receiver from its cradle. From memory she dialed Geoff Erickson's number.

"Hello?"

"Geoff, this is Mike's mom. Is he still there?"

"No, he left a while ago. I don't know, like ten or fifteen minutes, maybe?"

"Thanks," she said. After hanging up, Clare gave the sauce another stir, then put a pot of water on to boil for the spaghetti. Where was Mike?

When at last she heard his footsteps on the shabby wooden back porch, she took a slow deep breath and willed herself not to scream like a gull fighting over a fish. Restraint had never been harder.

"Hey, spaghetti for dinner," he said casually as he came into the kitchen behind her.

Without looking over her shoulder, Clare said, "It's almost ready. Go wash your hands."

She waited until dinner was dished up and they were seated. The quilted cloth she'd made hid the battered pine table, which she intended to refinish when she had time. Nothing could hide the peeling linoleum or the old metal kitchen cabinets.

"You were late," she said evenly.

"Was I?"

"I asked you to be home by five."

"What difference does it make? Dinner wasn't ready, anyway."

Clare laid her fork down. "I could have used some help."

The dark-haired boy completely ignored that. "Is there any garlic bread?"

"No. That was going to be your job."

He shrugged thin shoulders and Clare rolled her eyes. Even Mike's gestures seemed calculated to rub her the wrong way. Sometimes she'd have sworn he practiced in the mirror to achieve the maximum effect.

She managed to sound calm. "I think tomorrow you'd better stay home. Maybe that'll help you remember the time in the future."

He looked alarmed. "I can't stay home tomorrow. I'm supposed to go clamming with the guys. Ryan's dad said he'd take us to Tillicum Beach."

The thought of chowder made with fresh clams was almost enough to persuade her to back down, but Clare resisted the urge.

"I'm sorry. When I ask you to be home at a particular time, I mean it."

"That's not fair!"

"Your constant defiance isn't fair to me," Clare told him wearily. "I need help around the house and a modicum of cooperation. I don't think that's unreasonable."

"I do help. I mowed the yard this morning like you asked me."

Guiltily she realized she hadn't even noticed. "Thank you."

"Does that mean . . . ?"

"No."

For a moment she thought he was going to stomp away from the table, but hunger apparently won. Mike continued to eat in sulky silence. Considering how skinny he was, he sure put away an amazing amount of food.

She let the silence linger for only a minute before saying baldly, "Mike, Jake Radovich came into my office today."

His fork clattered to the plate as the sulkiness on his face was transformed into undiluted anger. "What'd he want? What's he doing here?"

Shocked by the intensity of her stepson's reaction, Clare said, "He's moving here. I don't know why."

Mike stood and shoved his chair violently back. "He doesn't have any right! He should stay away! Did you tell him we don't want him?"

She'd expected her stepson to be disturbed by her news, but furious? Never. Clare chose her words with care, wary of the tension that thrummed through him. "More or less. But this island was Jake's home, you know. We don't have any right to stop him."

"You want him here, don't you," Mike declared with flat suspicion.

"No." She looked down at the table and said in a stifled voice, "He made me remember. It was the first time since that afternoon . . ."

They were both silent for a moment. Clare could almost feel the heat of the fire, hear the roar, see the colors so unnaturally bright. And the look in Jake's gray eyes, the strength of his arms . . . That was the last time she'd seen or heard from him. She'd stayed in Oregon only long enough for the funeral. Jake hadn't come. She'd wondered why then, and now she wondered again. Had he felt guilty because he'd coveted his friend's wife? Would he have felt like a hypocrite, however much he might mourn Don? And why had she never realized he wanted her? Had she been blinded by Don's pain and anger? Or by her own secret hunger?

She looked at her stepson and saw how young and vulnerable he seemed. His anger had slipped away like a wisp of smoke. Somehow she had said the right words.

He met her eyes and gave an awkward shrug. "I think about Dad a lot, anyway. But it's mostly the good times I think about. I mean, I don't have to remember—" he sank into the chair, his shoulders hunched "—you know.

All the bad stuff. But it was partly Jake's fault, wasn't it? He talked us into moving, and Dad hated it. It wasn't fair. If we'd never gone—''

"No." Jake's arrival had shaken Clare, as well, but she couldn't let Mike blame him for the loss of might-have-beens that could never have been. "The move wasn't Jake's fault," she said gently. "Your father and I wanted the change. He needed peace and quiet. We found the quiet, but peace . . . Well, that's on the inside.''

The bleakness on Mike's young face made her ache. There was a moment's silence before he nodded and reached for his fork. He pushed spaghetti around on his plate without looking at her, then said suddenly, "Did you and Dad ever think about coming back here, instead? I mean, it's quiet, and Grandma's here and all.''

"We did talk about it," Clare admitted. "But your father thought it would be harder . . . where he knew everybody. And your grandmother has that heart condition, so we decided it would be better to start fresh, by ourselves. And when Jake suggested Oregon and told Don about the place next door to him . . . well, it seemed perfect.''

"It was lonely," Mike said in a small voice. "And scary.''

She touched his arm. "Yeah. It was.''

The boy's gaze shied away from hers and his cheeks reddened. "Hey, Clare, I'm, uh, sorry about being late today. Okay? I mean, I just . . . Sometimes I wish you really were my mother.''

Clare smiled shakily and reached over to give Mike a quick hug, which he didn't respond to but didn't pull away from, either. "I wish I were, too," she said. "But maybe . . . well, maybe it doesn't matter that much. We've gone through a lot together, haven't we?''

He nodded and the conversation ended there. But Clare went to bed that night feeling hopeful. Mike had opened up to her more in those few minutes than he had in months. Perhaps there was a silver lining to Jake's arrival, after all.

Her dreams were strange and troubling, with Mike and her running, running away from something—or somebody—so terrifying she couldn't look back. One moment she thought it was Don, the next Jake. But it was Jake they were running toward. She was certain of it. He stood up ahead, a solitary mysterious figure, dressed in black, his face shadowed and unreadable. Suddenly he was no longer there, he was behind—no, ahead again. Confused, she stumbled to a stop, pulling Mike with her. Smoke began to drift like a veil between them and Jake. Ghostlike, it swirled and shifted, deepening and thinning, burning her eyes and making her cough and clutch Mike. And the heat. She knew then what was behind them. She could hear the deep-throated dragon's roar with a despair that made her cry out.

For an instant Clare hung on to the dream, and she shuddered, staring into the darkness. Her throat was still tight. She could smell the smoke. And then she sat up sharply in bed, the dream fading. She *was* smelling smoke! And was that a glow outside her window?

Throwing back the covers, she jumped out of bed and ran to look out. Oh, God, she thought, snatching her bathrobe and racing across the hall to Mike's room. He was still asleep, but through the curtain she could see that glow. She yanked the curtains aside and stared out. Diffused by the dark wall of trees, there was still no mistaking that leaping orange-red glare. Not their closest neighbors, but a house not far beyond. Fire. A huge roaring blaze.

CHAPTER TWO

CLARE SWUNG AROUND. Mike sat up in bed, staring at her. Tinted with orange, his young face was a mask of fear.

He whispered, "Is it . . . ?"

"I have to call," she said, trying to think. "And then . . . there might be something I can do."

"Me, too." Mike was scrambling out of bed. "I'm coming." Clare didn't stop to argue. She ran downstairs. Her hand shook as she dialed the emergency number.

"Units have already been dispatched," the operator assured her, and Clare clumsily dropped the receiver back into its cradle.

Upstairs, she snatched jeans and a sweater. Tennis shoes without socks. Mike was waiting at the foot of the stairs.

With no discussion, they hurried down the wooden steps to the rocky beach. It would be faster than taking to the road. The softly lapping waters of the Sound, reflecting the inferno, looked like blood. The night was sliced by the scream of sirens, and Clare could feel the heat long before they rounded the point. She stubbed her toe against the top of a buried rock, ignored the pain. She prayed as she half-ran, half-walked, stumbling on the loose footing. Not the Petersens', please. They had small children whose bedroom was in the attic. And old Mrs. Brewer's—not hers, either.

"The Kirks' summer place maybe," Clare said. "Are they here this week?"

"I don't think so," Mike said, sounding uncertain and terribly young. "Their gate's been closed."

"Please, God," Clare murmured under her breath.

A moment later, "It is the Kirks'." Mike said it for her.

Clare didn't answer. Here the bluff was higher, the beach stairs steep. She was panting when she reached the top.

The sight there was nightmarish. The small clapboard cottage had already been consumed. The flames licked hungrily at the detached garage and the old orchard of apple trees. Volunteer firemen ran with hoses, calling incomprehensibly to each other, and streams of water shot up in crisscrossing arcs that glittered like fireworks.

Clare shuddered, hugging herself as she watched. She would never again enjoy the fireworks display on the Fourth of July. She glanced at Mike, to see a strange expression on his face. He stared unblinking at the blaze, mesmerized.

She touched his arm. "Mike." No response. She raised her voice. "Mike!"

With a jerk he focused on her. "Yeah?"

"Let's make sure there's nothing we can do. That the Kirks weren't here."

He nodded and followed her toward the dark huddle of spectators just beyond the yellow fire trucks in the driveway. The first person she recognized was Bart Petersen, her nearest neighbor, wearing an outfit as oddly assorted as her own. Sleeves of a pajama top poked out from beneath a sweatshirt, and a pair of expensive Nikes went oddly with the slacks he'd grabbed.

Beyond Bart were others: George Brewer, old Mrs. Brewer's middle-aged son who came over from Seattle every few weeks to check on her; Suzette Fowler, who ran the tiny bookstore in town, her face looking strangely naked without makeup; Tony and Phyllis Carlson, who'd bought the old Dwyer farm to try out self-sufficiency because they were convinced that civilization was near its end; Alison Pierce, who stared with the same horrified fascination as the others and didn't even notice Clare; Linda Michaels, who ran a bed-and-breakfast place. All lived along this stretch of the island loop road, just outside of town.

Clare had begun to turn back to the fiery battle when she realized who else she'd seen. Behind Linda stood Jake, the only one in the crowd who didn't look as if he'd scrambled into the first items of clothing his hand had touched. He wore the same black shirt and jeans. And unlike the others, he wasn't watching the fire. His eyes were shadowed, but Clare felt sure it was her he watched.

Clare was suddenly dizzy. Remembered fear touched her, and for an instant she lived again in her dream. Was Jake her refuge or her pursuer? She'd lied when she said he didn't haunt her.

She was startled when someone said, "Thank God the Kirks weren't here," and a murmur of agreement went through the crowd. Clare blinked and looked toward the dying flames. Tomorrow there would be nothing left but a black scar. Nobody had died—not this time. The house could be rebuilt. Nothing irreparable had been done. She'd overreacted.

Would she have been as terrified if Jake hadn't shown up today, made her remember and dream? A sudden surge of anger strengthened her. What right did Jake have to be here, to torment her this way? But when she looked back, he was gone. If he'd ever been there. Linda still stood in the same place, but beyond her were only shadows and a dark wall of trees. Had Clare summoned him from memory, as though he was inextricably connected in her mind with fire?

Despite the heat, she felt suddenly cold. Without looking at Mike, she said, "Let's go home."

JAKE EDGED his black Porsche into an empty slot along the street. He switched off the deep-throated engine, but didn't hurry to get out. It was ten o'clock, and tourists already strolled along the wooden sidewalk, peering into shop windows. Dorset had changed a lot since he'd left eighteen years ago. The tiny town was an odd mix. The supermarkets and the library, the gas station and the hardware store were for locals. The antique shops, the art gallery and the bakery/café were for visitors. Scrambling comfortably up the hillside, the town looked determinedly New England. The houses were saltbox, with small-paned windows, the clapboards painted white or red. White picket fences had old climbing roses sprawling over them. The marina, spiked with masts, nestled within the embrace of a rocky point.

Still Jake hesitated. Perhaps he should give Clare another day. Last night had been an incredible mischance. She'd hardly welcomed him with open arms, anyway, and the fire could only have brought her nightmares to life.

Jake saw again the expression on her face yesterday when he'd turned around and she'd recognized him. Shock and pain and longing and denial. He'd never dreamed she might blame him for her own torn feelings. He'd thought at least she would acknowledge their friendship, even if she hadn't been as haunted by its loss as he'd been this past year.

Maybe he'd been wrong to let her go the way he had. But he hadn't come to terms with his own feelings then, and she had needed time to mourn, to accept that she had given Don everything humanly possible to give. Neither of them had been ready to begin anything new.

Maybe she still wasn't. And maybe he was kidding himself that it was possible at all. He wasn't even sure what he himself felt. He only knew that he wanted to find out. Yeah, and maybe he was a selfish bastard, he thought wryly. Because Clare might be better off letting the past go. He'd probably be forever linked in her mind to Don.

But to have Clare claim she'd never recognized the tension between them! It was the ultimate irony. Jake shook his head. There had been electricity between them from the beginning. She *had* to have felt it, even if it was as unwelcome to her as it was to him.

Clare wasn't beautiful in the ordinary sense. She was small and slender, with a graceful dancer's body, not the type to turn most men's heads. High cheekbones and a square chin gave her face too much strength to be called beautiful. Her hair, chestnut brown, wavy and thick, would have fallen to the middle of her back if she'd let it hang free, but instead, she always wore it in a braid or loose knot. Hardly glamorous. Even her eyes, a deep shadowy blue, weren't the sort you'd call china-doll pretty. But Jake had wanted her all right. In his dreams he had tasted her and touched her and felt her shudders when he lost himself in her. Until he saw her again, he had forgotten just how badly he did want her.

He had to uncurl his cramped fingers from the steering wheel. So. Should he walk out of her life a second time? Let the past go and find his own tranquillity elsewhere?

Before he'd consciously made a decision, Jake was out of the car, locking it, walking across the sidewalk. It was time Clare confronted her own helplessness to save Don, and understood that she couldn't have done anything more than she had. His death was not her fault. She would be emotionally crippled until she accepted that. And if she needed to blame somebody, he was right here.

What a good samaritan, Jake thought sardonically. The truth was, now that he'd seen Clare, touched that long slender throat and heard her low husky voice again, he couldn't have made himself leave even if he was re-awakening painful memories for her.

The real-estate office fit the town perfectly. Pale gray, white trim, red geraniums massed in window boxes. Even a climbing rose tangling up a lattice-screened porch. Perfect to suck in the unwary tourist who'd been dreaming of an island cottage, he thought cynically as he opened the front door.

The receptionist looked startled when she saw him. Her glance turned involuntarily toward Clare's office, then back to Jake. He did his best to smile disarmingly.

"Will you tell Clare I'm here? She's expecting me today."

The young woman hesitated, then nodded. "Just a moment, sir."

He turned and pretended to look at the pictures of houses and waterfront acreage that adorned the bulletin board. First he heard the murmur of the receptionist's voice, then a moment later footsteps.

"Hello, Jake," Clare said.

He turned slowly, feeling the shock again when he looked at her. She had changed in ways he might never know. It had been too long. Today her expression was well schooled; he could have been a stranger.

She hadn't smiled yet. "Why don't you come into my office?"

Jake nodded and followed her, watching the quiet sway of her hips, sensing the tension in her neck and shoulders. She wasn't as indifferent as she pretended to be. He wasn't sure whether that gratified him or scared him.

He felt her warmth as she ushered him into the office. He'd always been a self-contained man, but having her so close made him want to touch her. Not with passion necessarily, or even possession. For reassurance maybe? He was angry at himself for his lack of patience as he strolled over and sat in the chair facing her desk, stretching out his long legs.

Clare closed the door, then made a wide circle around him and sat rigidly behind the desk. She picked up a pen and began to fidget with it. "Are you serious about buying a house?"

He lifted his brows. "Quite serious. But, Clare, before we start, I think we should talk about last night."

"No." The word was jerked from her. "Nobody was hurt. It... There really isn't anything to talk about. And I'd rather not."

He inclined his head in assent, but his gaze lingered on the shadows under her eyes.

Clare made a production out of reaching for her binder of listings, flipping it open, glancing at a note to herself clipped to the first page. This was harder than she'd expected. Damn Jake for that sheer masculine arrogance that allowed him to relax completely and watch her with dark unreadable eyes. Damn him for having a mouth that was too sensual for the harsher planes of his face, for possessing some quality that made her feel so painfully alive.

"What is it you have in mind?" she asked.

His mouth quirked as though he was tempted to answer flippantly, but instead, he replied, "Modern. I want big, with open spaces. Lots of windows and a view. And acreage, of course. I prefer not to have near neighbors."

Clare's stomach clenched. She said tonelessly, "They can be disturbing, can't they?"

His lean face looked suddenly bleak. "Very. Although I prefer disturbing to predictable."

"Then you don't know the hell life becomes when nothing is ever predictable," Clare said.

The silence between them was weighted with memories of the quivering tightrope Clare had walked for three years, once her husband had been diagnosed with schizophrenia. Each step, each word, each touch, carefully thought out. Each response, different and frightening. Clare had not forgotten. Random scenes often flickered before her eyes. Don, his face contorted with unbearable pain and rage. Burying his head under the pillow to shut out a world that assaulted him. Pacing, fists clenched, as he screamed his defiance at the voices that tormented him. Hurling his rage and his fears at her.

"I'm sorry," Jake said. His dark face showed the compassion she'd forgotten he was capable of. "That wasn't very... tactful."

Clare gave a small shudder. Her mouth was dry, her voice not her own. "No. You didn't say anything wrong. I shouldn't be so sensitive."

The look in his eyes was so potent then that she'd have sworn he touched her, except that he hadn't moved. "Don't toughen your skin, Clare," he said. "Sensitivity is a rare gift."

They stared at each other for an instant that stretched until Clare realized she'd quit breathing. She made herself look down at her desk, move in her chair until it squeaked. She'd imagined the heat, the urgency, the hunger. Of course she had. Neither of them had felt anything that intense.

Somehow she managed to sound almost normal when she said quickly, "We have a couple of houses I think might interest you. This isn't a big island—" She broke off. "Well, of course you know that. I'm sorry. I don't think of you connected with Dorset. It's easy to forget that you and Don... Anyway, there just aren't that many places for sale at any given moment. We do well with summer and weekend cottages, but they're small of course."

"I'd like at least three bedrooms. Preferably four."

Clare flicked a wary glance up to find that his expression was once again inscrutable, and she was able to relax by degrees. "Now this house—" she found the picture "—you might have noticed it from the ferry. It looks out on the shipping lanes. It's medium bluff waterfront, with the neighbors perhaps a little closer than you might like, but a magnificent view and a wraparound deck compensate for that. There's even a hot tub."

He'd sat up enough to glance at the picture, and now he shook his head. "I don't want neighbors looking in my windows."

"Waterfront lots tend to be narrow, you know. There's a fence, as you can see, and a good hundred feet between houses—"

"No."

"Well..." She thought desperately, refusing to consider the obvious choice. She couldn't bear to have him as a neighbor, not again. "The Boyer house might interest you. It's not modern, but it is charming, and there's no reason the interior couldn't be opened up. It has a barn, too, and of course is fenced."

"I know the Boyer place." Jake didn't move from his comfortable slouch. "It's not for me."

Frustrated, Clare forced a smile. "But you can't have seen it in years! Are you sure you wouldn't like to take a look at either of these places? Both have real appeal and—"

"Don't you have anything else?"

Driven to the wall, she hesitated. "Naturally we have listings on other islands. Does it have to be here? If you're not interested in the bigger ones, perhaps Shaw or Lopez . . ."

He simply looked at her and waited. She tried hard to control her impulse to babble, to fill the silence. She'd done that too many times with him. So she crossed her legs, tugged her skirt down, then pushed her thick bangs back from her forehead. Suddenly she realized she was fidgeting. Again. Sitting up straight, she glared at him. "You know, don't you? You came because you *knew* that house was for sale, didn't you?"

His rare smile was slow and amused. "What house?"

"The one on my road, of course!"

He didn't answer right away. Instead, he studied her face, the smile lingering in his eyes, as well as at the corners of his mouth. Finally he said, "You know, you really shouldn't poke at your hair like that. It's sticking straight up. You look like an angry cat with your fur all puffed out."

Her hand lifted involuntarily to smooth her hair, but she stopped herself in time, gritting her teeth. "If you think you can distract me, you're wrong!"

"I didn't know about the house. I don't even know where you live." The stark crease in one cheek deepened with his smile. "But now that you've let the cat out of the bag, so to speak . . ."

She felt as though the plastic-coated pages burned her fingertips as she turned them. Wordlessly Clare slid the binder across the desk to him.

For the first time, Jake reached for it. Dark head bent, he studied the picture and the spare information typed below it. Clare studied him in the silence.

Today he had on black jeans, obviously well-worn, and a gray corduroy shirt with the sleeves rolled up. She wondered if he'd look as secretive in red. If she'd had the right, she would have bought him a red shirt. She tried to envision him in an ordinary business suit and failed. Did he ever dress up for... whatever writers did when they weren't staring at a computer screen? How strange, she suddenly realized, that she didn't know what he wrote. He was a free-lancer, he'd said vaguely when she asked, and she was self-absorbed enough in those days to let it go at that.

"I'd like to see it," he said abruptly.

Maybe he would hate the Muellers' too-modern folly, she thought without believing it. Maybe he couldn't afford it. But he'd seen the price, and not even a flicker of dismay had showed on his face.

Just as abruptly she said, "Jake, what do you write?"

She did see something unsettling in his eyes as he set the binder down slowly. But then he smiled. "Does it matter?"

"I need to know whether you can qualify for a loan before I bother the Muellers," she said unconvincingly.

"Would you like to talk to my banker?"

"That's not necessary right now."

"Last year's tax return?" he asked mockingly.

Clare stared at him. "I asked a simple question. If you don't want to tell me, say so."

He was very still for a moment, but at last he shrugged as though in resignation. "Mysteries."

"Is that why you always wear black?"

Jake actually laughed. "You mean, as an affectation? Sort of like swirling a black cloak behind me? Lord, no. I just like the color. Is there anything wrong with that?"

She propped her chin on her hands and tried to take in this new facet of what was already to her a complex man. "Why haven't I ever heard of you?"

"Do you read mysteries?"

"No," Clare admitted. "But if you were famous like Elmore Leonard, I'd have seen your name at least."

"Did I say I was famous?"

"If you can afford the Muellers' house, you must be," she said simply.

For the first time she'd ever seen, he looked uncomfortable. "I don't write under my own name. I like fortune without the fame."

That didn't surprise her. Somehow she couldn't see him doing talk shows or smiling with rueful charm from the pages of *Us* or *People*. He was definitely the reclusive sort, which made it even stranger that he would choose to leave his magnificent perch on the Oregon coast to move back to his hometown, with all the gossip and coziness that made up a small island community. Did he have ties here, memories that had drawn him back?

"Did you sell your house?" she asked, watching him closely. It seemed to her that Jake was relieved at the change of subject.

"It's for sale. I have someone interested."

"So you'd need to buy on contingency?"

He shook his head. "I have investments I can liquidate."

He said it so casually. These days Clare would have regarded an extra month's income in the bank as an investment.

"Well, that certainly makes it easier." She smiled. "What name do you write under, Jake?"

His sudden tension showed in his fingers curling around the wooden arms of the chair. His tone was still casual. "Why? Are you planning to read my entire body of work?"

"It might be interesting."

"I doubt it," he said calmly. "If you're not a mystery reader—"

"Don't you trust me?" she challenged.

Jake looked at her with his dark unreadable eyes before he laid a hand on his heart and said lightly, "With my life."

"Then?"

He shrugged. "I write as Jacob Stanek."

Clare stared at him, stunned. She *had* read one of his books; who hadn't? Each one reached the bestseller lists. The book she'd read was far more than a mystery. It had been many layered, shattering in its emotional intensity, the characters stripped to their essence. The actual crime in the story existed only as a symbol, as a small next step for ordinary people. Clare had found the novel disturbing. She'd wondered about the author, who saw so clearly and cynically. But he was an enigma; the back flap of the dust jacket was a stark white, with no picture and only one sentence mentioning his previous novels.

"You're Jacob Stanek?" she said.

"I take it you've read one."

"Yes, a long time ago." She shook her head. "I don't understand. Why did you never say?"

He moved restlessly in the chair. "Because I didn't want you reacting like most people do. Knowing what I write makes them uncomfortable. They feel like I'm analyzing *them*. They expect to see themselves in my next book. And maybe they do, because we're all weak in one of a few ways."

"Are you?" she couldn't help asking.

His gray eyes narrowed, and Clare and he stared at each other. When at last he spoke, his voice was harsh. "Oh, yes, I have my weaknesses."

Was she one of them? Instinctively Clare rejected the idea. Whatever he now implied, Jake couldn't have hidden anything stronger than mild attraction all that time. He hadn't once touched her, except to lend a shoulder when she cried or a hand to help her over a log. He'd been almost impersonal, someone who listened and seldom commented, who expected no emotional return. Or had she been wrong? Had she simply not wanted to see?

She felt panicky, desperate. Standing quickly, she evaded his gaze. "I have a key. If you really want to see the Mueller place, why don't we...?"

He looked faintly surprised. "Shouldn't you call?"

"They're in Seattle this week."

"So we won't be bothering them."

Clare flushed, remembering what she'd said. "I'm sorry. But I am expected to get an idea of your financial situation before I show a house to you. And even though I knew you..."

Her words trailed off when he stood up in one easy motion. He was very close to her, looking down. She could feel his heat, see the crinkles at the corners of his deep-set eyes, the shadow on his hard cheeks, the slight flaring of his nostrils as he caught her scent. She wished she were taller; maybe she wouldn't always feel so defensive with him.

"...you were curious." Jake finished her sentence, then smiled with lazy sensuality. "I'm glad."

Mesmerized by the warmth in his normally cold gray eyes, she stood dumb for an instant. Finally, swallowing, she stepped back. Her voice sounded thin. "Shall we...?"

"After you." He gestured with one hand.

Walking ahead, Clare felt like a rabbit with a wolf at its heels. She wished she had a hole to bolt into.

She said automatically, "Joanne, I'm going to be showing a house. I should be back in an hour or two."

Wide-eyed, the young receptionist looked past Clare at the man silently following her. "Uh, sure, Ms. Talbot." She lowered her voice. "Shall I tell Alan?"

Alan was Alan Beckwith, her boss, and amused, despite herself, Clare suddenly relaxed. Good Lord, poor Joanne was scared to death of Jake. She must think he was taking her hostage or something.

"Heavens, no! Not unless he wants me. Jake's an old friend of mine," she added, trying to sound casual.

Joanne gave a funny little nod, her reluctant fascination unpleasantly reminding Clare of the way they'd all watched the fire the night before. Still, it reassured her, as well, to know that she wasn't the only woman intimidated by Jake's dark silent presence.

Outside, she had started across the sidewalk toward her car when Jake said from behind, "I'll drive."

Clare froze. The idea of his being in control was disquieting.

But that was absurd. What on earth was she afraid of? For heaven's sake, she knew half the people on the island. If she got mad enough at Jake, she could simply flag a ride from one of her neighbors.

The black Porsche looked familiar, although she'd never ridden with him before. The black leather seat was sinfully comfortable, the deep growl of the engine powerful. Jake's wide shoulder nearly touched hers, and his jean-clad thigh was too close.

Her gaze followed his hand as he reached for the stick shift between them. His fingers were long yet blunt tipped, his wrists strong yet supple, the contradictions a part of him. Clare remembered the graze of his knuckles down her cheek, the frighteningly gentle grasp of his fingers on her chin. A ripple of reaction ran through her, and she turned her head to stare out the window.

"Clare."

She made herself glance at him.

"Which way?"

Feeling foolish, she said, "Oh, sorry. Left. It's not far from Don's old house. Or from the place that burned last night. I suppose you must be staying at Linda's bed-and-breakfast."

He didn't react to that. "Tell me how you like living here."

Again it was amusement that relaxed Clare. "It's taken getting used to. Everybody knows everything about Mike and me. Total strangers know what brand of cereal we buy. The postmistress is married to the gas-station owner, so they compare notes. Mike's teacher grew up with Don. The woman who runs the bookstore is my neighbor, and she's having an affair with the principal of the high school. Of course we all know about them. At the moment the feeling is pro, because neither is married. If either was..." She sliced a finger across her throat.

Jake's sidelong glance was humorous. "Still conservative."

Clare considered it. "I suppose they are. Not necessarily politically. But if someone having an affair was married, we'd all know the spouse, too. That makes things look different."

"Yes, indeed." There was an odd note in Jake's voice.

Clare ignored it. "So I don't have to tell you that if it's privacy you're after..."

"Forget it."

"Find someplace else," she said bluntly.

"It isn't privacy."

Panic fluttered like a trapped moth in her chest. What did he want from her? Why now? He hadn't been there when she needed him after Don's death. If he'd cared at all, why had he disappeared then?

They passed the bed-and-breakfast, a remodeled Victorian surrounded by a lawn that sloped down to the bluff. Clare didn't have to tell him where to turn; he automatically steered the Porsche into the rutted lane past the cluster of mailboxes, reminding Clare that this was familiar territory to him. Where the Muellers' house now stood would have been woods then. As boys, Don and Jake must have played there. She tried to picture Jake as a boy, thin and dark, and succeeded disquietingly well. She tried to remember what Don had said about Jake, but it seemed to her it had been very little beyond their colorful escapades. Did Jake have family left here on the island?

Clare carefully didn't look as they passed the black remnants of what had been the Kirks', and then a moment later her house, shabby and aged. Next door was her mother-in-law's, a rambling, fastidiously cared-for cottage surrounded by the thorny roses that Anne Talbot cherished. Finally the lane narrowed and plunged into the woods; thick-trunked, moss-covered cedars and firs blocked the sunlight, and ferns grew in lacy profusion beneath. At last Jake reached the clearing, dominated by the huge glass-and-cedar house that commanded a sweeping view of the Sound.

He eased the car to a stop and turned off the engine, and they sat in silence for a moment. When he spoke, he managed to surprise Clare.

"Which house was yours?"

Her hesitation was brief. "The ratty one," she said.

"Do you own it?"

"I rent it from my mother-in-law."

"Are you short of money, Clare?"

She could be equally blunt. "Yes."

A frown drew his brows together. "I didn't know."

Clare stared straight ahead. "It wouldn't have made any difference if you had."

She felt him studying her, but he chose not to comment. Instead, after a moment he swung open the car door and climbed out. She did the same, not waiting for him to come around to her side.

The cedar porch of the house wrapped around the corner, angling into a huge deck that nearly overhung the bluff. Jake strolled out of sight while Clare unlocked the elaborately carved front door. When she followed him, she found him leaning against the railing, staring meditatively out. Across a deep channel was another of the islands, from this distance appearing uninhabited. Dark green plunged down to the glacially polished rock that tilted into the cold waters. An orange light buoy bobbed off a point, rocking in the swells.

Without looking around, Jake said, "I'd forgotten what it was like. Although I'll miss the surf."

"I did for a while," Clare admitted. Especially at night, when she'd stared into the darkness reliving all her mistakes, she could have used the eternal, soothing beat of the ocean. But she'd become used to the landlocked Sound; it had its own rhythm, quieter but no less natural.

"Well." He straightened and cocked a brow. "Shall we do the grand tour?"

Clare nodded, leading the way into the immense living room. A magnificent rounded-rock fireplace crowned with a thick slab of bird's-eye maple vied for attention with the wall of glass that took advantage of the view. Rich white carpet swept from the tiled entryway into the open dining room, and the furnishings were starkly modern and all in neutrals. The only color was added by a few wall hangings. Jake prowled in silence, running a hand along the silken wood of the mantel, standing before the huge windows, glancing through doorways.

Clare tried to remember how his home had been furnished, without much success. She had a vague memory of a certain starkness, but one created by lack of clutter, not colorlessness.

"The carpet would have to go," Jake commented. "Why would anybody put in white a few steps from the beach?"

"I don't think the Muellers go much farther than the deck very often. They're only here about half the time. This place is mostly for entertaining clients from Seattle. I'm pretty sure a designer is responsible for the decor."

"It shows."

What the kitchen showed was money, Clare thought wryly. Maple cabinets had narrow strips of mahogany inlay, the counters were granite, and the pale oak floor shimmered like a length of satin. The breakfast nook, enclosed in paned glass, was bigger than Clare's entire kitchen. The colors were all pale peach and blue, down to the placemats and the pleated blinds.

Clare had almost forgotten Jake until he said behind her, "No taste."

"It's not very... personal, is it?"

"I haven't even seen a painting they might have picked out themselves. Still—" he crossed his arms and glanced around "—I think the place could be made comfortable."

"Really," Clare said dryly, thinking of her own peeling linoleum, stained ceilings and inadequate furnace.

"Although I'd rattle around in it alone," he added thoughtfully.

"Why did you want three bedrooms?" she asked.

He didn't look at her. "For the future. Shall we go upstairs?"

It wasn't really a question, and he didn't wait for her to lead. In fact, she let him disappear up the skylighted staircase before reluctantly following. There was something altogether too intimate about bedrooms when connected with Jake. And the hot tub on the tiny deck off the master bedroom—it was all too easy to imagine him lounging in it, steam curling around his sleek, smoothly muscled shoulders.

"Damn," she mumbled under her breath, pausing at the head of the stairs. The house had four bedrooms, and she wasn't sure which one he'd vanished into. Still more reluctantly, she moved down the hall, glancing into each. She found him in the middle of the master suite.

Jake glanced at her when she appeared in the doorway. "Looks more like a ballroom than a bedroom."

Clare had to smile. "You certainly wouldn't want to sully the white carpet by actually having a fire in the fireplace."

"Mm."

She watched as he inspected the enormous bathroom, complete with sunken tub, a view of the Sound and a separate glass-enclosed shower. He moved on cat's feet, prowling like a black panther in an alien environment. Tension rose in her as she waited. It would be easy to be afraid of him, she thought. She couldn't imagine now how she'd ever found the courage to confide in him.

When at last he came toward her, her gaze flitted nervously to the bed before she backed into the hall. He smiled faintly, as though he sensed her edginess, before strolling past her and into the next bedroom.

It was the silence, she decided in her own defense. The big quiet house was like a mausoleum. The plush carpet deadened footsteps, and no outside noises penetrated. Clare felt unbearably isolated with Jake. She needed the reassurance of other people a room away, the traffic on the road. Something, somebody.

"What do you think?" she asked abruptly. Her voice sounded too loud in the silence.

Jake reappeared, pausing in the doorway with his shoulder propped against the frame, hands shoved into the pockets of his jeans. The long muscles in his thighs were outlined by the worn denim, and his ankles were casually crossed. Relaxed, imperturbable, he said, "I'll take it."

Clare blinked. "You'll take it? You mean, you want to buy it?"

"I like the view."

"But...don't you want to make an offer or something?"

"Naturally." He named a figure $20,000 under the asking price. "That ought to do it."

Clare was quite certain it would. Nonetheless, his confidence annoyed her. When she *had* needed him just to listen, she'd been grateful for his imperturbability. Now she'd have loved to see him jolted out of it. Really it was a pity that the Muellers, hungry for an offer, wouldn't laugh him out of the office.

Clare sighed. "All right. Are you ready to leave?"

He didn't move. "Is Mike home?"

Clare wanted very badly to lie, but what was the point? They would meet each other soon enough.

"He's supposed to be," she admitted. "I should warn you that Mike seems to be angry at you."

"Angry? Why?"

"I don't know." She hesitated. "He's at a difficult age."

Jake's gaze was sharp. "Do you get along?"

"Oh—" Clare shrugged helplessly "—we get by. It would be easier if I was his actual mother."

"Why?"

"He thinks I have him out of pity," she said simply. "I can't convince him I love him."

After a moment's silence, Jake said, "Poor kid."

She shrugged again. "We're managing."

"Do you have time to stop at your place, then?" Jake asked, pushing away from the door.

"If you do."

"For you, always." With the lightness of his tone, he seemed to mock himself.

Clare hardly knew how to respond. But Jake only gave that faint smile that made her feel as though he could read her mind, and then he tugged gently on her braid.

"Onward and upward."

"Down, actually," she said.

"Always literal," he said with amusement.

She startled herself by saying, "I used to think that if I ever went crazy, I'd be the kind who'd wash my hands over and over, something compulsive like that, instead of losing myself in nightmares. I never had enough imagination for that."

"You had enough to suffer for Don," Jake said quietly.

Shaken by the truth of that, Clare didn't respond. She couldn't understand what had possessed her to tell him what she had.

A moment later she locked the front door, and they drove the short distance up the narrow lane. Her own tumbledown house looked even shabbier in contrast to the Muellers'. The gleaming black Porsche didn't seem to belong on the dirt drive. But Jake didn't comment. Instead, he scooped up the gray cat that lounged between the asters in her narrow flower bed and followed her into the house, stroking the cat, who, after a surprised jerk, relaxed and began to purr.

"That's Misty," Clare said over her shoulder, letting the smell of cooking lead her to the kitchen.

The boy turned from the stove. "Clare! What are you— Oh." That flash of hostility showed on his thin face as he said flatly, "Jake."

Jake held out a hand. "It's good to see you, Mike. You've changed."

Mike made no move to return the gesture. "You haven't," he said with studied insolence.

Jake's mouth had a wry twist as he let his hand drop to his side. "No, I suppose not." Ignoring the stifling tension, he added quietly, "I've missed you and Clare. And your father."

The boy sneered. "Right."

Clare took a warning step forward. "Mike..."

But his belligerent gaze didn't shift from Jake. "Are you really moving here?"

"I hoped you'd be glad."

Mike's voice rose, cracking. "We don't want you here! You'll wreck everything! This was a cool place until—" Suddenly he stopped, his expression altering as he looked from Jake to Clare. "Wow, I almost forgot! Did you hear?"

"Hear what?" Clare asked with sharpened apprehension.

"Mr. Petersen called. The cops stopped by to talk to him this morning. You know the fire last night? They say it was arson. Somebody burned the Kirks' house down on purpose."

Clare felt a chill that raised goose bumps. It was like her dream. The dragon's roar of fire, and somebody there. Somebody behind who'd frightened her. She hadn't been sure, even in her dream, that it wasn't Jake Radovich.

CHAPTER THREE

"FROM WHAT I HEARD, nobody saw anything before the fire."

The others in the small cluster on the wooden sidewalk murmured their agreement; the island grapevine grew faster than roadside weeds, and everyone already knew who had talked to the fire marshal and exactly what had been said.

Clare wanted to walk right past, but she felt the same fascination they did. A neighbor's house had been burned, and they all felt threatened. If the arsonist wasn't discovered, he might strike again.

She hesitated only a second, then stepped toward them. Linda Michaels, the bed-and-breakfast owner, saw her. "Clare, has anybody in your office heard from the Kirks? I wonder if they'll rebuild or sell."

"Not a word," Clare said. "It's only been two days—they're probably still in shock."

"I suppose so," Linda agreed grudgingly. "Still, I hear..." She glanced toward an approaching tourist, then lowered her voice. "Word has it that Ed Kirk almost got fired at DataWare, but they settled for demoting him. Nobody knows why, but his income must have suffered. The insurance settlement wouldn't be too unwelcome."

"Are you suggesting Ed set the fire?" a more forthright soul demanded. "I can't imagine—"

"No, no," Linda said hastily. "I'm just glad this happened at a time when the Kirks might benefit, instead of suffer."

"How could he have set it, anyway?" The speaker was Reed Sargent, the bakery owner. "They weren't here. Somebody would have seen them getting off the ferry."

"They could have borrowed a boat," another one of the group pointed out.

Bart Petersen's wife, Sally, voiced Clare's troubled thoughts. "I'd rather not think it was somebody we know. There are still plenty of outsiders around. Look." She nodded down the street. "The inn is full. Isn't your place, too, Linda?"

"It was until Sunday, but the season's about over."

"Personally—" Reed shrugged "—I figure it was teenagers. They were probably horsing around and it got out of hand. Or maybe they broke in and stole some video games or something, then set the fire to cover up."

"Ed would've had gasoline in the garage for his mower, so they could've used that," said the owner of an art gallery two doors down.

"Makes sense to me," Linda agreed.

On that note, the townsfolk separated, most wandering back to work or the shopping that had brought them into town in the first place. Sally lingered long enough to say, "Scary, isn't it? I can't imagine any of the kids I know doing something like that."

"Maybe if it was a dare..." Weak, but Clare didn't want to think about the alternatives. She didn't want to think about fire at all.

She had tried to hide her repulsion from the fire marshal who'd knocked on her door yesterday evening. Coming from Friday Harbor, he wouldn't know how Don had died, and she would just as soon keep it that way. Brisk and matter-of-fact, she'd told him that neither she nor Mike had seen or heard a thing until the smell of smoke had awakened her.

"You're certain your son was home?"

"Of course I am!" Her tone was sharp. Mike, who had lost his father to an inferno, still had dreams as she did, nightmares in which he was always too late to save his father. To suggest that Mike might set a fire deliberately was ludicrous.

Impassively the marshal made a note. "So you called 911, then went over to see if there was anything you could do."

Her fingernails biting into her palms, Clare nodded. "That's right."

"Had some of the other neighbors gathered?"

"Yes."

"Who?"

She listed those she could remember: Alison Pierce, Linda Michaels, Bart Petersen with his pajamas beneath his clothes, the Carlsons, George Brewer. She found herself reluctant to add Jake's name, but the marshal must have already known who'd been there; he was merely confirming his facts, perhaps hoping for an addition.

So she concluded, "And Jake Radovich, who's staying at the bed-and-breakfast. He's buying a house down the road."

"I understand he grew up here."

"That's what I'm told," Clare said.

The marshal had left, apparently satisfied, leaving her to wonder why she'd had that first protective instinct where Jake was concerned. There'd never been any doubt that Don had set the fire to kill himself, so it wasn't as though the marshal would suspect Jake even if he knew

of that earlier tragic blaze. No, it was that ridiculous terrifying dream that made her reluctant to think of Jake
connected in any way with fire; that dream, and her
memory of him holding her.

Trying to put the gossip out of her mind, Clare spent
the morning checking the empty houses her firm managed. Some were rentals, others summer homes that
needed water shut off for the winter and an occasional
inspection for broken windows or downed trees. Her
boss, Alan Beckwith, had started worrying after the
Kirks' fire.

"I wouldn't want to have to call one of our clients to
tell 'em their house had burned down," he said. "Let's
just make the rounds, check the locks, look for signs of
entry, make sure no gas cans are left out."

Clare ate her sack lunch while sitting on the deck of
one of the empty houses, gazing across the water toward
the green bulk of San Juan Island. A fishing boat drifted
along the narrow rockbound passage, and a sea lion
poked its head out of the water for an inquisitive glance
around. The scene was so quiet, so peaceful, it was all
Clare could do to make herself get moving.

Perhaps she'd had a presentiment, she thought ruefully, when she spotted Jake's black Porsche parked
outside her office. Not that she wanted to hold up the
sale, what with such a welcome commission. She seldom
had the luck to be both listing and selling agent. But she'd
have been just as happy to conduct the entire business by
fax.

When Clare walked into the office, she found Jake
sitting on the edge of her desk holding a silver-framed
photograph of her, Don and a much younger Mike. Despite the artificiality of a studio portrait, they looked
happy, the three of them. She didn't have many pictures

of them all together that didn't betray the toll Don's ill-ness had exacted. But this portrait was from the time be-fore—before Don's explosive personality change, before Jake offered them a sanctuary. At the moment the shut-ter snapped, Don was half-turned from the camera, gaz-ing with tenderness at his new wife and his eight-year-old son. He'd been a large gentle man, auburn-haired and blunt-featured, not so much handsome as teddy bearish. *Before,* Clare thought again, deliberately blurring her memory of *after.*

With the office door standing open, Jake hadn't heard her come in. His expression was unreadable as he gazed down at the portrait, but after a moment he squeezed his eyes closed and bowed his head.

"Damn," he muttered. "Damn it to hell."

If Clare had thought she could escape without his see-ing her, she would have. But any second now he'd look up. As it was, she couldn't remember ever watching him unnoticed. It made her wonder again how much she'd forgotten or distorted.

She said, as lightly as she could manage, "Who are you damning? Don? Or me?"

Jake's head shot up, and his eyes, fierce for a mo-ment, pinioned hers. Then he was shielded again, able to set down the photograph with a steady hand and say sar-donically, "Myself, of course."

More guilt and another cryptic prod to her memory. "Give me a break!" Clare snapped, going behind her desk. She had startled him, she saw, before he hid that, too.

"In a bad mood today?"

"Not at all." She stowed her briefcase in a drawer. "Have you changed your mind about the house?"

One dark brow rose. "I rarely change my mind once I've made it up."

She let that pass. "The Muellers have made a counter-offer. Let's see." A quick shuffle through the pile of manila folders produced the paperwork. Clare passed it across the desk to Jake.

He glanced through it, then handed it back to her. "Fine."

Perversely she said, "They'd probably come down a little more."

"I'd just as soon not quibble." He stood and wandered over to the window, where he remained gazing out with his back to her. "What I'd like is to rent the house from them until closing."

Clare felt suddenly stifled. She'd expected to have a few weeks of peace before he moved in, before his car passed her own house daily, before she was likely to meet him on the beach or at the grocery store or the post office.

"Don't you have to pack and close up your other house?"

At something in her tone, he turned his head, showing his lean austere face in profile. "Trying to get rid of me?"

"Damn it, Jake!" Her tension needed an outlet, and she slammed a drawer shut with unnecessary force. "Must everything be personal? Has it ever occurred to you that I might not care what you do?" *If only it was true.*

The pause was long enough to be uncomfortable. Then Jake said in a voice devoid of emotion, "I apologize. My insecurities must be coming through."

Until the other day, she wouldn't have believed he had any, but that belief, like any number of others, was eroding. She heard him again: *Oh, yes, I have my weak-*

nesses. And here he was again, hinting at the same thing: that she was one of them.

She wouldn't think about it—what he implied about their shared past, her own guilt, the truth about Don's terror and rage. Already she was fumbling through her Rolodex.

"I'll call the Muellers right now."

Jake waited in silence as she phoned Mr. Mueller at work, told him that his counteroffer had been accepted, that the buyer wanted to rent until closing. Mr. Mueller was so thrilled to have an offer that wasn't subject to bank approval he'd have agreed to anything. He'd send a mover to empty the house immediately, he assured her.

Hanging up, Clare said, "Did I mention that we don't have an escrow company on Dorset? Usually we use Island Escrow in Friday Harbor. You'll have to go there for closing."

"Fine." Jake shoved his hands in his jeans pockets and sauntered toward the door. "I'll be back Friday to pick up the key."

"Fine," she echoed acerbically to the empty doorway. Only then, with him gone, did she wonder if she'd hurt his feelings. The idea that she might have that power was a peculiar one—disconcerting, but also gratifying in a way she didn't want to analyze.

With a groan, Clare shoved her fingers into her hair. Why had he come back? *Why?*

HE WAS AN IDIOT, Jake told himself. Don's mother might make a pretense, but she wouldn't welcome his return any more than Clare or Mike had. Any more than his own father would.

But he didn't get back into his car. He'd run away once, and where had it gotten him? Some people, some memories, should be faced.

Don's childhood home had changed. In the old days Mrs. Talbot, raising her son alone, had been too busy to garden. Instead of thorny roses, the yard consisted of beaten-down grass used as a miniature football field to go with the basketball court that was the driveway. The small house was close enough to the edge of the bluff that a tipped pass had sometimes gone over, a dreaded circumstance that meant scratches from the blackberry bushes that clambered down the steep drop to the beach.

Jake couldn't say those had been good days; he had too often nursed bruises and pent up rage, which gave him headaches. But if he'd felt safe anywhere, it was here. He had no idea whether Mrs. Talbot had known how brutal his father was, but she'd made plain that her home was a refuge for him. She'd been unfailingly gentle to the angry boy her son had befriended.

"What are you thinking about?"

Jake turned to see Mrs. Talbot approaching through a boxwood-edged path. With shock, he saw how much she'd aged. Good God, no wonder. He hadn't seen her in close to twenty years.

He told her only the literal truth. "How much I hated hunting for footballs that went over the bank."

Mrs. Talbot laughed and peeled off her gardening gloves as she stopped in front of him. "Do you know, I was cutting back the blackberries last year, and what did I find but a flattened football. What memories that gave me!"

"Does Mike come over to shoot baskets?" Jake asked, nodding toward the hoop above the garage door.

Her face softened still more. "He and his friends. Now they have to worry about the roses."

Jake took her outstretched hand, feeling the crinkles and fragility. "You must be glad to have him here."

"Yes, of course." She dismissed the subject of her grandson. "You'll come in?"

"You bet." He felt his own crooked half-rueful smile. "I'm surprised you recognized me."

"Clare told me you were back." Mrs. Talbot opened the front door, painted a bright red. "I was expecting you."

"I should've come sooner." He stopped just inside. "Years sooner."

"No, Jacob. Not until you were ready."

He'd written regularly, of course, or else he couldn't have faced her. He wondered if Clare knew they corresponded. And if Mrs. Talbot knew he hadn't gone to Don's funeral.

The kitchen hadn't changed: the old glass-fronted cabinets were still painted white; the same maple table, scratched and homey, stood in the bow window that formed a dining nook.

Mrs. Talbot poured them both lemonade, and they sat there at the table where he'd worked on innumerable homework assignments with Don. Being here, Jake could almost believe Don would walk in any minute. Not the man who had lost too much weight, whose eyes were dull from medication, whose movements had become shambling, but the boy who'd have grinned and said, "Jeez, not *you* again."

Mrs. Talbot nudged Jake back to the present. "Have you seen your father yet?"

"No."

"He can't hurt you anymore."

"So you knew."

She looked away, regretful. "I was never sure how much. Or whether I should do anything about it. I'm sorry now that I didn't."

"You did what mattered the most." He covered her hand with his as though it was the most natural thing in the world. He, who never talked about his emotions easily, had no trouble doing so this once. "You and Don let me know somebody cared."

But the words were no sooner out of his mouth than self-condemnation sliced through him. He'd owed Don an incalculable amount. And what was his payment? Loving Don's wife. Giving her what Don couldn't and thereby completing the destruction of the man. His best friend. This woman's son.

"You're not angry anymore," Mrs. Talbot said thoughtfully.

Guilt ridden, instead. "It was too many years ago."

She contemplated him for a moment. "Welcome home, Jacob."

"Thank you."

After he'd promised to come for dinner soon, she walked him to his car. He backed out and drove through the woods to the house that would soon be his own. Sprawling glass and cedar, too big for one man. The damned house was a gamble, a throw in the dark.

Has it ever occurred to you that I might not care what you do?

Oh, yeah, Jake thought. He just didn't want to believe it. She'd haunted too many nights, come back in small memories too many days. He couldn't go anywhere, do anything, without thinking of her. There'd been the log they'd sat on when she cried that day, one of the rare times she'd let him hold her. That painting had made her smile. That book she'd borrowed. When he'd seen sandpipers scooting after the waves, he'd remembered how she loved watching them. And always, whenever the fog rolled in off the ocean, an inexorable grayness that used to swallow them as Don's illness had, he'd wondered if she'd escaped the sadness.

Along the way he'd convinced himself that she, too, thought of him, waited for him. Knew that he would come.

"Arrogant son of a bitch," he told himself, slapping the steering wheel. That didn't stop him from pulling into Clare's driveway a minute later.

He didn't see her car, couldn't tell if she was home yet. But a mountain bike leaned against the shabby detached garage. Either Mike's or a friend's, which meant the boy was probably here. Jake found that he was very curious to discover why Mike had decided to hate him.

The wooden front stairs sagged and quivered when he stepped on them; unless Clare threatened to call the sheriff the next time he stepped foot on her property, he'd stop by and fix them.

He knocked and heard the thunder of feet from within. Don's son flung open the door. "You," he said flatly. "What d'ya want?"

"Your mom home?"

Obviously it was the wrong thing to have asked. Suspicion altered to outright hostility. "What if she is?"

"Actually I was hoping to talk to you, too."

Mike's lip curled. "So, talk."

Jake kept his voice calm, friendly. "May I come in?"

The boy's thin dark face showed an inner battle: manners versus dislike. Or was he, too, curious? At last he stood back grudgingly. "Yeah, I guess. Mom should be home in a minute."

Jake inclined his head and stepped past him into the small living room. The furniture was shabby, garage-sale finds, but she'd refinished some beautiful antique pieces, like the pine tavern shelves that hung above a blue-and-red plaid couch. A braided rug covered the center of the bare wood floor, which clearly needed stripping. The gray cat he'd seen on the other day was comfortably ensconced on a blue chair with a sagging seat.

Jake was opening his mouth to ask if he could sit down, when he heard a car. Something cramped inside him—anticipation, apprehension, damned if he knew. The slam of a car door, and he turned to watch Clare hurry toward the house. Her gaze went straight to him when she entered the living room. Sounding wary, she said, "Hello, Jake."

"Clare."

"Were you coming or going?" she asked, undoubtedly hoping the latter.

"Just got here."

"Oh." She pressed her lips together. "Well. What can we do for you?"

"I just visited Mrs. Talbot. Since I was coming right by here . . ." He lifted both hands and let them fall, knowing how weak his explanation was. Just yesterday Clare had rebuffed him as thoroughly as a woman could. So how to explain the compulsion that had brought him back for more, the refusal to believe she didn't feel what he wanted her to feel?

Jake was focused so completely on Clare he'd almost forgotten Mike, who asked belligerently, "What did you want with Grandma?"

Jake faced the boy. "Your father and I were best friends, you know. I grew up hanging around his house. I'll bet I've eaten more meals there than you have."

Mike chewed that one over for a moment, his face almost laughably expressive. He obviously didn't like the idea, and Jake couldn't blame him. He'd lost first his mother and then his father. He had so little he could claim as his own. He wouldn't like sharing any of that little.

A flash of self-loathing left Jake wondering again what the hell he was doing here. He'd tried; he wasn't wanted. How much plainer did they have to make it? But still, the certainty he'd nursed for so long flailed against cold reason. He couldn't have imagined the need he'd seen in her eyes, the hunger and softness.

"I think her health has improved lately," Clare said. "Did she tell you she had angioplasty last year to clear out a couple of arteries? Her color is so much better."

"She looked good," Jake agreed, wondering whether they'd discuss the weather next.

But Clare said, "Mike, I thought you were going to Geoff's."

"Nah." The boy didn't budge an inch.

"But you were determined . . ." When she saw that his expression hadn't changed, she shook her head. "Never mind. Why don't you both come back to the kitchen? I need to get dinner on."

The kitchen was homey and scrupulously clean, despite the old metal cabinets and yellowing linoleum peeling up at the seam. Clare dropped her purse on the table and went straight to the refrigerator. Studying its contents, she said over her shoulder in an impersonal tone, "Have a seat, Jake. Did you go by your house? Had the movers been there yet?"

"I drove over," he admitted, "but I didn't get out of the car."

That earned him a startled glance. "Whyever not?"

"The house isn't mine yet."

"For all practical purposes it is."

"Friday's soon enough." He paused. "Actually I'll probably make it Saturday, unless that's a problem. I'm flying to Oregon tomorrow to take care of things."

Clare started washing vegetables at the sink, her movements quick and sure. The line of her back was very straight, the heavy weight of her chestnut hair making her slender neck appear fragile in contrast. "Saturday's fine," she said in that determinedly pleasant voice. "Why don't you stop by here? If I'm not home, I'll leave the key in an envelope under the doormat."

"Thanks." He leaned against the end of the counter, conscious of the boy behind him watching suspiciously. Casually Jake turned. "You shoot hoops down at your grandmother's? Your dad used to slam-dunk. Bent the hoop one time. We straightened it out, but I noticed today you can still tell."

"Dad slam-dunked the ball?" For a moment, distrust was forgotten and his expression was eager. "Did he have any moves?"

"Did he have moves." Jake grinned. "He could do a three-sixty and just slap it down pretty as could be. Don was a hell of a basketball player."

"Then how come he didn't go to college and play ball?"

"Ah." Jake shrugged. "Made some money fishing in Alaska, met your mom. Didn't need the degree to get a job. He always said he wasn't quick enough to make it in the NBA, and if he couldn't have it all, he didn't want any of it."

That could have been taken two ways, and Jake regretted the words the second they were out. But Clare's back stayed turned and Mike didn't seem to notice the double meaning. He pulled a chair out and straddled it backward.

"I wish I could slam-dunk."

"I was never tall enough," Jake said. "You'll get there."

"Jake, you probably knew Mike's mother, didn't you?" Clare asked.

"I met her a few times." He watched narrowly for the boy's reaction. "Do you remember her, Mike?"

What he'd obviously remembered was that he didn't like Jake. His shrug was sullen. "Kind of."

"You look like her."

"At least she wasn't nutty as a fruitcake," he said rudely.

"Mike!" Clare exclaimed in shocked tones, turning from the sink with a knife in one hand and celery in the other. Water dripped unheeded.

"Well, Dad *was*." His dark gaze challenged his stepmother. "Or don't you want to admit you married somebody who was crazy?"

For a long moment their stares locked and Jake might as well not have been there. He had to admire Clare's self-possession when she said quietly, "Your father was mentally ill. I've never kept it a secret."

"Yeah?" Mike sneered. "Well, I think that's why you didn't come back here when Dad got sick. It's bullshit to say we moved to Oregon because *he* was such a good friend." Mike jerked his head toward Jake.

She flinched, and it was all Jake could do to stay silent and out of the way. Then, without raising her voice but giving it a rock-hard steadiness, she said, "We'll talk about this later. Right now you'll go to your room. I won't tolerate your rudeness."

The sneer deepened. "Getting rid of me so you can be alone with *him?*"

If he was fishing for a reaction, he got it. She snapped, "Go to your room right this minute!"

The kid lingered just long enough to be sure he'd made his point: she couldn't force him to do anything he didn't want to. Then he shot a dirty look at Jake, said, "Why don't you just stay away?" and sauntered out.

Clare didn't move until the footsteps on the stairs were followed by the slam of a door above. Then she sagged against the counter.

"I'm sorry," Jake said roughly. "I shouldn't have come."

"No, it's not your fault." She set down the celery and the knife. Defeat showed in the carriage of her shoulders and the shadowed blue of her eyes. "He's become so... volatile. We argue a lot. It's partly his age. I suppose he has to test me. But I think he's also trying to find somebody to blame for Don's illness."

"Maybe the trouble is that in his heart he already blames someone," Jake suggested. "His father."

"And feels guilty about it?" Clare tilted her head, a tiny line forming between her brows as she considered the idea. "I suppose that's possible. Lord knows I used to feel angry at Don sometimes, then horribly guilty because I knew it wasn't his fault, that he deserved compassion, instead."

"But you were an adult." Jake watched the emotions flitting across her face. "You knew the things you felt were natural. They didn't mean you were a terrible person. Maybe Mike doesn't have the maturity to realize that."

"It's possible." She tried to smile. "I'd forgotten how comforting you can be. You weren't a psychotherapist before you started writing books, were you?"

"No." He felt not the slightest trace of answering humor. Yeah, he'd been comforting all right. How easily he'd convinced himself that he could offer her that much without guilt, that Don would want him to. But with time he'd come to realize that his comfort was the trail of seeds used to lure a bird, to lull it and tempt it and tame it. Witness his shock now; he couldn't believe she wouldn't instantly fly to his hand.

"I've forgotten too much, haven't I?" Clare said softly.

Jake straightened. "I have to go."

"Don't run off," she said quickly. "You'd be welcome to stay for dinner—"

"No." Hearing how abrupt he sounded, Jake added, "Good God, you don't want to give your son fresh ammunition."

Clare made a face. "I guess not. Although I hate to let him have his way when he acts like that."

"I couldn't have stayed, anyway," Jake lied, then made it the truth. "I intend to catch a ferry tonight."

"Then let me walk you out to your car," she said, and he nodded.

Just having her stroll beside him made his heart cramp with painful pleasure and remembrance. She was small and slender and naturally graceful. On their frequent long beach jaunts, she'd often walked, as she did now, with her head bent, as though she searched for something—or didn't want to meet his eyes. On the beach she'd had an excuse—occasionally she pounced with delight on a sand dollar, creamy gray and filigreed. Once she'd found one that was fuzzy and purple, and, sure it was still alive, she'd insisted on throwing it back into the ocean, as though she couldn't admit it was doomed.

Jake gave his head a shake, trying to rid it of the incessant memories. He found that he'd stopped by the driver's side door, and Clare was gazing inquiringly at him.

Wondering what had shown on his face, Jake said neutrally, "I'll see you Saturday, then."

"Fine." There was something tart in her voice, but then she smiled, and her eyes were, for a moment, clear and bottomless. "Have a good trip, Jake."

In their acquaintance, her smiles had been rare, and this one sent blood roaring through his veins. To disguise his intense reaction, he turned away and opened the car door.

"Jake..." She sounded tentative.

He waited, shoulders rigid.

"Do you have a new neighbor in Oregon? Did Larry Forbes rebuild?"

"Yes." When he'd walked that way only six weeks after Don Talbot's funeral and seen a cement truck pouring a new foundation, Jake hadn't known whether to rejoice that the black scar that marked the place of Don's death had been healed, or outraged that it hadn't been left in remembrance. Now Jake had to clear his throat. "Not the same style. It's one-story, modern. A couple's renting it. He's a painter. She's doing her residency at the hospital."

"Are they nice?"

"I suppose so." He'd nodded at the man in passing, but hadn't tried to get to know them. He'd wanted Clare there, not these strangers.

"You won't miss your house? And the ocean?"

He couldn't keep standing here with his back to her. Turning back around, he shrugged and told her the bald truth. "It was too damned lonely."

She was searching his face, her expression grave. "You used to tell me you liked to be by yourself."

Until I met you.

He opened his mouth to take the easy way out, to say something offputting like, "I still prefer to be by myself." But he'd come here, home to the island, prepared to saw off the heavy cast that had protected the boy who'd fled all those years ago. So he made himself tell the truth.

"I got used to having you and Don and Mike there. You made me realize how antisocial I'd become."

She gave a low humorless laugh. "And we were there hiding from the world. It's ironic that we'd be the ones to draw you out into it."

He captured and held her gaze. "Maybe it goes to show that you can't hide from it."

Fleeting sadness touched her voice. "Very likely." She took a step back and nodded. "Until Saturday."

In the rearview mirror he saw that Clare stood looking after him, instead of hurrying back inside to see to either her dinner or her rebellious teenager. Not for the first time, Jake thought about what a raw deal that marriage had been for her. A year or two of happiness, then Don's descent into hell. Six or seven years younger than Don, she'd had to take over: earn a living, make the decisions, see that he took his medication, comfort him, raise his son. Plenty of women wouldn't have stuck around for the final act of the tragedy, but her doubts had never been about the right thing to do for herself. Her worries had all been for Don. Don, and the boy whose mother she'd unhesitatingly become.

Maybe, Jake reflected once a turn in the road hid her from view, that was what drew him so powerfully to her: Clare's love and loyalty, once given, never wavered. And, by God, under the force of Don's despair and rage, most people's would have.

Jake had been deluding himself that she would hand that love over to him. All because it had been to him she'd turned when she was lowest. Hell, he thought bleakly, he'd been there. Nobody else had. Now that she didn't need him anymore, she didn't like being reminded that once she had.

Which didn't mean he couldn't make her need him again. All he had to do was figure out how.

CHAPTER FOUR

IF ATTENDANCE WAS the goal, the Parent Association potluck was a whopping success for two reasons. First, the October weather was sunny and warm. Instead of being in the middle-school multipurpose room, the picnic took place at the county park, nestled on a gravel beach on the leeward side of the island. Along with tables, the park provided volleyball and tennis courts. On a day like this, why not come?

The second reason was the fact that everyone wanted to gossip. Right away Clare overheard one of the teachers announce that she'd talked to Jean Kirk, who'd said, "You can darn well bet we're going to rebuild! We've spent a lot of happy summers on the island, and we plan to keep spending them there!"

Another woman flipped a burger on the barbecue. "I thought they needed the insurance money. I guess it wasn't true, then."

Clare passed that group, clustered around the barbecue pits, and set down her chicken casserole on the table among the other offerings. Then she wandered on. But the adults watching the volleyball game were having the same discussion.

Bart Petersen, tall and sandy-haired, yelled encouragement to a boy who made a diving try at the ball. Then he shook his head at a comment Clare didn't catch.

"Maybe it was teenagers," he said, "but I'm not sure I buy that. We haven't had this kind of trouble before. The Kirks swear there wasn't anything in the cottage worth stealing. Didn't even have a TV."

"All you have to do is read the paper," argued a third man, whom Clare didn't know. "Cities are full of senseless crime. It's a contagion creeping everywhere. We'd be foolish to deny it's reaching us, too."

"Damned right!" snapped the one whose comment had apparently started the exchange. He turned his head, and Clare recognized Roger Mullin, the father of one of Mike's friends. Today a baseball cap covered Roger's receding hairline, and plaid shorts and a polo shirt displayed stocky, hairy arms and legs. "We may not have gangs yet," he continued, "but we have troubled kids, all right. We could all name a few. I say the cops should take a good look at them before somebody else's house gets torched."

"I'm not so sure I could name any," Bart said. "You got somebody in mind, why don't you tell us?"

All three jumped back to avoid an errant serve. Clare didn't get out of the way quickly enough. Roger stepped hard on her toes.

"Clare!" He grabbed her elbows. "I'm sorry. Are you all right?"

She wriggled her toes inside her canvas slip-ons and winced. "I'll live to dance again." When he started to repeat his apology, she shook her head. "That's what I get for eavesdropping."

"Lucky I didn't spout off more, then." His rueful grin looked a little forced to her. "Excuse me. I'd better go see what that kid of mine is up to."

Puzzled, she watched him hurry away. Had she said something wrong? Or was *he* the one who'd said something wrong?

But Bart distracted her. "Listen, Clare. I told Mike, too. Don't you hesitate to call if you hear anything strange during the night. I know you're a feminist, and I don't want to offend you, but fact is you don't have a man around. That fire being right in our neighborhood doesn't sit well with me. We need to band together just in case."

"Thanks, Bart," she said, smiling. "I'll do that. I take it the authorities aren't any closer to arresting anyone."

"Tom says not." His older brother was a volunteer fireman, Clare knew. "Somebody poured gasoline all over the back porch and tossed a match on it. Damn near exploded, dry as everything is."

"So it wasn't a break-in." Insofar as she'd let herself think about the fire, she'd been hoping it had been set to cover up a burglary. She'd rather believe that explanation than to think somebody had set the blaze just for fun.

"Doesn't look like it," Bart agreed. His wife wandered up just then, and he laid a casual arm across her shoulders. "Arsonist was taking a chance of being seen, right in sight of the road like that. If he'd already been in the house, why not start the fire there?"

"Not that big a chance," Sally protested. "It was pitch-dark and late enough—what, midnight, one o'clock?—that nobody was out and about."

"The Kirks had the kind of floodlights that sense movement," Bart said. "If I'd been going by and seen those lights on, I'd sure have glanced toward the house. Maybe done more than that, since I knew they weren't here."

The arsonist had taken a real risk. Midnight wasn't so late that some residents might not still be up. Old Mrs. Brewer was right next door. All she'd have had to do was glance out the window.

Yes, Clare's inner voice whispered, but if the arsonist was a local, he'd have known the old lady was in the habit of going to bed early. The only comforting part of that reflection was that he'd also have known the Kirks weren't there. Probably their absence was why he'd chosen their house.

Giving a shiver despite the warmth of the day, Clare said, "I don't even like to think about it."

Sally, a stay-at-home mother with two preschoolers and a first-grader, lowered her voice. "Bart and I were wondering about the Carlsons. You've got to admit, they're strange people."

Bart nodded in agreement. "They're always talking about doomsday and that end-of-the-world crap. Hell, maybe they thought they'd hurry it along. Or scare some people away so they could snap up more land."

"The Kirks' lot is only ninety-by-two-hundred feet," Clare pointed out. "It's not big enough to farm."

"Got that old orchard, though. And it's right across the road from the Carlsons' place. Would give 'em access to the bay."

Clare was shaking her head long before he finished. "Phyllis brought me homemade soup and bread when she heard I was sick. And Tony helped me get my car started last winter when the battery was dead. Arsonists aren't neighborly."

"How many arsonists do you know?" His wife's elbow in his ribs brought Bart to a stop, and a flush crept up his neck. "Oh, hell, Clare, I'm sorry. Talk about sticking my foot in it. You know I didn't mean . . ."

Just like that, Clare felt the sting of unshed tears. But her voice was steady. "Don't worry about it, Bart. And you're right. I only knew one."

"Clare..." Sally reached out a hand.

Clare touched it. "It's okay. Hey, look at the line forming. Shall we? I don't know about you, but I'm hungry."

She grabbed a paper plate and utensils and inserted herself between two near-strangers, which kept the conversation to common ground: whose kids had what teachers, whether the week-long achievement tests were a waste of valuable time or a useful indicator for the administration, whether the new math curriculum was revolutionary or nutty.

Clare succeeded in dodging the Petersens for the rest of the afternoon, but not the talk about the fire. Most of the community was here, not just those with children. Among others, were Suzette Fowler with the high-school principal and Alison Pierce with a man who looked like Bart Petersen, only taller and heavier; his older brother, Tom, she decided. Clare usually enjoyed these occasions; she'd grown up in a small town and liked the closeness of life here. But the gossip showed another side to it. She'd have been tempted to cut out early if she hadn't also been reluctant to be home when Jake came by for the key to the Mueller house.

Just knowing he was probably back on the island made her feel edgy, *alive* in an uncomfortable way. She'd almost felt let down these past couple of days, knowing she wouldn't see him. But the interlude had also been a relief, the chance to give herself a good talking-to. She was acting as though she was afraid of him, which was ridiculous. He'd been a good friend to her and—although her husband hadn't recognized it—to Don. Now Jake claimed to be attracted to her. But he hadn't shown it when Don was alive and hadn't acted on it. And while she'd been attracted to him, she hadn't acted on *her* feelings, either, and had done her best to hide them. So although she might feel guilty for being aware of another man while she was married, that was as far as it'd gone. Or ever would go. She'd be pleasant to Jake and leave it at that.

But she would just as soon not have to be pleasant today.

Although Mike had been grounded this week, she'd brought him along to the picnic, figuring it was for a good cause. Besides, she didn't want him home when Jake arrived, either. Now Mike horsed around with his friends, including Ian Mullin, played volleyball and stuffed his face. Other than discreetly keeping tabs on him, Clare ignored her stepson. God forbid that they had one of their increasingly disagreeable confrontations in front of the entire community.

But when she decided to leave, she let him know she was going. "If you'll promise to come straight home, I don't mind if you stay for a while."

His lip curled. "You want me to stay so you can see *Jake* alone?"

Clare felt a headache coming on. "You know better than that."

His eyes were hostile. "Do I?"

"Fine," she said from between clenched teeth. "Then come. I don't care." Clare turned to find that in addition to Mike's friends, they had another audience, including Roger Mullin, both the Petersen brothers and the women with them—Suzette and Alison.

Great. Now everyone on the island would know that Mike hated Jake Radovich and thought she—to use a crude term—had the hots for him.

She grimaced apologetically at the group, said, "Teenagers," and walked away, Mike on her heels. She could feel his sulkiness, as if it were her own vapor trail.

They didn't speak in the car until they'd nearly reached their turnoff. These days, this was a natural state of affairs. They hadn't had a normal conversation since Mike's outburst in front of Jake. *She* wasn't in the mood for conversation now.

But Mike said unexpectedly, "All the guys were talking about the fire."

She glanced at him, knowing she'd be an idiot to squelch his tentative attempt at civil relations. "Adults, too."

"Who do you think did it?" Amazingly he sounded as if he really cared.

"I don't have a clue," Clare admitted, slowing to make the turn. "Everybody else seems to have a theory, but none of them feels right to me. Who do you think?"

"I don't know, either." He frowned, looking straight ahead. "Ian says his dad thinks it's teenagers, but that can't be right. I mean, nobody's talking. Usually somebody brags. Like, what's the point of doing it if nobody knows you did?"

"That kind of destructiveness is generally a bid for attention," she agreed. "Having everyone know you did it *is* the point."

Silence again. They were passing the bed-and-breakfast when Mike said in a subdued voice, "Do you think Dad was really trying to kill himself? Or was he trying to get attention?"

"Neither," she said, then, "Oh, hell," at the same time as her stepson exclaimed, "He *is* here!"

"You know he had to pick up the key to his house." Clare strove for a disinterested tone. "I expected him to have come and gone by now."

But Jake's Porsche undeniably sat in her dirt driveway, albeit carefully parked on the verge to allow room for her to pass. She pulled in, and there he was, rebuilding her porch steps. At the moment he was wielding a circular saw on a slab of lumber braced on two old sawhorses. Sawdust collected beneath it.

"Did you ask him to do that?"

Clare turned off the engine. "No, I can't say that I did."

They sat there. Sounding very young and less sure of himself, Mike asked, "Well, then, why's he doing it?"

"Because we used to be good friends?" she ventured. "Because he feels guilty for abandoning us there at the end?"

"Abandoning us?" Mike looked baffled. "What do you mean?"

So that wasn't the explanation for Mike's anger at Jake.

Slowly she said, "I never saw him again after that day." The hurt and bewilderment were as fresh as they'd been a year ago, when her phone calls went unanswered and Don's best friend couldn't be bothered to come to his funeral. She hid her sharp emotions. "Didn't you ever wonder where Jake was?"

Mike's voice was tentative. "I guess maybe I was too upset."

"Well, I wasn't." If she sounded grim, so be it. But rather than leaving Mike with that, she touched his arm. "About that question you asked earlier. I don't think your dad was trying to get attention *or* kill himself. I think he was trying to cure himself.''

Mike's head swung toward her. ''What?''

''You know how he heard voices and always thought somebody was watching him. I think he was trying to kill whoever it was tormenting him. He may have really believed he'd be left on the other side of the fire, cleansed. Sometimes he didn't . . . reason very well.''

''Oh.'' The one word was said in a small voice. Clare watched as Mike thought it over. They'd talked about his father's death shortly after the fire, and Clare had said much the same thing as she was saying now. But back then, still in shock, Mike probably hadn't taken it all in.

That was fine, but what she still didn't get was why he was angry at Jake, too.

Taking a deep breath, she got out of the car, retrieved her empty casserole dish from the back seat and walked toward the house.

''Afraid one of the steps would collapse the next time you came over?'' she called to Jake.

He'd been working as though he was unaware of their arrival, which she didn't believe for a second. Now he straightened, his wary gaze meeting hers. ''I noticed it needed doing,'' he said simply.

''You should be tinkering with your new house.'' Clare stopped beside him. She could sense Mike right behind her.

''What's to do there?'' Jake said mildly, that remote expression on his lean face giving absolutely nothing away. Shrugging, he added, ''The movers won't be here until Tuesday. I was bored.''

He was bored. Great. Edging his way back into her life was apparently to be his entertainment. And she, guiltily conscious of how she'd used him, how desperately she'd once needed him, couldn't say, "Go find something else to do. Don't come back."

Instead, good manners produced a stilted response. "This is thoughtful of you, Jake."

A muscle twitched in one cheek, only that flicker telling her he was no more comfortable than she was. Then his gaze moved from her to Mike and he said easily, "Want to give me a hand?"

Clare braced herself, but—not for the first time—her stepson surprised her. He tried to sound sullen, but some little-boy eagerness crept through. "I guess. It's not like I have anything better to do."

She wasted no time in making her getaway. "I'll just leave you to it, then," she said with the kind of false cheeriness she normally despised.

Jake didn't comment. By the time she awkwardly clambered up onto the porch and the screen door slammed behind her, he was already explaining how to use a circular saw. Which renewed her feeling of inadequacy as a parent. There were all too many 'guy' things she had to hope her stepson picked up from some friend's father. The idea of Jake's teaching them, instead, boggled her mind.

Except, she thought, frowning as she ran hot water and poured soap into the crusty casserole dish, that Jake *had* done things for Mike before. She had a sudden picture of the two of them clamming at a low tide, both in old sweaters and jeans and enormous rubber boots, heads together as they peered into their bucket. Mike had been eleven then; Don hadn't yet decided that Jake couldn't be trusted. They'd all eaten together that night, clam chowder and homemade bread, her contribution, and they'd laughed. Don had seemed almost his old self. She remembered her feeling of hope, her congratulations to herself that they'd made the right decision.

Clare gave her head a shake, but failed to clear it of memories. There had been other times. Jake faithfully went to Mike's basketball games, for example, although that last winter Mike hadn't seemed to want him there. And the two had made a birdhouse together, with a copper roof and a grinning cat's face on the front. In that last sad expedition, when she and Mike had wandered through the blackened ruins salvaging what was left from the fire, they'd found the birdhouse, singed but intact. They'd taken it down from the garage and brought it with them. Mike had intended to repaint it. She wondered what had happened to the birdhouse, and whether Mike remembered making it with Jake.

Sinking onto a chair at the kitchen table, Clare heard the buzz of the saw outside, followed by a quiet deep voice. In her determination not to think about that time, she'd put the good things out of her mind, too. The truth was, Jake had always been there for Mike, although Mike had begun to reject him that last year when things got so bad. When Don started hiding his medicine again; when he decided to hate her, too.

Wrapped up in her own troubles, she'd taken for granted Jake's willingness to step into Don's shoes when Mike needed a father figure. Taken it so much for granted she hadn't thought about the fact that Jake had surely spent as much time with Mike as he had with her. She recalled how, the day she'd shown Jake the Mueller house, he'd asked, oh so casually, "Is Mike home?"

Maybe Jake hadn't come after them because of her. Maybe it was because of Mike. After all, Jake and Don had been best friends. Jake had told her once that he owed Don.

Maybe he'd decided the time had come to pay back that debt. Maybe *she* had nothing to do with it.

And why, she asked herself, was the thought so unsettling?

HE SHOULDN'T HAVE STAYED for dinner. Mike had—almost—relaxed and accepted him while they worked outside. The minute Clare stepped out onto the porch, the boy reverted to sullenness. He didn't want his mother anywhere near Jake.

Smart kid. He was reading the undercurrents better than she was. If Jake had had any self-control, he wouldn't have stayed. But, damnation, he'd waited so long, and here she was, almost in his grasp. Sitting at the table, he could've reached out and touched her hand as she set down a serving bowl. Such a small hand, delicate, yet strong.

He shut his eyes on a stab of pure sexual hunger. When he opened them, Mike was staring at him with hate, just as pure. And Clare was looking from one to the other, her expression bewildered.

Jake cleared his throat. But his voice was still hoarse. "I'd forgotten how good your lasagna is."

The boy's eyes, brown like his father's, narrowed.

"It's only leftovers." She poked at the food on her plate. "Just today I was remembering how good your clam chowder was. You and Mike went clamming a couple of times."

So she was spending more time dwelling on the past than she wanted him to know. Or else for some reason she had chosen to help his cause with her stepson.

"I was supposed to go clamming with Geoff." It was at his mother that Mike looked accusingly. "And you wouldn't let me."

"Beast that I am," she said lightly.

Jake hated seeing her so tense. She'd hardly eaten a bite herself, she was so busy making sure everyone else had food and contributing the kind of conversation that wouldn't light flares. Seeing her now, back perfectly straight, fingers playing with the edges of her napkin, smile trembling almost imperceptibly, Jake was angry at the fates that had cursed her to living with perpetual uncertainty.

He heard her again. *You don't know the hell life becomes when nothing is ever predictable.* He'd assumed she meant life with Don, but now he wondered. Mike was obviously a pain in the ass. She'd admitted to financial insecurity. Here he'd spent the past year imagining her regaining the inner serenity he'd seen slowly erode. But maybe things weren't all that much better, even with Don gone.

Hell, face it, he told himself. *You wanted to think she'd be better off without you. You were too damned scared of Don's ghost to help her then, when she needed you.*

"Thanks for dinner." He blundered to his feet. "I'd better be going."

He couldn't blame Clare if that was relief he saw mixed with her surprise.

"Already? Well, let me at least walk you out and admire the steps again."

Damned if the boy didn't shoot to his feet, too, and trail them, an oppressive chaperon. Out front, Clare dutifully approved their work, trying to include the sullen kid in her praise. Mike's only response was a sneer.

He didn't, however, follow them up the drive, only stood on the porch and watched. Jake stopped beside his car. Jerking his head toward the house, he said, "Is Mike always like this?"

Clare bit her lip and said in a low voice, "No, thank goodness. We've had our...troubles, but sometimes we're friends. Actually it's a little dizzying. I never know whether I'll be coming home to the nice kid or the snotty teenager." She looked down, evading Jake's gaze. "To tell you the truth, he's been worse since you came back. I don't know what's going on."

Was she really oblivious, or did she not want to acknowledge with words the sexual tension between them? Jake had no trouble figuring out what was behind the boy's behavior. To test his belief, he reached out and lifted her chin. Her jawbone was so fragile, her skin so soft, that his intention blurred, and he damn near forgot the boy. Her eyes, huge and deep blue, captured his, and the tremble of her lips was an irresistible lure. His head bent and he ached to feel that quiver with his mouth, to release a small part of the anguished longing that had gripped him ever since he'd gotten to know this woman, his best friend's wife.

But with his peripheral vision he saw Mike launch himself down the porch steps two at a time, outrage personified, and Jake froze before he had the chance to taste her lips. "I think," he said gruffly, instead, "your stepson is about to yank you away from temptation."

Clare sucked in a breath and leapt back. "I..." Her voice was high, breathless. The next instant it was furious. "Damn it, Jake!" She cast a hunted glance toward Mike, who skidded to a stop. Her breasts rose and fell with a deep steadying breath. "Goodbye," she said firmly, even coldly.

Without waiting for a response, she turned and stalked toward the house. Mike gave Jake one more narrow-eyed hate-filled look, then followed her.

Jake waited until he was in his car before he swore, slowly and bitterly. Don's ghost might be exorcised, but his son was a considerably more solid obstacle standing between himself and the woman he wanted.

DURING THE NIGHT, Clare heard the long undulating wail that summoned the volunteer firemen. Her eyes snapped open and she stared into the dark, listening to the sirens. Oh, God, she thought, and climbed out of bed to go to the window. Outside was only night, layers of black on black, still and mysterious. Clare didn't smell smoke, saw no distant glow of orange.

From the silent hall she could see only darkness through the window in Mike's bedroom. She heard no stirrings; he must still be asleep.

Shivering, though the night wasn't cold, Clare slipped back into bed, curling on her side as though to hug to herself warmth or primal reassurance. Although the sirens died, she had trouble falling asleep again. She tried to convince herself that the emergency was a medical one. Maybe somebody had had a heart attack and needed an aid car. Bad enough, but not arson. Yet every time she closed her eyes, she saw the Kirks' place, the glittering arcs of crisscrossing water powerless to quell the fiery orange breath of the beast. Or *was* it the Kirks'?

For the first time in months, Clare let the memories come....

A THIN LINE of dark smoke rose above the trees, etching the blue sky. Clare had only idly noticed it as she drove home from town with her groceries in the trunk of the car. At the moment there was no county ban on outside burning, so there was nothing unusual about seeing smoke. This was a deep oily color that made her think it would give off an unpleasant smell, but with luck the fire was downwind of her house.

As she slowed to turn off the highway, Clare felt a familiar knotting in her stomach. Almost home, her brief pretense at freedom gone. She was suddenly aware that she'd been humming as she drove. She hadn't hummed or sung aloud to herself for so long that now the contrast was painful. Those few minutes of mindless contentment made her dread seem sharper.

The narrow country road she'd turned onto was shadowed by tall firs. A few driveways cut up the ridge through the woods to houses that perched above. One more turn. Suddenly she smelled the smoke. At almost the same instant, she came out of the trees. Directly ahead, thick black smoke roiled now in an angry cloud, darkening the sky. Even with the windows rolled up, the smell was stronger—burning wood, with a bite of something else. Gasoline?

A new fear clutched at her, and Clare pressed the accelerator. As the narrow road climbed the last hill, the ocean came into sight first, then the rocky point. She was driving far too fast, knowing what she would find even as she refused to let herself accept it.

She passed the first driveway plunging into the trees, then the second. Had somebody called in an alarm? But she couldn't stop. This close to the fire, the smoke had turned day into night. When she steered the car into the narrow track that led to her rented oceanfront home, she knew there was no longer any doubt. And when she emerged from the trees, she had to slam on the brakes. What had been a cedar-shingled glass-fronted home was now an inferno, a blast of red flames. Through the fire she could see the stark bones of the house being eaten alive, and it was like a glimpse of hell.

"Oh, God."

The car lurched and then died as her foot slipped off the clutch. Clare scrambled out, flinching as the wall of heat hit. Now she could hear the crackle and a deep-throated roar that made her think of dragons or demons. She barely felt the first tears that slipped hotly down her cheeks, but she knew when she started to scream.

"Don! Mike! Oh, God!"

She was running. Not toward the house—that was impossible. But around it, praying even as she screamed their names that she would find her husband and stepson standing on the beach side, holding each other as they waited for help.

Burning cinders rained on the lawn and Clare felt a sting on her cheek, which she brushed at as she stumbled and kept going. "Don! Mike! Please..." She coughed as her feet sank into the sand and she looked frantically around. No one. Surely, dear God, no matter what Don had done to himself, he wouldn't have let his son die this way!

Clare couldn't tear her eyes away from the house even as the heat seared her face and the smoke stung her lungs. One wall fell with a groan, tearing the roof with it. The colors were so intense, orange and blue and red, incandescent against the thick blackness of the smoke.

Suddenly in the far distance she heard sirens. The smoke could probably be seen all the way in town. Another wall went, and her body echoed the shudder of the house.

Clare sensed more than saw the figure that appeared from the trees. For a moment she didn't turn her head. What did it matter? If Don or Mike had gone to a neighbor's to call, they would've been back by now. But when she did look...

"Mike?" She couldn't manage more than a whisper.

The boy walked toward her, staring at the fire. "Wow," he said when he got close enough. "What happened?"

Clare looked incredulously at him. "What happened? My God, Mike. Our house..." Her throat seemed to close and she couldn't go on.

He tore his fascinated gaze from the flames, raising his voice so she could hear him over the crackle. "Well, we didn't own it, anyway. I mean, it's awful, but look at those colors. I wish I had my camera."

"Mike—"

"Where's Dad? Did he go call the firemen?"

She couldn't have answered to save her life. The fire trucks were almost here. Too late. Much too late.

The thirteen-year-old's thin dark face had changed. First he looked angry. "*Where's Dad?* How come he's not here, too?"

She could only shake her head.

He shot a look at the conflagration, then at her. "Clare..." Mike was pleading, and when she didn't answer he stumbled back. "He was with you. He went to town with you. He said he was!"

"He...he didn't go."

A wail rose in his throat and he lurched toward the burning house, which was crashing inward on itself. Clare grabbed his arm and held on when he fought desperately.

"Let me go! I have to find Dad! I have to! Let me go!"

Only when strong arms pinioned Mike did she release him. Holding the boy effortlessly, the dark-haired man who'd magically appeared turned his intensity on her. "Clare, where's Don?"

Her gaze swung toward the blaze. Beyond it, hazily, she could see the fire trucks, with streams of water directed not at what had been her home, but at the trees and garage. When she looked back at her neighbor, she knew he could read the answer on her face.

For the first time in the year and a half she'd known him well, she saw raw emotion in his dark gray eyes. Pity, and pain for her. And perhaps more, despite everything, for Don. It was the last thought that allowed her to go into Jake Radovich's arms. She held Mike and Mike held her and somehow Don's mysterious friend held both of them. Jake's strength was almost enough to shut out the horror. Almost.

CLARE AWOKE with a start and struggled to sit up. She was trapped, her nightgown twisted around her waist and the sheet tangling with her legs. Pale morning sunlight, not blocked by the blinds she hadn't drawn, lay in a wide band across her bed.

With a whimper, she fell back against the pillow. Memories and dreams were as tangled as her bedding. Don's death... But there was more, a nightmare. That same nightmare in which Jake was her savior or her tormentor, she was never sure which. Always the fire and the smoke confused her, made her turn to him or run from him. And sirens—they had cried in her sleep like a lost child, haunting her.

No, she remembered suddenly. The sirens weren't in her dream. She *had* heard them in the middle of the night; they were as real as her memories.

It was still early, but she got up and showered, anyway. As she dried herself with a thick towel, Clare caught a glimpse of her face in the mirror, cheeks pale, shadows like bruises beneath her eyes. She was letting all this get to her—the fires, Jake's return, Mike's defiance. Good God, the fires had nothing to do with her! Mike was just going through a difficult stage, and Jake she could ignore.

So why, her inner voice whispered, *had she invited him to dinner last night?*

Clare shook off that voice and went downstairs, brewing coffee and nibbling on toast slathered with homemade jam. It was Sunday, but they'd go to the late service this morning so that Mike could sleep in. She had time for a walk on the beach, which always soothed her.

This morning the tide was low, with gulls fighting over tidbits out on the slick rock-studded flats. Sharp in her nostrils was the pungent smell of fish and salt water and seaweed. Far out, the bay was unusually still. It wasn't until she'd nearly reached the Muellers' house—no, Jake's house—that Clare realized which direction she'd unconsciously chosen. She almost stopped and turned back, but innate stubbornness kept her feet moving. She would not let Jake's presence shape her life. The beach wasn't private, and she especially liked the views this way.

The house, brown and angular and glittering where morning sunlight touched tall windows, came in sight first. A second later, Clare saw the police car parked in front.

Why it was there was none of her business, but she started up the steep steps, anyway, even if she had no idea what she would do when she reached the top. Knock on Jake's door and insist he tell her what was going on? Sneak up and peek through the window? Press an ear to the door?

But she had to do neither. Jake and a uniformed officer came out the front door just as she topped the bank. Both men saw her immediately, and she had no choice except to walk across the lawn toward them.

She almost succeeded in sounding casual. "Is something wrong?"

Jake stayed silent, but she felt the anger crackling beneath his closed expression. The police officer glanced at him, then back at her. "And you are?"

"Clare Talbot. I'm a neighbor."

"Ah." His tone told her that he knew something about her, though she couldn't guess what. "Well, Mrs. Talbot, we had another case of arson last night. The bookstore in town."

"The bookstore?" She didn't know why the idea was so surprising. "Then why...?"

"Why is he here?" Jake sounded no more than ironic, but again she read the undertone and knew he was nowhere near that detached.

"I'm sorry." They must have thought her inexcusably nosy. "It's none of my business."

"Everybody will know soon enough. It seems," Jake said, in the tone of a mere observer, "that the arsonist used a pile of copies of my latest book to set this fire. Interesting critical comment, wouldn't you say?"

CHAPTER FIVE

YELLOW CRIME-SCENE TAPE blocked the front entrance to More and More Books. After parking her car, Clare was drawn like a dozen other townsfolk to gawk into the soggy charred interior of the shop.

Actually, she was surprised to realize, most of the damage she could see was from the water. One of the front windows had either exploded from the heat or been broken by the firemen, and just inside, in what had been a cozy reading area, was a blackened semicircle centered on a small heap of what were recognizably books. Flung atop each other, fanned open, they were still dense enough to have burned slowly. One on top was scarcely singed. Far larger than the title was the author's name, proclaimed in huge black type: Jacob Stanek.

Suzette Fowler, a fire fighter and two men dressed in civilian clothes were huddled around the damaged area. Clare recognized one: the marshal who'd interviewed her after the fire at the Kirks'. Suzette was shaking her head vehemently and waving her hand at the heaped books while the men, no doubt detectives, watched her, their expressions curiously impassive.

With an unpleasant shock, Clare realized that Suzette was now automatically a suspect, just as the Kirks had been. If Suzette was well insured, both the authorities and the gossips would wonder whether she needed the money. Clare hadn't heard her complain that business was slow this year, but that didn't mean Suzette wasn't in financial difficulty. She wasn't the sort to whine. In fact, there were those who didn't like her, who considered her unfriendly. Despite having lived here all her life, she tended to keep to herself.

Well, not entirely to herself. She and the high-school principal were having a torrid affair—versus mere dating—if rumor was to be believed. Clare *had* believed it, and all because the principal's car had been spotted in front of Suzette's small beachfront cottage in the early hours of the morning. Clare didn't even remember who'd seen it.

With a shiver she retreated. Always before, the whispers and the gossip had been about trivialities, harmless, an accepted part of living in a small community. But now those same whispers could shatter a life. Would Suzette guess what people in the crowd were already murmuring?

After a morning spent brooding, Clare marched back over to the bookstore at lunchtime. The yellow tape was gone; a Closed sign hung on the doorknob, but the door opened when Clare tried it.

"Hello?" she called.

"We're not open," a voice answered.

Clare followed it through the store and into the alley out back, to find Suzette in jeans, T-shirt and work gloves, heaving boxes full of books into the Dumpster.

Suzette Fowler, along with Bart Petersen, Alison Pierce and Jake, had been in Don's high-school class, which meant that Suzette was in her midthirties now. She was a small, plump woman with an intense way of looking at you when you talked. Clare found it most unnerving. She always felt as if her polite but unexciting conversation must be disappointing Suzette.

But now Clare said to the other woman's back, "Hi. I wondered if you could use a hand cleaning up."

The bookstore owner jerked around. "Oh, Lord, you scared me!" she exclaimed. Then, "Do you mean it? Bless you, if you really have the free time."

"Not a soul has walked into the office all morning," Clare said. "I was getting bored."

"I have some extra gloves." Suzette headed briskly back into the store. "Wet books are going straight into the Dumpster. Dry ones go over here."

Clare looked with dismay at the children's section where Suzette had steered her. "They're all going to be thrown away? What a waste!"

"No kidding." The other woman's voice had hardened as she gazed around. "I don't know whether to be madder at the arsonist or the fire fighters. If they'd used their brains, I could've salvaged more."

"I figured you had sprinklers."

"Nope. What's the point? Water is as bad as fire in this business."

"Will insurance pay for your inventory?"

"More or less." Suzette blinked rapidly, and Clare was startled to realize that she was fighting back angry tears. "It's just so damned personal! Why me? Why not the hardware store or your real-estate office or...?" Her face twisted and she wiped her wet cheeks with the back of one gloved hand. "I sound like I'm wishing my misfortune on someone else, don't I?"

"I wouldn't call it a misfortune. This wasn't exactly an act of God."

"That's for damned sure!" Suzette snapped.

"Does the fire marshal have any idea who...?"

"Lord, no. Obviously it was set. Somebody broke in through a rear window, dumped a bunch of books on the floor and set the fire. The spent match is still lying there. But I do have a smoke alarm, so the fire itself didn't get very far. Even so, the arsonist was long gone by the time the fire trucks arrived.''

"He didn't use gasoline, like at the Kirks'?''

The tears were gone. Suzette Fowler had herself back in hand. "Nope. Probably figured the books in here were plenty flammable. Either that, or he's an opportunist. There was gas in the Kirks' garage. I don't have any reason to keep gas around.'' She sighed. "Well. Let me get you those gloves.''

They worked in silence but for Clare's occasional request for guidance. She got angrier herself as she checked books off the inventory list, then dumped armful after armful out.

After seeing Suzette, Clare didn't want to believe that the woman had tried to burn down her own store for the insurance money. Yet it was conceivable, wasn't it, that she was furious, not at the waste, but at the fire fighters, who'd responded so quickly that the store hadn't been completely destroyed.

And what was the alternative? That somebody had set the fire for fun?

Clare returned from a trip to the Dumpster to hear Suzette talking to somebody up front. Clare knew that deep quiet voice even before she saw Jake, dark and looming against the brilliant square of window without glass. He stood with his hands shoved in the pockets of his jeans, his head bent as he looked down at the burned books.

As Clare approached unnoticed, he said, "I think this was aimed at me, not you.''

Suzette poked at the pile of blackened books with one toe. "They're not all yours.''

"Where were mine shelved?"

"That's just it. They were handy. I had your latest displayed right here in front." Suzette gestured ruefully at the bay window, where a few soaked books lay amidst shattered glass. "Your others were over here in the fiction section."

Clare had already looked. "You don't have a single copy of a Jacob Stanek left."

Both Jake and Suzette turned sharply. Jake's eyes narrowed for a heartbeat. "Clare."

Suzette appraised her speculatively. "You know he's Stanek?"

"I didn't realize *you* knew."

"We're old friends."

Clare looked at Jake, her head held high. "Was I the only one who was oblivious?"

"You had reason." Had his voice softened?

"To be completely self-absorbed?" Deliberately Clare swung her gaze back to Suzette. "I don't know whether you had any of his books in the paperback mystery section, but there aren't any now."

"Yes, a couple copies each of, oh, four or five titles." Suzette's years suddenly showed in lines on either side of her mouth. "I didn't think to look this morning, even though the marshal was interested in the fact that Jake's were on top. Clare, are you sure?"

Suzette moved toward the back of the store, disappearing behind freestanding shelves.

"What are you doing here?" Jake asked roughly.

"I figured Suzette could use some help." Clare tried to smile. "I know what it feels like to pick through charred ruins."

"You couldn't have found much to save after *your* fire." She hated the pity in his dark gray eyes. "I looked the next day."

"Did you?" she said. "I didn't see you."

"I saw you." Just like that, his voice was raw.

Clare stared incredulously at him. "You were there, *watching?* Then why—"

She was interrupted by Suzette's return. "You're right," Suzette said flatly. "They were all burned."

"Hell." Jake rubbed the back of his neck. "Suzette, how many people know who I am?"

"Not that many. Those of us who do keep our mouths shut. Even me, and I'd profit from spreading the word."

"If it's you he's after, Jake, why didn't he burn your house?" Clare asked. "Why the Kirks'?"

"Maybe he doesn't know I've bought a place or that I've moved in so fast."

"But still," she said stubbornly, "what do you and the Kirks have in common?"

"Good point," Suzette said. "Maybe our friendly local arsonist doesn't happen to like your writing, and this was just another bad review."

Jake gave a bark of laughter. "It isn't any worse than the last one the *L.A. Times* gave me."

Clare wasn't really listening. Frowning down at the stark graphics on the jacket of his latest hard cover, she said consideringly, "Maybe it isn't *you* at all. Maybe it's something you wrote about. Like arson."

"No arson." Nonetheless, he sounded thoughtful. "But I suppose it's possible that somebody saw himself in one of my books and didn't like the reflection."

"Suzette, I just heard—" The man who burst in the front door of the store stopped when he saw Jake and

Clare. Then he took a quick look around. "Oh, my God. It's true."

Suzette went to him. His arms closed tightly around her for a brief embrace. Then she faced the others again, her expression softer. "Stephen, do you know Jake Radovich and Clare Talbot?"

"Clare I've met." He gave her a smile, which she returned. The high-school principal had really been very nice when Mike and Geoff were caught toilet-papering the girl's rest room. "Jake."

As the two men shook hands, Clare thought what a complete contrast they were. Stephen Hadfield was several inches shorter than Jake and thin, built like the runner he was. Blond, he had open friendly features. Next to him, Jake looked large, dark and reserved to the point of coldness.

"Shall we conduct an experiment?" Jake asked. "Stephen, what do you know about that author?" He nodded at the book in the ashes.

Hadfield glanced at it. "I know he's a local—" He stopped, then said on a note of astonishment, "You're Jacob Stanck?"

Jake raised a brow at Suzette, but she was already shaking her head. "I didn't tell him. Jake, listen." Her tone was urgent. "I didn't tell the police this morning, either. I have no idea how they found you."

Only the furrow between Jake's brows gave away his distress. "Bart Petersen?"

"Oh, hell," said Suzette. "That must be it. He'd have told his brother, and Tom is a volunteer fire fighter. I suppose he was here last night. Tom might have even told other people. Your homecoming is the most exciting thing that's happened around here since . . . good Lord, I don't know when."

Jake didn't comment, but the frown still darkened his brow.

Suzette's expression was oddly beseeching when she said, "I swear, Jake—"

"I don't doubt you." The gruff statement was typical of him, as though he hated admitting to faith in anybody. Rotating his shoulders to relieve stiffness—or tension—he added, "Suzette, I'm sorry. Let me pick up the bill."

"Don't be ridiculous, Jake!" She sounded like a parent, brusque and fond at the same time. "My insurance will pay for it. We have no way of knowing for sure you were the target. Although if you were—"

"I'll be hearing from our arsonist again." His voice was flat, though his mouth was a hard line. "I'll be waiting. In the meantime, shall we get to work cleaning up after him?"

"DID YOU KNOW Jake writes?" Clare tried to make the question sound casual.

Her mother-in-law, washing vegetables at the sink, glanced at her serenely. "Yes, of course. Jake and I have stayed in touch. He was a nice boy."

Nice. It wasn't a word Clare would have associated with the dark secretive man she knew. But that wasn't what she got snagged on. *Stayed in touch?* "You mean...even this past year?"

Mrs. Talbot carried the celery and tomatoes to the cutting board. "I heard from him every couple of months."

He could write her mother-in-law, but he couldn't even say goodbye to *her*. On a hot jolt of anger—or, dear God, was it jealousy?—she snapped, "Did he tell you he didn't come to Don's funeral?"

She was immediately ashamed of herself. Who was she trying to hurt?

But her shame came too late. Mrs. Talbot's hands stilled and crinkles appeared on her forehead. "What do you mean? I thought you'd all stayed close."

"I shouldn't have told you."

"Was he away?" Don's mother sounded bewildered.

The least Clare could do was lie one more time. "I don't know. I was hurt that he didn't come. I've never asked him why he didn't."

"And he hasn't said?"

"We . . . didn't talk about it."

Mrs. Talbot came to the kitchen table and sank heavily onto a chair. "I should have found a way somehow to come."

Clare was even more ashamed of herself. Her throat constricted, she set down the spoon she'd been using to stir chowder and turned off the burner under the pan. She felt as though she ought to put an arm around the older woman, but physical affection had never felt natural between them. In lieu of a reassuring touch, she said, "I'm the one who chose to have the funeral so quickly. I wanted desperately to be done. I thought it would be easier for Mike, but I wasn't fair to you. I should have waited until you were out of the hospital."

Her mother-in-law looked at her with disconcerting steadiness. "I meant that I should have been there for your sake. Not Don's. What difference would it make to him when and where we mourned?"

"I was fine," Clare lied yet again. Half in despair, she wondered if she ever told the truth anymore. Why was it so important that everyone think she could cope no matter what? Why was she so unwilling to reveal her terrifying vulnerability?

She knew the answer. As long as she could pretend, the pretense was reality. When she was confident that she gave the appearance of competence, she had the strength to handle that day, and the next, and the next.

It was why Jake was such a threat. He knew, had always known, how afraid she was beneath her veneer.

You were never weak, Clare. Never. But she was. Had been. If she'd been stronger, she would have gotten Don help before his desperate attempt to help himself ended so tragically.

"Well, we can't undo what's done. I hope you know how much I admire your strength, Clare." Mrs. Talbot used the support of the table to stand.

It scared Clare, seeing the older woman's momentary weakness. What would she do without her mother-in-law? And then she was ashamed again of the selfishness of that thought.

"Why don't you sit and let me finish dinner?"

"Don't be silly. I've never liked twiddling my thumbs."

How true. And how like Don. A man who didn't enjoy quiet pursuits, either, he'd worried because his mother wouldn't slow down after her heart attack. Instead, she insisted on digging up her front lawn to put in the huge thorny roses she'd always wanted to grow.

"Gardening may be hard work," she'd declared stoutly, "but it also relaxes me. Besides, if I don't do it now, I may never have a chance."

It would have been so much easier to return to Dorset Island when Don became ill. They'd lived in Seattle and had been married only a couple of years when he'd first begun showing symptoms of mental illness. First confusion and insomnia, then the bizarre suspicions followed by anger. The other fishermen were trying to put him out of business, he'd declared. He'd decide at three in the morning that he had to check on his boat, and would come home in a fury, face mottled, certain somebody had been on it, that it had been sabotaged. In his rages, he would bellow and kick furniture and throw anything that came to hand, terrifying her and Mike.

Thank God he hadn't hated her yet. She'd been able to talk him into seeing a doctor. Medication helped for a while, but it was obvious he couldn't head to Alaska for the fishing season. That was when they sold the boat and moved to Oregon. Don hadn't wanted to go to his mother for help, and Clare hadn't known Mrs. Talbot all that well then. Now she wasn't so sure their decision had been the right one. Her mother-in-law was a strong woman, however weak her heart.

Clare had never had the slightest idea what Mrs. Talbot thought of their move. She'd suggested they come here, but she hadn't reproached them when they decided not to. Did she think it was Clare who hadn't wanted to return to the island? What an irony that would be, considering Clare had come running the moment Don's death freed her!

And how sad that they couldn't seem to talk about any of this. Clare had a feeling that, too, was her fault.

Now both women worked silently for a minute. It was Clare who said finally, "Are Jake's parents still alive?"

"His father is. His mother died of a stroke a few years back."

Clare poured the corn chowder into the soup tureen. "Do you know if Jake's father still lives here? Or why Jake decided to come back now?"

Mrs. Talbot set the salad on the table and said pleasantly, "Why don't you ask Jake? Please don't take offense, dear, but he's such a private man I don't like to gossip about him."

Heat rushed to Clare's cheeks. Was that what she'd been doing? Gossiping? She, who'd always detested gossip, so often cruel?

"I'd better call Mike to dinner," she said, grateful for the excuse to slip out for a moment.

JAKE KNEW how much fodder he was providing for the gossips, but these days he didn't give a damn. Which was progress, he supposed. He could still close his eyes and feel the humiliation and impotent rage that had been his constant companions when he was a boy. He'd show up at the bus stop with another black eye or bruised cheek, or holding himself stiffly because of the welts on his back, and he'd hear the whispers, the same ones that followed him down the hall at school.

All that anger in desperate need of an outlet. He'd been in fights constantly. All it took was a taunt—"Let your old man beat you up again, Radovich?"—and he'd launch himself into battle, trying to regain the self-esteem his father had pummeled worse than his body.

It had taken him years to learn that he didn't feel any better after a fight, even when he bloodied a nose or slammed an opponent onto the asphalt.

What he couldn't figure out was why Don Talbot had befriended him. Jake remembered the exact moment. A whole gang of older boys had decided it would be fun to torment the thin angry kid. They'd circled him, saying mockingly, "Daddy's little punching bag. He's such a little chicken shit, all he does is turn the other cheek."

The rage and shame had risen in his throat until it burned, the hot tide drowning rational thought. All he wanted was to strike back, however uselessly. He'd gone at them swinging, only to have them circle around and close in from behind. A quick blow to his kidneys and he crumpled to his knees. The next thing he knew, another kid was there swinging in his place, only this one was bigger, his anger less blind.

The two of them hadn't won the fight, but they'd acquitted themselves well enough to win some respect. And out of it had come a friendship that had endured until Jake committed the most basic of betrayals: he lusted after his best friend's wife.

Why Don had thought him worth saving in the first place was what Jake had never understood. He couldn't have been very likable. But thank God for that friendship. It had been his salvation.

It had let him come back now, not giving a damn that people still whispered.

He'd thought he didn't give a damn about his father anymore, either, but now, sitting here in front of the house where he'd grown up, Jake discovered that the hurt boy still lurked inside him. Just the sight of the house— peeling white clapboard, lawn brown from the dry autumn, huge gnarly crab-apple tree scratching at the front window—was enough to make his pulse pound.

He was here only to ensure that their first meeting wasn't in public, giving the gossips something else to whisper about. He was tempted to forget it, come back some other time. But he'd run away once, and damned if he'd do it again.

Jake climbed out of the car and started up the cracked cement walk. Weird how his feet knew every step, how his hand wanted to reach for the dented aluminum screen door, instead of the bell.

The chime rang inside, followed by a bellowed, "Just a minute!" and the sound of heavy footsteps. His father was a shadowy bulk in the hallway, and a hardly recognizable face blurred by the screen door.

He made no move to open it. "Well. It's you."

"I figured you'd have heard I was back."

"I heard."

"May I come in?"

Heavy shoulders shrugged. "Why not?"

He turned and lumbered back down the hall. Jake took it as an invitation and opened the screen door, following his father into the kitchen.

Since he'd last been here, the linoleum had been replaced and the old-fashioned wood cabinets had been painted yellow, instead of green. They were greasy now, and the floor dingy. Crushed beer cans overflowed a couple of brown paper bags in one corner, and a new case of beer sat on the counter. Jake didn't suppose this kitchen had been really clean since his mother had died.

His father pulled out a chair and sat stiffly. He'd aged of course; Jake hadn't seen him in damn near twenty years. That would make Adam Radovich—Jake calculated quickly—about sixty-five. He looked older than that, hair gray, cheeks sunken beneath a couple of days' growth of beard. Mostly he looked smaller. The beefy hands were gnarled now like the crab-apple tree. His large frame didn't carry as much flesh. He still bore welding scars from the auto-body shop he owned.

He spoke first, gruffly. "Fancy car you got out there."

Jake made himself sit. "I can afford it."

"Your mother always said you were smart enough to make something of yourself. I didn't believe it."

"You didn't want to believe it. What, you were afraid your own son would show you up?" Jake's bitterness surprised him.

His father spoke without heat. "I was never afraid of a little punk like you."

"Then why did you beat the shit out of me? For fun?"

Their eyes met then, and Jake saw some fleeting emotion in his father's. Was it wishful thinking to imagine it was shame?

Adam Radovich leaned back in his chair and reached for a mug that appeared to have the dregs of coffee in it. "If that's what you think, get the hell out of my house."

"Fine." Jake stood. "I'll do my best to avoid you."

His father stayed sitting. "It was for your own damned good. You always had a mouth on you. Never could learn when to keep it shut."

"Not like Mom," Jake said softly. "She learned, didn't she?"

"She was smarter than you were."

"Weaker," Jake corrected his father, and turned and walked out, letting the screen door slam shut behind him.

Funny. He didn't feel a thing.

So why did he have this compulsion to drive straight to Clare's house and think up some excuse to get himself in the front door?

Fighting it, he made it past her place. But Mike was next door at his grandmother's, shooting baskets in the hoop above the garage. Jake lifted his foot off the accelerator, hesitated, then parked on the shoulder. Mike never even turned around, just shot, caught the rebound, dribbled out and shot again with the machinelike intensity of a teenage boy who had something on his mind.

Jake remembered doing that on this same hoop. Don had always had to work harder for grades than Jake did, and he'd spread his books over the kitchen table while Jake played endless games of horse with himself.

Today Jake approached, ignored if not unseen. He waited for his moment when the ball bounced off the rim, then snatched it out of the air. Whirling, with Mike right in his face, he went up for a shot.

And missed by a foot.

"Hell," he muttered. "I forgot her driveway slopes."

The kid had the gall to mock him. "Yeah, right. Excuses."

"Give me ten minutes to warm up, and I'll take you one-on-one."

"Ten years, maybe." Mike grinned. "So, shoot."

Jake's touch came back. The game was one of those things, like riding a bike, that never leaves you. And he knew this driveway, this hoop, as well as the contours of his own face.

The contest started out as fun, but somewhere along the way it changed. Mike quit laughing when he missed, started using his shoulder to move Jake out of the way when he drove to the basket. He blocked one of Jake's shots and gave a nasty grin. "In your face!"

Despite having grown a foot in the past year, Mike was quicker than he used to be. And he wanted to win with a passion, one that vibrated from his lanky frame. Jake was tempted to let him win, but if there was one thing the kid wouldn't forgive him, that was it.

Dusk was starting to settle, soft gray and still, the warmth of the day lingering in the air. Jake used the hem of his T-shirt to wipe sweat off his forehead as he carried the ball out of bounds. Mike waited in front of him, knees bent, ready to go. The score was eight-six for Jake.

That was the moment when Clare stepped out onto her porch and leaned against the railing to watch. Jake felt her presence on a subliminal level and turned his head. Just the sight of her wearing snug jeans and a T-shirt with some kind of lacy edging, her heavy hair falling out of a knot at the nape of her long graceful neck, slender arms crossed on the railing, and Jake had an intensely sexual reaction.

"Come on," Mike said impatiently, shifting his weight on the balls of his feet. He gave no sign of noticing their audience.

Jake wrenched his attention back, if not all of it. But what he'd lost in focus, he gained in determination. Damned if he was going to let a kid, barely fourteen, drill him, not in front of Clare. That need to impress his woman was so damned primitive Jake could hardly believe he felt it. But, hell, a man had his pride, right?

IN THE DEEPENING DUSK, man and boy were becoming indistinct, features unreadable, clues to their emotions made up of larger gestures. It was a sort of dance they were engaged in, Jake driving for the basket and Mike falling back in front of him, the one a shadow of the other. The slap, slap, slap of the basketball hitting concrete just reached Clare's ears, the only sound, though they must be grunting with exertion and exclaiming in triumph or frustration.

Clare knew Jake had seen her, but still in the blue-gray depths of oncoming night, she felt invisible here in the darker overhang of the porch.

They played so intently, so intensely. One would spring upward and the ball would eject, seemingly in slow motion, off his fingertips. The other would turn, in a pantomime of the game, and both would gaze upward as the ball hung, weightless, undecided, on the edge of the metal rim, before falling back or dropping gently in. And then man or boy would take the ball outside their imaginary out-of-bounds line again and they would start all over.

She knew it had ended when Jake made a shot from well out, and both froze watching it. It was getting so dark that Clare could scarcely see the long arc the ball made, but she saw Jake's fist go up in triumph. Mike grabbed the ball and, with a frustrated gesture, bounced it so hard it slammed against the backboard.

Now she heard their voices. Mike's, not quite as deep as it would someday be, "I'll beat you next time."

"Don't bet on it." The lower rumble belonged to Jake, who clapped him on the back. "But you're welcome to try."

"Now?" Eagerly.

Jake nodded toward Clare's hiding place and said something indistinguishable.

Mike groaned. "Oh, jeez..."

"Dishes and homework," she called.

Her stepson tucked the ball under his arm and headed across the lawn at a trot, calling over his shoulder, "Guess I'll see ya, okay?"

"Sure." For a moment she thought Jake intended to leave without speaking to her. Mike passed her and went in, letting the screen door slam behind him. Clare hesitated. Good manners insisted she be pleasant, but she was reluctant to antagonize her stepson by inviting Jake in. When he ambled across the lawn toward her, indecision held her in place at the top of the porch steps.

"I'd forgotten how often you two used to play," she said, the words surprising her.

Jake stopped at the bottom of the steps. "He was easier to beat in those days."

"His feet have grown two sizes this year. I don't know why he doesn't trip over them."

This time, Jake didn't say anything, just waited her out.

Tension indefinably altered her voice. "Have you talked to the fire marshal? Does he think this fire was aimed at you?"

"It occurred to him." Jake sounded laconic. "My guess is he doesn't really think so. Apparently Tom Petersen did tell everyone and anyone my pseudonym. The marshal figures, with me a local celebrity—his words—the arsonist using my books wasn't surprising. He did say they're considering giving all the volunteer fire fighters polygraph tests. In case one of them was just stirring up some excitement."

"What an awful thought." She'd read somewhere that arsonists often had a background in fire fighting.

"Not too many palatable alternatives," Jake said.

"No." Clare gazed past him to the moon, a sliver rising above the jagged black line of treetops. Fruitlessly she said, "I wish it would rain."

"It's dangerously dry," Jake agreed.

Silence opened between them. Clare wished that she could see him better, that she'd turned on the porch light or even the hall light just inside. Below her, he was large and dark and inscrutable, the man who walked her dreams and her memories, not the one who confessed to weaknesses of his own, who could disappear in a crowd.

Abruptly he said, "You're not thinking these fires have anything to do with you?"

"Of course not!" Another lie? she wondered. "But that doesn't mean I don't feel threatened. Any of us could be the next target!" Clare hated the way her voice took on a note of hysteria.

Jake moved then, in that unnerving way he had, taking the steps two at a time. Clare backed up, but still he was just in front of her, so close she crossed her arms to form a defensive barrier.

"Are you really afraid?" he asked.

Of you? Sometimes.

"Afraid?" she echoed. "I wouldn't put it that strongly. But yes, I'm unsettled. It's my worst nightmare revisited. Can you blame me?"

"Do you have a gun?"

"Heavens, no! I'd probably shoot the cat or Mike. I'm okay, Jake. Bart next door told me to call if anything scares me. And of course I have Mike. It's not as though I'm alone." She suddenly sounded so upbeat, so...fake. Jake wouldn't be any more convinced by her reassurances than she was.

She felt as much as saw his frown. "Do you trust him?"

"Trust *Bart?*" Her first instinct was to laugh, but Bart had been a volunteer fireman, too, she remembered. At the thought, her sense of security crumbled just a little more, as though it were shoreline being eroded by constant waves. "Shouldn't I?" she asked anxiously.

"I don't know," Jake said. "There were some fires, just small ones, when we were in high school. Bart was there."

"So were you," Clare said tartly.

Another uncomfortable silence fell. Clare hugged herself more tightly.

"True," Jake said at last, his voice dark and silky. "I guess you'll just have to decide who to trust."

"I trust you." Right now it was the truth. Tonight, in her dreams, it might not be.

"Good. Clare..." His voice had changed again, become as richly textured as a hand-stitched quilt wrapping her in the darkness. Her alarms sounded, but too late. Already he gripped her chin with one hand, lifted it...

When his mouth closed over hers, Clare was paralyzed by astonishment and something more complex. Fear was there, and a shiver of excitement. Outrage that he should assume she'd drop into his hand like a ripe blackberry now that Don was gone. And bitterness—she could taste its sting. When she'd needed him afterward, where had he been?

But his lips felt like nothing she'd imagined. She'd known, somehow, despite her denial, that he was capable of passion, but she'd expected him to be the kind of man who ruthlessly claimed what he wanted. Instead, his hand slid around to rest lightly on the back of her neck and the kiss was gentle, even tender. Perhaps because of the unexpectedness, something melted inside Clare, letting her feel a trickle of sweetness that, strangely, pricked her eyelids with tears. The impulse to relax, part her lips, let herself drown in that sweetness was powerful. She didn't have a chance.

A muffled exclamation of shock made Jake lift his head and Clare swing around. The hall light fell across Clare and the man who slowly released her, and in the open doorway stood Mike.

When her eyes met his, Mike said furiously, "Dad was right!" Then he turned and disappeared inside.

CHAPTER SIX

"MIKE . . ." RESTING her forehead against her stepson's closed bedroom door, Clare tried again.

"I don't want to talk about it!"

"It wasn't what you think." She wished she were sure she knew what he *did* think.

"I don't care!" he cried, voice muffled by the door. "Go away."

At last she did so, her distress magnified by Mike's unwillingness to talk about his shocking statement.

When Mike had been so hostile to Jake, she should have remembered that Mike had to have overheard his father railing at her or seen him sneaking from window to window to watch Jake's every move through binoculars. Was it so surprising that Mike might have soaked up his father's intense suspicion?

In the kitchen Clare steeped herself a cup of tea and then sat at the table, depression settling on her, as heavy as an armload of groceries she couldn't afford.

The trouble was, she'd been confident Mike understood that his father's bizarre accusations were products of his mental illness, not reason. They had been allies, she and Mike, practiced at handling Don's rages and confusion. So why would Mike have internalized this one absurd fear of his father's?

Because it wasn't absurd.

Agitated, Clare stood and paced to the window to stare out across the dark water to the sprinkling of lights on Orcas. She'd been so ashamed of her feelings back then, so determined that nobody would ever know she was attracted to her husband's best friend. She could look at it rationally; probably she wouldn't have been attracted to Jake had Don still been the man she married. But by that time she felt as though she had two children, not a husband and a stepson. What sex life she and Don had by then was sad, not arousing. Don would turn to her with such desperation, and she would cradle him in her arms and try to pretend he wasn't sick, frightened, lost. Was it any surprise that Jake, sexy and kind, had awakened feelings she'd almost forgotten?

Oh, yes, rationally she could forgive herself. It was on some deeper level that she couldn't. It was when she remembered Don's ugly accusations and saw the pain in his eyes. How joyously, certainly, she had taken her vows! Hadn't she betrayed them in her heart, even if not with her body?

And, dear Lord, had everybody seen what she felt? Not just Don, but Jake, and even her young stepson?

Were Mike's fears about Jake not the product of Don's rantings at all, but *her* fault, because she had felt things she shouldn't have?

"JAKE SAID SOMETHING the other day about fires when you guys were in high school." Clare took a sandwich out of her brown paper bag and unwrapped it. "Do you remember anything about them?"

She was at the bookstore again helping Suzette. They were taking a lunch break after a morning spent moving freestanding bookshelves into the back room so the carpet could be torn up and replaced.

"That's funny." Suzette glanced up from the apple she'd been polishing on the hem of her baggy T-shirt. "I was thinking about those fires just last night myself. Well." She grimaced. "I suppose that's inevitable under the circumstances, isn't it?"

"Jake didn't say much about them."

"For the most part none of them were any big deal—paper set on fire in wastebaskets, that kind of thing. The only one I remember that was more serious was in the chemistry lab, when a fire in a metal wastepaper basket right next to one of the tables made something in a test tube explode. The janitor who discovered it burned his hands. I seem to remember the fires stopped after that. Or we graduated. I'm not sure which."

"And they never discovered who was responsible?"

"Nope." Bouncing the apple in one hand as though she'd forgotten she intended to eat it, Suzette had an unfocused look to her eyes. "There was talk of course. Some of it vicious. Jake—" She stopped abruptly and shook her head hard. "He wasn't very popular."

"You mean...people thought *he'd* set the fires?" The idea was unexpectedly shocking, considering her subconscious had been hinting at it.

"Oh, his was just one of the names tossed around," Suzette said almost too hastily. "Mine might have been, too, for all I know. The thing is, I can't see how this connects to what's going on now. Do you know how many years have gone by since we graduated from high school?" She answered her own question ruefully. "Too many. Most of us have scattered halfway around the world. And as for those of us still on the island... I mean, if I really loved setting fires back then, wouldn't you think I'd have kept doing it?"

"Yes," Clare admitted. "Unless something triggered you to start again. Or—" she hesitated, then said it, anyway "—if you *have* been setting them all these years somewhere else. And now you've just come back to Dorset."

Suzette's brows drew together. "Like Jake, right?"

Clare looked away, hating the doubts that entered her mind as insidiously as inhaled gas fumes. "I don't know!" she said vehemently. "Maybe there's someone else—"

"Alison," Suzette interjected surprisingly. "She just moved back recently. Maybe there arc others. Let me think."

"Won't the fire marshal investigate people? Find out whether there have been unsolved arsons wherever they lived before?"

"Not if he doesn't know about the fires back when all of us were in high school. Otherwise, what would he do? Investigate everyone on the island?"

Clare had completely lost her appetite. "Should we tell him?"

Suzette was probably one of those people who hid her worst pain behind wryness. "I have to admit I'd as soon he didn't know. It's *my* bookstore that burned, remember. He already suspects me."

Recalling the clinical way those detectives had listened to the bookstore owner, Clare didn't protest, even though good manners probably insisted she should. Instead she said thoughtfully, "But why would you burn the Kirks'?"

"To divert suspicion from myself, of course." The other woman's response was prompt and dry. "Or else the two were unrelated. Maybe teenagers burned down the Kirks', and that gave me the idea of picking up some insurance money. Copycat crimes are not uncommon, you know.''

''No, I suppose not.'' Clare looked down at her untouched sandwich. The conversation was becoming increasingly awkward and disquieting. She didn't know Suzette well enough to automatically dismiss any suspicions. Maybe the fire *was* helping Suzette financially. And she *had* gone to the high school back when the small fires were set.

Deciding she'd as soon change the subject, Clare said, ''I don't know Alison very well. I gather she came back when her father died and she inherited his estate. What's she been doing all these years?''

''Do you know, I don't have a clue.'' Suzette frowned. ''She's engaged to Tom Petersen, I hear. I don't see much of him. He's not a reader.''

''I've only met him a few times,'' Clare said. ''Isn't he older than Bart?''

''A couple of years. He went off and joined the air force. Fought in Vietnam. He's a pilot now. He charters small planes, does those sight-seeing flights.''

It was Alison she wanted to hear about, not Tom or Bart, despite Jake's insinuation. Clare wanted to know why Alison Pierce was so guarded. Had she changed since high school in ways that went beyond just growing up? Did other people like her? There wasn't any sensible reason to connect Alison to arson, but here was a rare chance to ask someone who'd known Don and his high-school sweetheart about their relationship.

''Were Don and Alison serious about each other in high school?'' she asked.

''He didn't talk about her?''

''Not much. More about Sheila.'' Mike's mother had sounded like a nice person. Clare had suffered some of the usual second-wife jealousy; how could she not, when reminders of the other woman were constant and unavoidable? Because of Mike, Clare had to gracefully accept the way Don continued to talk about her, the framed photos that stayed out. Eventually she found she didn't mind, even coming to think of her predecessor as someone she, too, had known. To this day she found herself reminding Mike about some trait or interest of his mother's that he shared. She and Sheila had touched the same lives, occupied the same place in them.

Where Don was concerned, so had Alison, about whom Clare knew almost nothing. So why, Clare wondered, did she feel as if she would've liked Sheila, while her instinctive reaction to Alison was so negative?

Suzette took a big crunch of apple as though the changed subject allowed her, too, to relax. Around the bite, she said, "Yeah, they were pretty serious. They went together for a couple of years. He was the big football star, she was a cheerleader. But I think for him it was just a teenage thing. You know? Meantime, she was planning their wedding. He was it for her." Suzette made a face. "After graduation, Don went off to Alaska on a fishing boat for the summer. That's where he met Sheila. Next thing we knew, he wrote that he'd gotten married. A few weeks later, he brought Sheila home. Alison hid it in public, but she was hurt and bitter. Who could blame her?"

Who indeed? The story stuck with Clare over the next couple of days, giving her pause at idle moments. She'd known the basic outline, but never heard it told so baldly. The truth was, Don had been a crud to Alison, unless there was more to it from his point of view. Could they have broken up before he went to Alaska and Alison had kept it to herself, convinced they'd make up? But that wasn't even the way he'd told it, to Clare's best recollection.

She could picture him leaning back against the kitchen counter, watching her cook, so big and vital and untamed, a man made for hauling in nets as salt water stung his face and the sea rolled beneath the boat. He was ruddy-cheeked, his hands rough with calluses, the smell of fish and the ocean always clinging to him. He had a confidence about him that had drawn her, a directness and strength unlike any other man she'd known. But sometimes that confidence had come out as sheer masculine arrogance, and this was one of those times, though Clare wasn't sure she'd recognized it then.

She must have asked him about his first wife, because he'd grinned jauntily. "I had a girlfriend back home, but I forgot her in a second when I met Sheila. Damn, Sheila was pretty. No prettier than you," he'd had the good grace to add, along with a swat at Clare's behind. "But it wasn't just that. She was... I don't know." He moved his shoulders awkwardly. "Soft. Gentle. Sweet." Another grin. "I like my women to be women."

Alison Pierce hadn't struck Clare as soft or gentle, but she might have been once. Being dumped by the man she loved would have a way of hardening a woman. Clare herself had eventually learned that gentle was sometimes only another word for weak.

The last person Clare expected to find herself talking about Alison with was Jake. After the kiss, he'd stayed out of her way for several days. But then she came home from work one afternoon to find him waiting on her doorstep, long legs stretching halfway down the sturdy new steps. His old leather tool belt was dumped on the porch at his side.

He rose to his feet when she walked toward the house. His expression was carefully shuttered. ''I won't stay, but I heard water dripping under your sink the other night. I figured I'd take a look.''

She should have thanked him and told him she'd already called a plumber—which would have been a lie of course. But pride didn't fix leaks, and she'd once been happy to accept his help. So she found herself unlocking the front door and stepping aside to let him in, even as she hoped anxiously that Mike wouldn't be home for another hour or two.

Let him be late today, was her silent plea.

Clare set about preparing dinner while Jake, head and shoulders under her sink, sprawled on her kitchen floor— mopped, thank heavens, only yesterday. His jeans were soft and worn, molding the long muscles in his legs and making her conscious of other parts of his anatomy. Every once in a while he would grope with one long-fingered hand for a wrench or flashlight, and Clare felt this peculiar piercing pain under her breastbone, a form of wanting that could have been sweet under other circumstances. She had to do something to combat this agonizing awareness of Jake she'd sworn to Don she didn't feel. She'd always figured circumstances—her isolation, her need—had created her fixation on Jake. So why hadn't that awareness gone away?

Needing to think about something else, anything else, she heard herself ask, ''Did you know Alison Pierce well?''

''Alison?'' More clanging came from under the sink. ''On the surface.''

Clare chopped celery. ''She seems very... reserved.''

''Yeah, I always wondered...'' He grunted. ''You need new pipes.''

"And insulation and flooring and probably wiring. Tell me about it."

He levered himself out of the cabinet. "Wiring?"

Seeing the look on his face, she said hastily, "I don't know. It's an old house, that's all. It needs work."

Another grunt. "I'll take a look one of these days." And he vanished underneath the sink again.

Her mind reverted to the previous topic. "What did you always wonder about Alison?"

"What her home life was like. She reminded me of myself."

Startled, Clare stopped chopping. "What do you mean?"

The long silence made her wonder if he didn't regret his unguarded remark. But at last, "Careful," he said. "Didn't hang herself out to dry emotionally."

"But she must have with Don."

"He was the one and only. She didn't have many friends. I don't think she liked the fact that he did."

What an irony if Alison had driven Don away by being possessive, considering that in the end he became pathologically jealous of any man who even looked at Clare.

"Is that why he went to Alaska, do you suppose? He got tired of it?"

"Yeah. He didn't say so, but yeah." Jake backed out from beneath the sink. "Your plumbing is in crappy shape, but the leak's from your garbage-disposal unit. You need a new one."

In dismay Clare said, "I suppose Anne will help pay for one. Although I hate to ask her."

"Anne?" He frowned. "Oh. Don's mother. I forgot she was your landlady. Why in hell didn't she spend some money on this place before you moved in?"

"Because she can't afford it, either." Clare mechanically returned to her dinner preparations. "This was just a summer cottage, not meant for year-round living. She had it for sale when Don died. My moving in was supposed to be temporary."

"Aren't you making a living?" He was gathering up his tools, not looking at her. Maybe that was what made it possible to tell him the truth.

"I guess I am, and the sale of the house to you really helps. But I was so broke to start with—we're still behind. You know how little I worked that year. It's a miracle Coastal Realty kept me on at all. I sold one place, a duplex, the entire time we lived in Oregon. One. But Don hated it when I was out—" She stopped herself. Old territory. "The fact that Don deliberately burned the house down meant that our rental insurance was useless." How composed she sounded. "We lost everything. And we'd been living on our savings. Don hadn't carried life insurance, and once he was diagnosed as schizophrenic, he couldn't get any. My father is remarried and not in any position to offer financial help, even if we were closer. The result was that Mike and I came here needing everything—clothes, dishes and pans, sheets for the beds..." She gestured helplessly. "We had the car. That's it."

Partway through her admission, Jake had lifted his dark gaze to her face and kept it riveted there. In those eyes, usually so unreadable, she saw shock and building anger.

"Damn it, Clare, why didn't you come to me?" The movement explosive, he flung his tool belt onto the table. "For Mike's sake if not your own?"

He was angry because she hadn't come crawling to him for help? It was almost funny. Would have been funny, if she hadn't been swamped by a memory of herself and Mike, alone at the graveside in the drizzle.

"Why would I have? Because you were such a good friend to Don?"

His posture was rigid. "I'd have done anything for him."

"Except come to his funeral," she said acidly.

Between set teeth, he said, "You know how I felt!"

"No, I don't!" The words came in a flood, unstoppable. "You weren't there to tell me. And you sure as hell weren't there making certain Mike and I were taken care of, were you, Jake? Hell, no, you were holed up wallowing in guilt and anguish! Just what Don would've asked of you, right, Jake?"

Too late, she saw her stepson standing in the kitchen doorway behind Jake. A glance at the clock told her Mike was right on time. Didn't it figure? she thought half-hysterically. But, hey, there was an up side—Mike wanted her to hate Jake. He ought to be pleased by her tirade.

Instead, he looked shocked, even scared. It made her wonder what depths of despair and bitterness her face revealed.

Jake had followed her gaze to see Mike. The three of them stood frozen, caught in one of life's uglier moments. How had all that spilled out? How many times had she vowed never to let Jake know how his desertion had hurt, to keep her pride even if she had nothing else?

Mike was the one to break the tableau. He turned jerkily and vanished. Moments later she heard the front screen door slam.

A long breath sagged out of Clare. "Here we go again."

"Clare—" Jake's eyes glittered with intensity.

"No," she said quietly. "I shouldn't have said all that. I wouldn't have taken money from you, anyway. It hurt that you didn't come to Don's funeral, but you didn't owe me anything. You were as much a friend to Don as he'd let you be. And you were good to me too, Jake. It only goes to show how pathetic I'd become that I resented suddenly being on my own."

"Pathetic?"

"I was so young when I married Don." Was she trying to excuse herself or explain? "It's been good for me to be on my own."

"You were so patient, so strong, so loving." His voice was gravel scraped on bare skin. "Watching you with him damn near killed me."

Her breath stopped in her throat at his expression of raw need. Oh, God, how much harder it would've been then if she'd had any idea. How much harder it was now.

"I promised him for better or worse." It was the simple truth, the one she could never get beyond.

"He was a lucky man." The terrible loneliness in Jake's gray eyes held her still, stunned her. "And I'm a son of a bitch." He turned and strode out.

"Jake!" she cried, but then she heard the front screen door slam again. The finality of the sound killed her impulse to chase after him. New guilt corroded her self-esteem. Why had she accused Jake of failing her, when he'd done so much for all of them? Because he hurt her feelings by shutting her out after Don's death? Maybe she should have tried understanding his.

"Just when I thought things couldn't get any better," she said to the empty room.

FIRE, HOT AND ORANGE. Jake, no more than a dark silhouette against the leaping blaze, was watching her, just far enough away that she couldn't cry out to him, couldn't have heard if he'd called her name. Why hadn't he been burned? Fear choked her throat, seared like the smoke, but she didn't know whether the fear was *for* Jake or *of* him. But he drew her; she couldn't seem to run away.

Hollow-eyed come morning, Clare reflected on her nightmare as she took her last few swallows of coffee. Was it really Jake she was dreaming about, or was he a stand-in for Don, who had both set the fire and died in it? Or was the whole idea to make sure she suffered the agony of indecision night after night as she had day after day during her marriage? *Should I commit Don to an institution, or shouldn't I?* had become *Do I trust Jake and my feelings for him, or don't I?*

Whatever her mind was trying to tell her, it was getting wearing. And why had her subconscious stayed blissfully silent until Jake had come back into her life? Was she supposed to resolve something? If so, it would be nice if her dreams would tell her what.

Sighing, she called, "Mike, do you want a ride to school?"

"Sure." He appeared with his backpack already slung over one shoulder. He'd walked on eggs around her since overhearing the scene with Jake. Her one tentative attempt to discuss it had been rebuffed, for which she'd been grateful. God knows what she would have said. In the meantime, she and her stepson had reverted to the careful polite way of dealing with each other that had so discouraged her before Jake's arrival.

On the way to school, she said, "I have a potential buyer for the marina. He's coming on the eight-o'clock ferry, and I'm going with him to take a look. Keep your fingers crossed."

"Would it mean lots of money?"

"It'd be the biggest sale, hands down, I've ever made. Maybe we could move."

"Why do you want to move so much?" Mike asked.

"Because I don't like living on charity, even if it's courtesy of your grandmother," Clare told him. "Besides, wouldn't you like someplace a little nicer?"

"I like being next to Grandma."

"That *is* handy," she admitted, pulling up in front of the high school. "We'll see. Wish me luck, anyway."

"Yeah, okay." He stopped with the car door half-open. "Hey, listen. You bought that new disposal, didn't you? Do you think we could figure out how to put it in ourselves?"

Mike sounded so elaborately casual it was hard to interpret his question. Was he hoping for a cool family project, a little togetherness in an acceptable form? Or was it that if they could do it themselves, they wouldn't need Jake? Maybe neither was true and he was just sounding her out, not wanting to ask directly whether she'd talked to Jake.

"Yes, I bought it, but I know absolutely zilch about plumbing," Clare said ruefully. "I'm all for World History, but I think high schools should offer Home Maintenance, too, and make it mandatory. To tell you the truth, if I don't hear from Jake, I'd better call a plumber. And if I were Jake, after the stuff I said to him, I wouldn't offer my services again. So let's hope the guy this morning thinks the marina is the perfect business to sink a million bucks into."

Mike nodded and hopped out, loping toward the school. Clare wondered if she'd satisfied his curiosity.

The potential buyer did indeed seem very interested, asking endless questions and taking a hard look at the figures. He was an attorney who'd decided to opt out of his high-pressure partnership in a Seattle firm. He owned a boat himself and had docked it here, he told her; Dorset was a favorite destination for weekend boaters. The marina had the facilities to cater to them, and the town had the charm, elegant dining and intriguing shops to be a magnet.

Feeling hopeful, Clare saw him off on the one-o'clock ferry to Seattle.

"I need to think about it and talk to my wife," he told her. "I'll be in touch."

Clare hardly ever let herself hope for anything as much as she did this sale. But dollar figures danced pleasantly in her head all afternoon, making up for the hours wasted putting on, at the owner's insistence, an open house for an overpriced beachfront cottage. From there she collected her signs and went straight to the grocery store.

She'd made it all the way to the checkout line before she saw Jake there ahead of her. He waited, looking disinterested, while a woman in front of him juggled coupons and a whiny toddler. The very sight of him doing something so mundane as shopping for food—lettuce and tomatoes and bread and a few prepackaged entrées, she saw, craning her neck—was enough to freeze Clare in place.

She hadn't even noticed the man who stopped a few feet away until he said sarcastically, "Well, look who's here."

Jake turned slowly, his face so expressionless she didn't know why she was sure he'd braced himself. He inclined his head.

With the two men face-to-face, Clare saw the resemblance immediately. Bigger-boned than his son, his features coarser, Jake's father must have been a handsome man twenty years ago. He wore a T-shirt that revealed muscular arms, but his belly hung over his jeans and his bloodshot eyes matched the broken veins in his nose. An alcoholic.

"Goddamn it, you said you'd stay out of my way," he said in a voice loud enough to be heard several check-stands away.

Jake looked bored. "I'll refer to your schedule next time."

His father slammed a hand against Jake's cart. "You got nothing better to do than drive around in that fancy car and make sure everybody sees you're back? Shit. That's all I hear about. You're making me look like a goddamn fool."

Jake's lip curled just a little. "I'm not trying to make you look like anything. I have no interest in you," he said dismissively before turning to push his cart forward.

His father moved suddenly, aggressively, grabbing Jake by the shoulder to spin him around. "Don't turn your back on me, punk!"

"You're making a scene," Jake said icily. "Go home."

Clare held her breath. Jake's stillness was dangerous, the contempt in his eyes a warning. The clerk behind him was reaching for the phone when Jake's father, glowering, lifted his hand from his son.

"Why don't you go back wherever the hell you came from?" he spat. "There's nothing for you here."

Jake didn't even dignify his father's departure by watching it. He reached for his wallet from his hip pocket and nodded to the wide-eyed clerk.

Very quietly, Clare backed up, taking her cart with her. Her mother-in-law was right. Jake was a private man. This wasn't a scene he'd have wanted her to see.

But what disturbed her most was her realization that here was somebody who hated Jake. Did his own father hate him enough to use his books to start a fire?

AT THE KNOCK on the door after dinner, Clare said, "Mike, can you get that?"

He returned a moment later with his grandmother. "Hello, Clare, I won't stay but a minute." Then she saw the new garbage-disposal unit sitting untouched in its box on the floor. "Oh, dear," she said in dismay. "I didn't know you were having trouble with your disposal."

"It's leaking, Jake tells me. I just bought that one yesterday."

"I'll run right home and get my checkbook. Goodness! You should have said something."

Clare met her gaze. "No. You've done enough for us."

The smallest of frowns touched her mother-in-law's brow. "You're paying me rent. It's my responsibility to maintain this house."

Stubbornly Clare said, "I'm paying you an absurdly low rent. The least I can do is handle basic stuff like this on my own."

Mrs. Talbot set down the covered plate she'd been carrying. "I like to help," she said quietly.

Clare knew on one level that she should gracefully give way. But her pride made her stiff and ungracious. "I'd rather take care of it."

Hurt was hidden behind dignity just as stiff. "Very well. I'll just leave these cookies and get out of your hair."

Clare felt lower than a slug. "Please, don't go yet! Would you like a cup of coffee?" The phone rang before her mother-in-law could refuse. "Don't go anywhere," Clare said quickly.

As she answered, Mike said, "Wow, those are cookies? Can I have one?"

"Of course you can, dear. Now I'll just be on my way. I can see that your mother's busy."

Phyllis Carlson was explaining to Clare that Jean Kirk had asked her if she'd like the apples in their small orchard. "I was wondering if you'd want to join me Sunday after church. We could make applesauce and slice and freeze bags of apples. There's plenty for both our households."

"Can you hold on a second?" Clare asked, then covered the mouthpiece, feeling harried. Her mother-in-law was almost out the kitchen door. Clare called after her, "Anne, please, stay for a cup of coffee. We'd really like the company."

"Oh, is Mrs. Talbot there?" Phyllis asked. "She'd be welcome to join us if she could use any of the apples."

"Phyllis Carlson wonders if we'd both like to can applesauce with her Sunday. From the Kirks' trees."

Predictably her mother-in-law said, "Oh, I'm sure the two of you would have a nicer time without an old lady like me."

"You know what a big job it is," Clare coaxed.

"Well." Anne sniffed. "Fine."

With it settled that she would bring her long-handled fruit picker, canning kettle and jars, she departed. Clare watched her go, feeling combined irritation and shame.

Into the phone she said, "Thanks for including me, Phyllis. I'm looking forward to it."

Since the fire in town at the bookstore, Clare hadn't overheard any further suggestions that the Carlsons might be the arsonists. Admitted survivalists, they were a little strange, but they had been generous neighbors.

Here they were trying for self-sufficiency, and still they shared bounty like this apple harvest.

"Why didn't you let Grandma pay for the disposal?" Mike asked from behind her as she hung up the phone.

"Because, as I've said half a dozen times, I don't like—"

He rolled his eyes and mimicked her tone. "Living on charity. Yeah, but jeez. You hurt Grandma's feelings."

"I know." Clare let out a long breath. When had she started hating the necessity of accepting help? "I suppose," she admitted, "I was selfish."

Mike's eyes shifted away from hers. "I don't know," he said awkwardly. "I mean, if you can afford it... Does she *know* you can afford it?"

"Your grandmother doesn't know what my income is, if that's what you mean."

"Well, maybe you should tell her," he suggested. Apparently losing interest in the subject, he opened the refrigerator. "Can I have some milk with the cookies?"

"Why not?"

Clare wasn't so sure she needed to share the precise state of her finances with her mother-in-law, but Mike was right that it was past time she and Anne had a real talk. Somehow their relationship had never progressed past a certain point. They got along just fine; between Mike and community affairs, conversation was easy. What they'd never done was talk about feelings. Clare had no idea whether her mother-in-law even *liked* her. Because of Mike, they needed each other, but need was a good culture for resentment. Which, she supposed, explained some of her complicated feelings for Jake.

And, she realized uneasily, Mike's for her.

Instead of cleaning the bathroom, her appointed task for the evening, Clare took herself to the beach to consider the disquieting parallels between her relationship with Don and Mike on the one hand, and Jake and her mother-in-law on the other. Need versus love. When did the one corrode the other? Why was it so much easier to give than receive?

She settled on a little pocket of gritty sand, her back against a driftwood log, and wrapped her arms around her knees. It was almost dusk; the quality of the light had changed, bringing a stillness that she liked. An incoming tide lapped over the cracking, sun-dried layer of seaweed earlier exposed on the rocky beach. The salty smell was sharp and distinctive, as familiar to her as smog to an urbanite.

Resting her chin on her crossed arms, Clare sighed and let her thoughts drift like the loon bobbing offshore. Had Don ever realized that, if not for her, he would have been institutionalized? When had love and gratitude become the childlike dependence that a healthy man would despise feeling? Even toward the end, she sometime saw flashes of the man she'd married. In those flashes, did he see himself and what he had become, and her and what she had become?

And what was that? she wondered with a sting of self-doubt. Had she liked being needed so desperately? Refused to commit Don because she hadn't wanted to give up the sweet power of knowing she and she alone could provide comfort, hold off the ravening demons? Was she determined to raise Mike, not because she loved him or because she owed it to Don, but rather because she'd become addicted to being needed?

If so, no wonder she hated conceding that power to someone else, becoming the recipient, instead of the giver.

But oddly enough, she couldn't remember being anything but grateful that Jake was there to lend an ear, some dispassionate advice, occasionally his strength. She'd been disturbed by her physical reaction to him, but that was because it was something forbidden, a woman's secret fantasy, hidden away. She'd been careful never to let herself wonder whether *he* might be attracted to *her*.

Maybe her relationship with him had stayed simple because she'd never let him become a real person to her. He was like a child's imaginary friend: there when she wanted him, invisible the rest of the time, his own personality and needs suppressed, hers all important. Oh, yes, she'd been childlike in her single-mindedness, in the way she grabbed what Jake offered without ever thinking about the cost, without ever speculating about *him*. About the dark quiet man who gave such an extraordinary amount to her, a stranger who happened to be married to his best friend.

Just as she had always felt his presence with a prickling consciousness she'd been dismayed to recognize as sexual, Clare knew he was approaching now even before she heard the crunch of footsteps on the sand. Nor was she surprised by his appearance; he'd always had a gift for knowing when her emotions were most disturbed, when she had a need to talk.

There it was again, that word. *Need.*

Clare lifted her head and watched his approach. More déjà vu; how many times had she seen this man striding along the beach, breeze lifting that straight dark hair, his hands shoved in the pockets of his jeans? He was watching her, too, of course; he always had. But where once she'd been comforted by that watchfulness, by the very dispassion in it, now it struck her as vaguely unsettling. What did *he* want? Need?

Jake stopped in front of her. "If you bought that disposal, I could put it in tomorrow while you're at work," he said abruptly.

"You mean, like the shoemaker's elves?"

His gaze stayed level. "Something like that."

"You don't strike me as a self-sacrificing man."

One eyebrow went up. "How do I strike you?"

The answer should have been instant; she should have known him well enough to speak without hesitation. Instead, she found herself studying him as though they'd never met. Jake rocked back on his heels and withstood her scrutiny with apparent calm, but somehow his lack of expression no longer convinced her. Before, she hadn't really looked. Now that she did, she saw the rigid control disguising emotions as turbulent as anyone else's.

"I see," she said slowly, "a forceful man who doesn't like being the beggar, who is determined never to be out of control."

A flicker of something powerful passed like a shiver through his eyes before his mouth quirked in a wry smile. "You're right. But then I have no intention of begging. Relationships should go both ways, or they're not worth having."

"Do any of them do that?" Clare asked with a tinge of bitterness. She let her chin drop onto her arms. "Mike needs me. I need Anne. Don needed me. I needed you. And, oh, God, he hated knowing that."

Jake eased himself down beside her, not so close as to scare her off, but near enough to be companionable. The feeling was achingly familiar. She'd missed him, never let herself understand how much.

Quietly he said, "It must have been different once, when you first married Don. He knew what it felt like to have you turn to him."

"I suppose so." She made a face. "It's easy to forget what normal marriage was like."

"And sex." Jake was looking out at the water, but his voice had roughened. "Isn't that the most naked expression—if you'll pardon the pun—of the need between a man and a woman, need that cuts both ways?"

Of course, she hadn't actually *had* sex in longer than she cared to think about. Her relationship with Don had become closer to that of mother and child than husband and wife. Which might be why, at this very moment, she was so acutely conscious of the bones and muscles and controlled power of the man whose shoulder almost touched hers.

There was no safe answer to Jake's remark, so she didn't say anything. She heard him exhale.

"I suppose Mike's out for my blood."

No safe answer, so he'd found a safe subject.

"I'm...not sure," Clare admitted. "He won't talk about—" On the brink, she came to a screeching halt.

Jake glanced at her with raised brows. "The kiss? Or my...absence at his father's funeral?"

She chose bluntness. "Mike was too distraught at the funeral to care whether you were there or not. But I think he believes that, if you're kissing mc now, you probably were back then, too."

Jake swore. "Did you tell him...?"

"He won't listen to me."

"Don's been dead more than a year. You're entitled."

"To some sexual release?"

"To a life," he said.

She had a flash of longing, of what could be. All those things that Jake's kiss had hinted about him: the tenderness, the passion, the complexity. The way she could talk to him, had always been able to talk to him.

An ache lodged behind her breastbone. Looking away from Jake, she said dully, "Mike's just a kid. He's lost both his parents. I'm all he has. The idea that I might have...betrayed his father hits pretty close to home, you know. If I could do that, how can he trust me?"

"Goddamn it, you didn't!"

She met his eyes. "Didn't I?"

"You don't know what betrayal is!" Suddenly Jake loomed above her, on his knees, instead of sitting. All that turbulence she'd sensed was in his eyes, the twist of his mouth, the restrained harshness of his voice. "But I do! Don't you know that? I *wanted* you to betray Don!"

"No," Clare whispered. "If you had, you'd have kissed me or touched me or—"

Face tormented, Jake was deaf to her reason. "*This* is what I wanted. *This* would've been betrayal!" And he snatched her into his arms.

God help her, she met his mouth with hunger as frantic. It shocked her, this electric wave of *need,* mindless and so utterly physical. He yanked her up and pressed her body to the length of his, his tongue plundering her mouth as his hands massaged her back, her hips, squeezed her buttocks. Her own fingers were tangled in his hair, tugging, insistent. With a whimper, she let her head fall back, and his lips, hot and damp, moved down her throat. She felt his teeth, his breath, his hands cupping her breasts, flattening them, rubbing—

"No!" Clare fell back against the log. "No. Jake, please..."

His hands curled into fists and his eyes glittered. "You feel it, too. I know you do."

"Don—"

"Is dead, for God's sake! Dead!"

Her voice shaking, she stumbled to explain. "I just can't. I'm not ready."

His hands dropped and he rose to his feet. Looking down at her, he said harshly, "Do you want to spend your life with a damn ghost?"

A second later, his feet crunching on the gravel, he left her alone in the gathering dusk.

CHAPTER SEVEN

A FIRE-DEPARTMENT CAR was sitting in front of the bookstore the next day when Clare headed home from her office. The marshal was back to talk to Suzette, who must have been looking better and better as a suspect with no more fires having been set. Island gossip was running against her, too; Suzette was outspoken and unconventional enough to have antagonized some people. Both blazes had brought infusions of insurance money, but which owner had needed it more? And how likely was it that one of the Kirks had managed not only to sneak up here to set their own place on fire, but the bookstore, as well?

This second fire had achieved something else, too, Clare saw. A large sign in the new front window promised that Jacob Stanek would be autographing books two weeks from Saturday at three in the afternoon. A coup of major proportions in the Pacific Northwest bookselling community. He must be doing it to help out Suzette. Since his books had been used to fuel the bookstore fire, Jake's identity had become a poorly guarded secret, locally, anyway.

Pulling into her drive, Clare wondered whether the authorities were working their way up to arresting Suzette, or whether they were just pressuring her, hoping she'd crack and confess all. Had she taken a lie-detector test? Clare's gut instinct said that Suzette Fowler was no arsonist. But if not her, who?

When she stepped in the front door, she called for Mike.

His bellowed response came from upstairs. A minute later he bounded down the steps, two at a time. "Hey, Jake came and put in the disposal."

Dropping her purse on the side table, she kept her voice casual. "Is he still here?"

"Nah." Mike lounged against the newel post. "He left a while ago. Said to say you're welcome."

"Oh." Clare forced a smile, hoping she didn't sound as hollow as she felt. "Well, that's something."

"Yeah, it's cool. It works."

"Didn't you trust him?" She regretted the words the minute they slipped out.

Just like that, her stepson's mood changed. "Should I?"

"Mike, Jake was good to us."

He looked at her insolently. "Yeah, he was really good to you."

"He never once kissed me or laid a hand on me, whatever your father may have believed." It mattered so terribly that she convince Mike, though she knew in her heart that she wouldn't succeed, that he wasn't ready to listen.

It was resentment that burned now in Mike's eyes, dark like his father's. "Well, he was sure more interested in you than he was in me."

Oh, Lord, had she been wrong? Was simple jealousy the trouble? Had Mike seen Jake as the father he no longer had and was hurt now because Jake was also interested in her?

"Mike—"

"I don't really want to talk about it," he said quickly. "Besides, it doesn't look like he's so hot for you anymore." His tone was gloating. "I mean, he came on purpose today when you wouldn't be here, right?"

She couldn't even defend herself by saying, "He doesn't want to hurt you," because that *would* have hurt him.

"Are you done?" she asked quietly.

He flushed, and she was glad to know he was decent enough to be ashamed of lashing out that way. But all he did was shrug. "Can I go to Geoff's?"

"Have you finished your homework?"

"I didn't have much."

Not quite an answer; she had a sneaking feeling that his schoolwork was plummeting along with his attitude at home. But so far no teachers had contacted her, and considering the tension between her and Mike, this didn't strike her as the moment to call him on it.

So she nodded. "Fine. Be home by five-thirty."

That evening, her mother-in-law phoned and suggested that she take Mike to a movie and that he spend the night with her on Friday.

"It'll give you a break," she said.

Clare couldn't deny that she could use one. "Bless you. Things have been ... tense lately." That was as close as she'd ever come to really talking about problems with Mike. She'd been half afraid Mrs. Talbot would hear it as criticism of her grandson. Clare told herself it was only right that her mother-in-law's loyalty and sympathy should belong to him, rather than her. She just wished she didn't feel so isolated, that she, too, had someone who put her first.

In response to her comment, Mrs. Talbot said gently, "Yes, I've gathered that. He seems ... angry at you."

"Has he said why?"

"No. I've been puzzled."

"It's a long story," Clare said ruefully.

"I'm always here to listen."

Did she dare believe it? But Clare could hear Mike in the next room, so she said only, "Maybe I'll take you up on that one of these days. Would you like to speak to Mike now?"

"Why not?"

From her end, Mike sounded enthusiastic about his grandmother's proposition. "Cool!" Clare heard him announce. "Geoff's seen it. He says his mom had her eyes shut through half the movie."

When he handed the phone back to her, Clare said, "Better you than me."

Mrs. Talbot laughed. "I'll shut my eyes, too."

The house was unnaturally quiet when Clare came home the next day. She found a note from Mike on the kitchen table that said, Did my homework. Grandma and I are going out for pizza. She says to tell you she has lots of canning jars, and not to buy any.

On impulse she called her friend Sharon, the high-school librarian, who said, "Dinner? You're a lifesaver. I was just contemplating frozen lasagna. Where shall we go?"

They chose a small seafood restaurant so popular with tourists that locals didn't even try to get reservations during the summer. But tonight the two women were seated by the window, where they watched the ferry depart for points east, leaving Dorset again to its isolation. Of course, they knew half the other diners, which involved some visiting before they actually got around to ordering.

They even saw Alison Pierce, who paused by the table with Tom Petersen. He was the one with the big mouth, the guy who'd spread the fact of Jake's alternate existence.

But then, Clare had to admit Tom hadn't had any particular reason to guard his knowledge. He'd probably considered Jake's profession a mildly interesting bit of local color.

After introducing Tom to Sharon, Alison looked at Clare. "Suzette tells me you helped her clean up after the fire. I'm worried about her. The police seem so interested in her."

Alison seemed softer tonight, more relaxed. Maybe her coldness was no more than aloofness. Or—was it possible?—shyness.

"Without evidence, they'll have to give up," Clare said.

"Yes, of course. It's just that I know she always runs on such a shoestring. That doesn't look good for her."

A little shocked, Clare said, "Are you implying she might have actually set the fire?"

"Of course not!" Alison denied. "I'm just concerned that if the gossip hurts her business any, she'll have to shut down. And it *is* her livelihood."

Most people would have interpreted the whole exchange as concern for a friend. Clare wondered. That pointed reference to Suzette's financial precariousness had been made altogether too innocently. Was Alison making sure people didn't dismiss Suzette as a suspect?

Or—Clare probed her own psyche—was she reading something into Alison's remark that wasn't there simply because she didn't like the woman?

At last Tom steered Alison to a table in the far corner of the room. Sharon and Clare's dinners arrived about then, and over her crab fettuccine, Clare pleaded, "Tell me about your life. Let's talk about anything but the fires."

"Done," Sharon agreed. "Do you want to hear about my budget problems?"

Like plenty of school districts these days, Dorset had failed to pass the last maintenance bond issue, which meant "nonessentials" like new books disappeared from the budget. "I ask you," Sharon said, "are books nonessential in a school of all places?"

"Mike was grumbling just the other day that he's supposed to do a report on the Suez Canal, and he couldn't find anything in the library."

"I could use twice the books I have. But the money's just not there."

"Maybe we could do something about that," Clare said thoughtfully. "How about some kind of fund-raiser just for the library?"

Sharon set down her fork. "Like what? Another bake sale? It's hardly worth the time."

The idea must have been lurking in the back of her mind, because Clare didn't even hesitate. "How about about an authors' day? Maybe a young authors' conference, but readings and programs for adults, too. You know how many writers live in the San Juans. Surely we could get a few to volunteer for a good cause. And besides, we have a big draw right here at home."

Her friend's eyes narrowed. "Then it's true?"

"Yes, and I'll ask him," Clare said recklessly. "Jake was a good friend of Don's. He's already doing a signing at the bookstore. If he's coming out of the closet, so to speak, why not go all the way?"

"He might not agree."

"He went to school here. It's time he contributed."

Sharon didn't look totally convinced, but her voice quickened with enthusiasm. "If he'd do it, we could have a big money-maker. Then if Suzette would sell the authors' books, we could finish with an autographing. Clare, it's brilliant! Do you really know Jake Radovich?"

Oh, how she was tempted to say, "He kissed me the other night. I'm scared by how he makes me feel." But she wasn't ready to admit as much, to try to explain the complexities of their relationship, the pain that lay beneath the surface facts. So all she said was, "I just sold him the Mueller house. I'll talk to him. You find out if we can use school facilities."

"Deal." Sharon grinned. "Your turn. How's life?"

Talking about her problems with Mike would have involved explaining many of the same complexities. Part of Clare wished she could; heaven knew, she needed a friend she could tell anything. Sharon had heard the basics of Clare's marriage, of course. But the only person who knew how inadequate Clare had felt and how guilty about her failures was Jake—ironically, the man who'd reawakened her old fears.

Even so, she chickened out and confined herself to telling Sharon about the possible sale of the marina. "Keep your fingers crossed for me," she concluded.

Maybe they hadn't had a heart-to-heart, but Clare still went home feeling cheerful thanks to the evening out. The TV reception on the island was no great shakes, but they did get a couple of channels, and for once there was actually a movie she wanted to see on one of them. She curled up on the couch with an afghan, a glass of wine and the cat on her lap, and luxuriated in the chance to watch something Mike would have hated.

Neither wine nor the romantic movie made her quite forget how quiet the house was. She told herself it wasn't unreasonable after two arson fires to feel just a little vulnerable alone at night.

At bedtime she stepped out onto the unlit porch and stood listening to the night sounds. She heard the lone cry of a heron and a scuffling just out of sight, probably the raccoons that regularly tried to get into her garbage cans. A car passed up on the road; a light went off upstairs at the Petersens'.

Comforted, Clare went to bed.

Sometime during the night, her nightmare began—fire and confusion, this time with Don laughing and laughing as she tried to find her way through the smoke. For a moment she hovered in that half-awake state where she tried to push the dream away and burrow back into sleep. But it wouldn't go—she still saw the smoke, smelled it.

Oh, Lord. Even as she snapped awake, fear rushing through her, Clare knew the smoke was real.

Feet cold on the floor, she hurried to the window and lifted her blind. Nothing. But through Mike's bedroom window she saw it, an orange glow, past the Petersens'.

"Oh, God," Clare whispered, and grabbed for clothes. Downstairs she called the emergency operator; once again, she wasn't the first.

She took the beach route, stumbling alone in the dark. A glance over her shoulder showed her that her mother-in-law's place was still dark, but the approaching sirens would undoubtedly wake Mike and Mrs. Talbot, along with the rest of the neighborhood.

She passed the Kirks' scorched property, then one more house. The bluff was becoming lower, and without even climbing the crude steps, she could see that the blazing cottage above, often rented out weekends, was a goner.

Sliding glass doors shattered as she watched, and a part of the roof fell in.

The first screaming siren abruptly died, to be replaced by men shouting and then by the powerful whoosh of the hoses. More sirens, more voices, arcs of water leaping like spray from a brilliantly lit fountain.

Clare stayed on the beach staring upward, shaken by horrific memories. Not again! The dragon's roar, the burning cinders that sprinkled the beach as though a giant had flicked his cigarette. The colors, unreal against the velvet black backdrop, the soft shush of the water behind her. Herself, alone.

"It's not the same," she said aloud. "Somebody's doing this for fun. Nobody has died."

But if it was a game, it was a frightening one.

There was no point in standing here, and she didn't want to go up and see which neighbors stared with shocked fascination at the blaze. Shivering despite the heat, she turned and started back, going too fast, fleeing past and present.

She stubbed her toe once, ignored the pain, rushed on. Once she rounded the point, the bluff rose higher, blocking lights from above. When she looked back, an orange glow, like the far-off halo above a city, was all that told what she was running away from. Even that fleeting look was a mistake. Before she found her night vision again, she tripped over a rock and crashed to her hands and knees.

Clare heard herself sob, but there were no tears in her eyes. Whimpering, she scrambled to her feet. And in the pause before she took a step, heard the crunch of a foot on the gritty sand.

Her heartbeat took a sickening leap, and she froze. "Who is it?" she called.

Darkness out of darkness, Jake was suddenly just *there,* only a few feet away, squarely in her path.

"Damn it, Clare," he said harshly, "is that you?"

Relief made her dizzy. Or was it apprehension? This was a little too much like one of her nightmares. Fire behind her, Jake ahead, and no way of knowing which was the greater danger. No, that was crazy. He was her bulwark, not the fire storm.

"No, I'm the tooth fairy! Of course it's me."

"Where's Mike?"

"He's spending the night at his grandmother's. Now, if you don't mind..." She edged a few steps to one side.

"What in hell are you doing out here by yourself?"

She might ask him the same question. "I smelled the smoke," she said defensively.

He swore. "Some nut is starting fires and *you* go wandering out to investigate? Don't you have any sense?"

Clare shivered and hugged herself. "He doesn't attack people."

"Not yet." The grimness in Jake's voice echoed her own fears.

"Well, if you're trying to scare me, you have!" Aiming for tartness, she sounded closer to hysteria. "I think I'll just head on home and lock myself in."

"I'll walk you," Jake said implacably.

She started past him, but his hand on her arm stopped her. "Hey. Slow down. Take it easy."

"Take it easy?" Definitely hysteria. Her teeth wanted to chatter. "We had eight houses on this road, and two of them have now been burned down. You'll pardon me if I'm starting to get a little anxious."

"You're trembling." His fingers tightened and he turned her toward him. She sensed him searching her face, though she couldn't imagine how he could see enough to tell anything. But apparently he had, because, voice rough, he said, "God, Clare, I'm sorry."

"What are you sorry about?" she managed, refusing to look above his dark shirtfront.

"Everything." His arms closed around her, comforting and confining at the same time. "Sorry I yelled at you. Sorry I wasn't there when you needed me."

It was unexpectedly easy to lay her head on his chest and wrap her arms around his waist, to feel how solid he was and how safe. Just to be held like this, to be able to lean, was heaven. Oh, God, how she'd missed him!

"Maybe," she whispered, "you *were* there when I really needed you."

Under her hands and cheek she felt his muscles lock. A second later, his arms dropped to his sides. "Yeah, and when was that? After your husband burned himself to death right in front of you and left you destitute? Good thing it wasn't then. I couldn't be any use to you. I was too busy consigning myself to hell for being glad Don was dead."

He'd meant to shock her, but only half succeeded. After all, he was talking to somebody who'd had enough ignoble thoughts of her own. Clare peered up at his face. "Were you really glad?"

Jake turned slightly away. "Any price for you to be free." If he meant to sound mocking, he failed; the self-hatred was too close to the surface.

"We all have dark thoughts. Yours did nothing to cause Don's death. It was what he wanted," she said almost steadily.

"Do you think I don't know that?" Jake snarled, and she felt the frustrated rage coming from him in waves. "That I don't regret it? That I wouldn't give anything—" He broke off.

Throat tight, Clare touched his rigid arm. "Jake, it's done. Over. We can't go back and we probably couldn't change anything if we did. You know I have my regrets, too. Sometimes I tell myself if I'd been stronger, I'd have gotten help sooner, but maybe Don wouldn't have wanted to live that way. Maybe he really was sacrificing himself for my sake and Mike's."

"You know what the trouble is?" Jake faced her again, his voice sounding as though it had been torn out of his throat. "I think it was all a goddamn mistake! Maybe Don was flirting with death, but I don't think he meant to die or to burn the house down. Mike was supposed to be home! Would Don have taken a chance of killing his son, too?" Jake grasped her upper arms. "And this is the good part. As much as Don hated the idea of you and me together, would he really have conceded the field?"

She'd thought the same things; oh, God, how many times had she thought them? Maybe that was why it had been so hard to let go, to say a peaceful goodbye, to tell herself she'd done all she could. Because in her heart, she'd never believed that was the time or the way Don would have chosen to die.

"He heard voices." It was her own best explanation. "He used to throw things, even though he couldn't see who was speaking. He said he'd do anything to make them go away. I always thought—" she had to clear her throat "—maybe he was trying to kill *them*, whoever the voices belonged to."

"Maybe." Jake spoke flatly, released her arms. "Come on. I'll walk you home."

Clare nodded and started along the beach, Jake striding silently at her side. Why had he suddenly backed off that way? For her benefit, in an effort to become again the man she'd once known, the comforting listener who admitted to no needs? Or was he running from his own dark admissions?

Twice she stumbled; both times Jake caught her arm and released her the moment she was steady again. Of course *he* never stumbled. It wouldn't surprise her if he saw as clearly in the dark as a cat does.

They were almost to her steps when she said, surprising herself, "It was scary back there. I mean, the fire. I don't know why it hit me more tonight."

"Last time you didn't know the fire had been set on purpose."

She blinked, reassured by his reasonable explanation. In the next instant, she felt a spurt of irritation at herself for falling instinctively into the same pattern of seeking comfort from him. Always, she was the needy one, the taker, and Jake the giver. Well, times had changed, and just because he'd dismissed the subject of his own regrets and guilt didn't mean *she* had to.

"Jake." She took a deep breath and rushed into speech. "What counts is how a person behaves, not what he thinks and feels. You're not guilty of a crime just because something you secretly wished for came true. Don't you think there are times I wished myself free? I may condemn myself for inaction, but not for those moments Don never guessed at." Except, she silently amended, for her secret hunger for a man who wasn't her husband. Maybe because Don *had* guessed? "Why should you be different?" she concluded. "You're human, too."

Jake was silent for so long she didn't think he was going to answer at all. But at last, gutturally, Jake said, "He gave me so much."

"You tried to help him."

Jake offered a mirthless laugh. "Did I?"

The pain in his response was so stark she had to understand it, confront head-on the source of his guilt. Part of her didn't want to know the answer, but it was past time the question was asked.

"Did you really want me that much?"

He made a ragged sound. "God, yes! I'd have sold my soul for you. Maybe I did sell it."

"No."

Her protest went unheeded. His big body suddenly loomed again, and his hand tangled in her hair. "Why don't I show you?" he suggested hoarsely, a second before his mouth captured hers in a kiss as hungry as flames licking at dry wood.

If she'd had any defenses, the fire had scorched them. Now they crashed down as though they'd collapsed from within. When Jake yanked her hard against his long frame, she pressed closer; when his tongue drove into her mouth, hers met it eagerly. The kiss was hot and hungry and the next thing to painful, but she didn't care, was past thinking and agonizing and battling her conscience. All she knew was that his hands burned where they touched her, that the slam of his heartbeat and the groan deep in his chest thickened her blood and ignited the coals of a kind of need she'd never felt before.

If this is betrayal, God forgive me, she thought, and lifted her hips helplessly when Jake insinuated his hard thigh between her legs.

She whimpered as he devoured her mouth with passion so out of control her heart splintered into little pieces. He let her mouth go long enough to string heated kisses across her cheek and down the sensitive skin of her throat. She snatched in a breath, then pressed her lips to the top of his head, to his forehead and temple and across the harsh angle of his jaw to meet his mouth again, her own open and desperate.

A shudder ripped through him and he lifted his head, his fingers biting into her arms. His voice was raw. "Will you come home with me?"

She never even considered saying no. She'd spent the past two years refusing to accept what she felt for Jake Radovich. She was done with cowardice.

"Yes."

His fingers tightened painfully, as though in a spasm, before loosening. "You mean that?" he asked roughly.

"I..." Her courage was fast fading, but that desperate need coiled inside her like a trap waiting to be sprung. Waiting to free her. "Yes," she repeated, only a little tremulously.

"Your house is closer."

"Yes, but what if Mike comes home?"

Jake swore under his breath. "I want you right now. Right here."

I'd have sold my soul for you. Maybe I did sell it.

The words whispered in her head, and she was shocked to realize they were an aphrodisiac. She—only she—had such power over this taciturn guarded man. How often in her life did a woman have the chance to give or withhold heaven? Maybe this was wrong—oh, God, maybe she was betraying every promise she'd made when she married Don—but she couldn't turn away now.

"All right," she said through a tight throat, and waited.

His body jerked, and she knew she'd shocked him. Perhaps he'd been trying to shock *her*. Scare her away. Why? But she didn't have a chance to think that one over. His breath hissed between his teeth, and then he had her arm in a firm grip and was hauling her along the beach.

"We might just make it to my place if I don't kiss you again." Jake sounded grim.

The five minutes it took to wend their way along the rocky beach and find and negotiate the steps that led up the bluff to his house should have been as nightmarish as any of her dreams. Behind them a house burned, torched for reasons as incomprehensible to her as had been the demons who'd tormented her husband. Even this far away the smoke was sharp in her nostrils, recalling another time, another horror.

But Jake's hand was hard and warm, his steps sure. He had Clare half running, gasping for breath and concentrating on where she put her feet. If she'd been surer of herself, she might have teased him. "Where's the fire?" she could have asked. The idea made a bubble of half-hysterical laughter rise in her throat.

He fumbled trying to unlock the door, swearing under his breath the whole time. Jake, clumsy. Nervous. Maybe as terrified as she was. The realization calmed her, gave her legs the strength to carry her the last step into his house.

A lamp provided a pool of warm light in a far corner of the large room, and she had a quick impression of color and books where there had been bland neutrals. Then Jake closed the door and swept Clare off her feet.

One look at the strain on his face, and she started to tremble inside. Desire swept through her, stealing her air and her strength. She wrapped her arms around his neck and held on for dear life, unable to look away from the glittering intensity of his gaze.

Not once did either of them look away as he carried her up the stairs and down the hall. Somehow she'd known, when she'd shown him the house, that if she ever saw his bedroom again, this would be why. In the light of a small lamp, she saw a huge bed covered with a black spread. Books were stacked ten high on the floor, as though he read here more than slept. But not tonight. As he let her slip down his body, he kicked the pile of books to one side.

She expected passion, but for the longest time he didn't move at all. The intensity in his eyes had metamorphosed into heart-stopping hesitancy and wonder.

"I can't believe you're standing next to my bed."

Me alone, of all women. "I'm so ordinary," she argued.

"Never." His big hands came up to frame her face. His eyes didn't waver from hers, even as he softly explored the contours of her cheeks and jaw, as his thumb shaped her mouth and she shivered in reaction. "I must be dreaming," he muttered.

She didn't want to think about dreams or nightmares. "No. I don't know whether I should be here, but I am."

His hands stilled. "You're entitled."

"Let's not think about it. About him."

Jake deliberately misunderstood. "Mike would be peppering that window with a BB gun if he had any idea."

Mike. Clare quelled the shudder of dread with a dose of realism. Give him a year or two, and he'd be trying to make it with some girl in the back seat of the junker he was saving his money for. He had a life ahead of him. She should, too.

"Would you kiss me?" she asked in a voice that didn't sound quite like her own.

"You're sure?" His was like the rasp of a shaven jaw against the soft skin of her breast. Something she hadn't felt in so long she'd begun to wonder if such contrasts even existed.

Clare tried to speak and failed. Did the next best thing and smiled, though her mouth trembled as much with trepidation and outright terror as promise.

Jake groaned and kissed her, his lips achingly tender, piercing her with such sweetness her knees buckled. She never gave a thought to saving herself from falling; somehow she knew he'd catch her. Hadn't he always in one way or another?

Not always, a corner of her mind reminded her. Once, he let you fall.... But she refused to listen. He was human, too, wasn't he?

And of course this time he did catch her, the solid strength of his arms a dangerous memory she'd tried to forget. She wanted to take some of that strength into herself, take *him* into herself. Her body knew how to do that, and she was shocked to realize how ready she was.

His tongue stroked her lips, and she whimpered as she let them part. Her hips moved restlessly, especially when she discovered the way even those small movements made his muscles contract with pleasure and a groan work its way out of him.

About the time the groan vibrated in his throat, his kiss changed. Seduction became raw hunger; suddenly he was using his teeth and his tongue and his mouth as though he wanted to consume her. One hand kneaded the back of her neck; the other lifted her hips to meet the frantic grind of his.

When he raised his head, she saw his eyes, wild with savage need. His fingers shook as he peeled off her sweater, wrestled with the front clasp of her bra. He succeeded and it slithered off her shoulders to fall unheeded at her feet. A rumble of satisfaction came from him. She gazed down as his big brown hands engulfed her pale breasts. She'd never before felt a touch so intense it seared her to the soles of her feet. He bent to rub his mouth against the swell of flesh, to kiss and nibble and gently suckle, and Clare was distantly shocked to hear herself uttering small cries of need.

When her knees buckled, Jake lowered her to the bed and followed her down. She struggled to pull off his T-shirt as he stripped her of her leggings and panties. "You, too," she whispered, when he started to bend down for her mouth again.

He gave a laugh that was close to a groan and shucked his jeans. Oh, Lord, his body was beautiful, long and sleek, muscles rippling under tanned skin as her hands explored. His face was almost unrecognizable, all sharp angles and predatory male. His eyes blazed and a flush ran across his cheekbones. His hair was disarrayed and his mouth twisted as he gazed down at her. How she used to dream of seeing Jake's formidable control shattered! Of shattering it herself.

"Lovely," he said huskily. "You have a dancer's body." Clare arched upward and he came down to meet her. "I should take this slow."

"Don't," she said. "Please."

His probing fingers found slick heat, and the next moment he was growling, "Wrap your legs around me. That's it. Oh, God, that's it."

She took him inside her, as deep as the fears that walked her dreams at night. He filled her, was—for this brief time—part of her.

She had never made love like this, rough and desperate and out of control. Each time he withdrew was agony, the long inward stroke ecstasy. She called his name, let the pleasure sweep over her in crashing waves. But for sobbing breaths, Jake was silent until the end, when he breathed her name as though it was a prayer.

HE USED TO THINK that if he had her just once, he could die happy. That had been as idiotic as telling himself that if his father just once approved of him, his self-esteem would be magically restored. As a child needed years of approval, he needed a lifetime of possessing Clare before he went to his reward—or damnation.

The last thought was an uncomfortable one, giving him a brief vision of red-hot fires, spiritual and real, and of the friend who'd died in them. The friend who had loved Clare and claimed her first.

Jake wanted her to break the silence now, to whisper an idle endearment or even to say, "I feel guilty." But she remained quiet, her head nestled on his shoulder and her fingers splayed on his chest. He breathed in her scent, lavender and Clare, and moved his lips soundlessly against the silky waves of hair tumbled across his neck.

He should say something if she couldn't. *That was everything I dreamed it would be.* Or even, *I love you.* Was love, simple and eternal, what he felt? Or was it something far more complicated, having to do with his affection and jealousy for the friend who'd been his lifeline?

The truth was, Jake knew himself for a coward. What if he spoke and still she stayed silent? What if she'd been swept away by desire, but wasn't ready to admit to love? If indeed she felt love, or anything approaching it, at all. Maybe she was like that wild bird he'd imagined himself coaxing, luring, tempting. At last she'd alighted on his finger for the briefest of moments, but never with any intention of staying. If her heart was still wild, could he close his hand around her and hold her captive?

At last he felt her stir. Away from him. Her hand on his chest curled into a fist, and she shifted an inch or two back, the boneless trust of her body retreating into wariness.

A chill settled in his gut and he said roughly, "Clare—"

"I'd really better go." She sat up and swung her legs to the floor. Her voice was quick and high. "You never know. If the sirens woke Mike, he might go home. I should be there."

Jake wanted to ask her to stay, tell her he needed her. The words wouldn't come. *I see,* Clare had said, *a man who doesn't like being the beggar.* And in this relationship, whatever she thought to the contrary, he *was* the beggar.

"I'll walk you home," he said.

CHAPTER EIGHT

MIKE'S GREETING was so sullen when he came into the kitchen the next morning that Clare had to wonder whether he'd discovered her absence during the night.

"Did you hear the sirens?" she asked casually—probably too casually, considering the subject.

His head came up and his eyes darkened with alarm. "Sirens? You mean, there was another fire?"

She took a sip of tea. "I can't believe you slept through them."

He thrust out his chin. "Are you calling me a liar?"

Why was everything she said to him suddenly so inflammatory? "Of course not. I didn't mean it that way. I'm just surprised you and Grandma were able to sleep through the racket. Yes, there was another fire. That summer cottage beyond the Kirks'. The one the Bishops rented last year."

"Did it burn down?"

"Yeah." Clare looked out the window toward the water, blue with a metallic sheen today. What she'd give to see it gray and storm-tossed, battered with rain! But here it was October, and still one dry Indian-summer day followed another. "It was just like the Kirks'," she said. "I walked down there, but I didn't stay once I saw which house was on fire. I thought it might be Mrs. Fowler's or even the bed-and-breakfast..." Presumably she could leave unstated the subtext: she'd been afraid somebody might be *in* the burning house. "Anyway, once I realized it was that cottage, I just sat on the beach for a while."

His expression said, *So?* Clare shut up. He was going to start to wonder why she was explaining her movements.

"Do you have any plans today?" she asked.

"Why?" His tone was sulky. "Do you have a list of chores I'm supposed to do?"

She was exasperated enough to be tempted to come up with one on the spot. But the two of them didn't need any new battlegrounds.

"Nothing but the usual." She raised her eyebrows. "Am I such a slave driver?"

"Geoff doesn't have to do stuff in the house like dishes. All *he* has to do is mow the lawn."

"Geoff's mother isn't a single parent. What's more—" Clare allowed some acerbity to creep into her voice "—I don't believe in those kinds of traditional roles. I wouldn't marry a man who refused to help with housework, and I'm not going to raise my son that way." *So there,* she almost added.

He rolled his eyes to express his disdain for her philosophy. Or was it her parenting?

She gritted her teeth and smiled again. "I have to cover the office today. Give me a call if you're going anywhere. Just leave a message if I'm not there. Oh, and put some hamburger out to defrost this afternoon, okay?"

"How can I go anywhere if I have to do that?"

"Well, then, stay here," she suggested, and left before she said something she'd regret.

Unfortunately, despite a slew of weekend advertising, calls were few and she had plenty of time to brood about last night.

Okay, so she'd been honest with herself and admitted how much she wanted Jake Radovich. Great. She was an adult, for God's sake! Adults knew they couldn't have everything they wanted. Aside from Mike—and her stepson was a big issue—she had too many confused emotions where Jake was concerned. In the heat of passion, she'd blocked out all those emotions, but they hadn't gone away.

Pushing back her chair, Clare went to the window, barely seeing the ferry easing up to the dock.

Was it dumb, she asked herself, to suffer qualms based on the fact that Don had been so bitterly jealous of Jake? She had trusted Mike to understand that Don's paranoid fears were irrational. Why was she letting those same fears give her an undeserved guilty conscience?

So what if she was attracted to Jake then? She hadn't acted on that attraction. Jake might be tormented by guilt now, but he hadn't acted on whatever he'd felt for her, either. Her husband had been dead more than a year. Would Don, in his right mind, really begrudge them a passionate affair?

Clare made a face and went back to her desk. How easily she reasoned it out! So why couldn't she close her eyes without seeing Don's face, contorted with rage and suspicion, without hearing the furious obscene words he flung at her as he accused her of screwing his best friend? Why did she have such trouble remembering the easygoing man she'd married, the one who'd said, ''I won't lie to you. I loved Sheila. Chances are, I'll be better at loving you because of how I felt about her.''

The truth wasn't hard to come by. Rage and suspicion were symptoms of his illness. The heartbreaking insecurity she had also seen on his face wasn't. Part of him, locked inside, knew what he had become, knew he was no longer lovable. That part of him was so terrified she would leave she could never do it. She'd built her life around reassuring him, around trying to give him back the sense of security that was his saddest loss.

It would be different if she was falling in love with a man she'd just met, making a new start. Instead, last night she'd finally acted on those deep-seated longings she'd suppressed for the sake of the man she'd married and promised "for better or worse." She'd made lies of all her denials.

Even if she could live with that knowledge, all she had to do was look into Mike's face to see that same insecurity. Don's son, who'd lost both his parents, had to feel vulnerable in a way most teenagers didn't. How could he be expected to have faith that she, too, wouldn't leave him?

If Mike felt that in liking or even loving Jake, he was betraying his father, he would never accept a relationship between her and Jake. Which meant she had a painful choice to make.

Her stepson or Jake. A child who needed her versus a man who didn't. There was really no choice at all.

CLARE SIGHED and, to her cat's displeasure, flipped over in bed, sneaking another look at the green numbers on her digital clock—1:03 a.m. She wasn't the only one having trouble sleeping, either; she'd earlier heard the creak of footsteps on the stairs and the sound of the refrigerator door opening and closing. All a snack would've done for her was upset her stomach. Mike's, of course, was cast iron.

She flopped onto her back again and stared at the dark ceiling. Why hadn't Jake called today? Had he lost interest now that he'd satisfied whatever obsession had brought him in pursuit of her? Or had she somehow disappointed him?

Clare groaned. She ought to be grateful Jake *hadn't* called, considering she had no idea what to say to him.

And somehow she didn't think he'd been any more disappointed than she had been. All she had to do was close her eyes and remember the look on his face, the stark need and shattering desire, hear the way he'd called her name at the end.

Clare gave a little whimper and flipped over again. Misty, who'd put up with enough tossing, made a grumbling noise and thumped to the floor. Clare hardly noticed.

If Jake loved her— Did he love her? Was that what he'd been implying? If he did, how could she say, "No, sorry, Mike needs me more"?

How could she not?

At the first whiff of smoke, she stiffened. Was Mike cooking? In the middle of the night? He wouldn't have left a burner on and gone back to bed, would he?

She couldn't smell smoke at all in the dark hall or when she stood at the top of the stairs. Had she imagined it? Maybe she'd been starting to fall asleep, and her nightmare had been waiting.

But she smelled smoke again, stronger, the moment she stepped back into her bedroom. Heart in her throat, she hurried to the window, which was open a crack. Her mother-in-law's cottage was dark; Clare couldn't see any orange glow beyond it. Oh, God. What should she do?

Last night's jeans and a sweater lay on a chair; she pulled them on, thrust her feet into sneakers and went downstairs, carrying the flashlight from her bedside drawer. Outside the night was moonless, and she paused, listening.

Silence. But something was burning, and not far away. Should she have called 911 before she came out? It wouldn't take long to check Mrs. Talbot's. She wouldn't try to stumble through the woods to Jake's. If she saw nothing at her mother-in-law's, she'd go back and call him.

Aiming the narrow beam of light ahead, Clare hurried across the grass. Damn, it was dark. She'd been leaving on her porch light, but Mrs. Talbot apparently hadn't done the same tonight.

One second Clare didn't have to think about breathing; the next she inhaled smoke and doubled over coughing. Still gagging, she stumbled forward.

Smoke was thick around her. It was like her dream. Worse than her dream. She couldn't see anything. Her eyes stung and watered; the breath she was holding ripped at her chest in a desperate bid to escape.

"Mrs. Talbot!" she screamed. "Anne!"

Staggering, she collided with something. No, some-one, Clare realized on a spurt of panic. She wrenched backward just as hands closed on her arms. Her flashlight beam swung wildly, and through the swirl of smoke she saw Jake, teeth set and eyes streaming.

For an instant, her nightmare mixed with what was happening now, and she was confused. He *had* been chasing her, and now he'd caught her. She let out a squeak of terror, saw the recognition of it on his face. Then he let her go. Abruptly he turned and, bent over at the waist, ran toward her mother-in-law's house.

If this was a nightmare, it was a waking one. Dizzy, lungs burning, Clare followed him. A rosebush tore at her arm, another snagged her ankle, but she hardly felt the pain, only knew that those were real flames ahead.

Her eyes watering so that she could hardly see, she ran into Jake's solid body again on the small lawn, where he'd stopped. The smoke had shifted away so that they could breathe in gasps. But at the sound of shattering glass, Clare lifted her horrified gaze to see fire leaping out of a downstairs window.

"Oh, my God," she whispered.

"Is her bedroom still upstairs?"

"Yes." In her terror, it was hard to think. "There's a ladder just inside the garage. On the right wall."

"Throw some rocks. See if you can't wake her up." Jake disappeared back into the smoke.

Clare ran to the side of the house. The downstairs window gave a view through the kitchen. The flames were in the hall. Frantically she shone her flashlight around until she found a rock.

She flung it as hard as she could. It smashed through the upstairs window, and she yelled, "Anne, wake up!"

Smoke curled through the hole in the window, and she cried, "Jake! Oh, God, hurry!"

Had it been a mistake to break the window? Would the fresh air suck flames up the stairs? She shot a glance into the kitchen, to see fire licking along the floor.

The next second Jake was there, leaning the ladder against the house. "Hold it, will you?" he snapped, and started climbing.

Clare locked her arms around the ladder and braced it, feeling it shift and sink in the soft soil of the flower bed. Above, Jake swore and broke out pieces of window glass, dropping them into the bushes. He must be slicing his hands, she thought fearfully. The ladder suddenly went still, and she knew he'd climbed into Mrs. Talbot's bedroom.

She let go of the ladder and picked up her flashlight, aiming the beam at the window ledge. All she could see was thick smoke. Could Jake hold his breath long enough? She prayed incoherently, counting the seconds. One thousand one, one thousand two, one thousand three... Where was he? *Please God, please God, please. Not Jake.*

A dark shape appeared above, and a foot came over the ledge. Clare dropped her flashlight and grabbed for the ladder, just as it started to slide sideways. She put all her weight against it and squeezed her eyes shut as pain hit her collarbone.

A breath rasped, the ladder shook, and Jake reached the bottom, the limp form of Mike's grandmother draped over his shoulder.

"Damn it to hell," he said in a strangled voice. "Why don't I hear sirens? Does everybody in this neighborhood sleep like the dead?"

Clare looked past him into the kitchen, where the flames had almost reached the stove. The gas stove.

"Run!" she screamed. "It's going to explode!"

In front, the porch was collapsing with a groan. The blaze leapt toward the roof, illuminating the maze of rosebushes and narrow paths in an eerie orange light. They stumbled up the sloping driveway to the road, where Jake stopped.

He laid Mrs. Talbot on her back and bent his head. "She's not breathing," he muttered.

Behind them, a deep boom shot flames thirty, forty feet high. Cinders rained down on the road. Oblivious, Clare dropped to her knees and felt for a pulse as he tilted her mother-in-law's head back and began mouth-to-mouth resuscitation. With that weak heart...

Amazingly she found a pulse fluttering hesitantly in Mrs. Talbot's throat. "Her heart's beating!" she exclaimed.

He nodded and kept up the rhythm.

The undulating wail she usually dreaded started up, and she breathed a thank-you.

"Clare!" Mike bellowed from a distance. His voice was frantic. "Mom! Where are you?"

"I'm here!" She stood and waved.

He raced over, barefooted and wearing nothing but pajama bottoms. "Grandma! Is she all right?"

Clare wrapped her arms around her son. He hugged her back, his thin body trembling.

"I think so. I hope so. Thanks to Jake."

"I called 911." Mike sniffed and swiped at tears on his cheeks. "Why haven't they come?"

Other sirens had joined the first lonely one, and she said, "Listen. They're on their way."

The first truck rumbled down the road, passing them. Right behind it was the ambulance, which slammed to a stop and backed onto the gravel shoulder right beside them.

It was astonishing how quickly an all-volunteer fire department could respond. Men called from their beds were somehow here within minutes, maneuvering enormous yellow fire trucks into position and snapping orders as others uncoiled fat hoses and trained streams of water on the blaze. Medics had taken over from Jake, and Mrs. Talbot now had an oxygen mask on her face. Within seconds she was on a stretcher and being lifted into the back of the aid car.

Clare pulled herself together. "We'll follow her to the clinic. Get some clothes on, Mike."

He nodded and headed for the house. Clare turned to see Jake arguing with the emergency medical technician.

"I'm all right. Just get going."

"Sir, you should be checked for smoke inhalation, and your hands are bleeding."

Jake had a forbidding frown on his face, but Clare ignored it. "Don't be a macho idiot. Go. Mike and I are coming. I'll give you a ride home."

He glowered at her, but then gave a reluctant nod and climbed into the back of the aid car. The EMT slammed the door, and Clare hurried down her driveway.

Mike was already tying his high-top shoes, but she had to hunt for her purse, then her car keys.

"Why don't I always put them in the same place?" she exclaimed in frustration, stabbing her fingers into her hair as she tried to remember what she'd done with them.

"Here they are." Mike dangled them in front of her. "Why don't you?"

She snatched them from him. "Because I don't think! Are you ready?"

Dorset was too small to have its own hospital. The limited medical care was one drawback to island living. When his mother developed heart trouble, Don had wanted her to move. She wouldn't hear of it.

Stubbornly she'd said, "If I actually have a heart attack, my odds of surviving it are pretty miniscule, anyway. For that, I should leave a waterfront house and my garden to move to a condo on a busy street in Anacortes? No, thanks."

Lights blazed in the small clinic when Clare pulled into the parking lot. The basics of emergency treatment were offered here, while patients in need of more drastic care were airlifted to the mainland. Inside, a nurse met them in the lobby.

"Mrs. Talbot is breathing on her own," she said. "The doctor is looking her over right now. Given her age and heart condition, she'll be flown to the hospital in Anacortes as a precaution, but I imagine you can see her first. Let me go check."

"And Mr. Radovich?"

"Right in there." She nodded at the other examining room. Its door stood open.

Clare peeked in to see Jake getting his hand bandaged by a white-coated man who had his back to the door. Blood-soaked gauze littered the examining table, and the water in the basin below Jake's hand was pink. He was filthy, soot streaked across his cheek and smudged on his forehead, his eyes bloodshot and his hair sweat-soaked, but Clare wanted nothing more than to walk in and wrap her arms around him.

Only then he lifted his gaze and saw her. The remoteness in his gray eyes was chilling.

"Are you all right?" she asked hesitantly.

The male nurse caring for him glanced over his shoulder. "Clare. Hell of a night. Fortunately these cuts are pretty superficial. Mr. Radovich wrapped his shirt around his hands before he broke the glass."

Clare lifted her chin and met Jake's cool stare. "Don't let him tell you he's not a hero," she told the nurse, whose wife was a grocery checkout clerk. "Thank God he was there."

Jake's voice was hoarse from the smoke, but otherwise dispassionate. "How's Mrs. Talbot?"

"They say she's breathing. Jake—"

"Don't make me into something I'm not."

"You saved her life."

"I owed her." The brusqueness of his voice said, *It had nothing to do with you.*

Clare's cheeks flushed hot, but she remained conscious of the nurse. Whatever she said and did would be common gossip tomorrow. So she kept her chin up and said with dignity, "Let me thank you, anyway, Jake. If you hadn't been there—"

"You're welcome." End of discussion.

What had she done to make him look at her so coldly? He was clearly angry. Was it that moment when she'd been afraid of him? But surely she had reason, she thought defensively. In the smoke and confusion, shouldn't she have been scared?

Not once she recognized him.

She wanted to open her mouth and say, "I never thought you started the fire. It's my own feelings that scare me." But of course she couldn't, not with a witness. Maybe not even without one.

So she nodded stiffly and retreated.

CLARE DIDN'T GET out of bed again until almost noon on Sunday. By the time she reached the kitchen, Misty was bumping her ankles insistently, wanting to be fed. Ignoring her, Clare called the hospital in Anacortes right away and talked to Mrs. Talbot, who sounded dopey but claimed to be fine. The doctors wanted to keep her for another day or two, however. Clare let Mike talk to her and was pleased at how gentle his voice sounded.

They spent a lazy afternoon that might have been pleasant had the house not been permeated by the smell of smoke, which constantly reminded them of the charred ruin next door. And thinking about that set Clare to wondering why Jake had looked so cold and angry, then to remembering a moment when he hadn't looked angry at all. She should have said something at the clinic. But what? "I love you"? "I don't dare love you"?

She succeeded in wrenching her mind away, only to start all over again, like a tape that had barely had time to rewind: that one frightening instant when she'd realized it was Jake there in the smoke; the even more frightening one when he'd disappeared into the burning house after Mrs. Talbot; her mother-in-law, still as death. And later, the chill in Jake's eyes, which dragged her back to remembering the passion and tenderness and even uncertainty she'd seen there just the night before. The way his hands had trembled, the triumph and gratitude in his voice when he called her name...

Oh, Lord, couldn't she think about anything else? Dinner. She'd make dinner, she decided, glancing at the clock. That would distract her. Even if she wasn't hungry, Mike would be. Clare was heading into the kitchen when she was galvanized by a memory that, for the first time all day, had nothing to do with Jake. Phyllis. Today was the planned apple harvest.

"Be back in a minute," she called to Mike. She hurried down the road to find the Kirks' trees stripped of apples. Phyllis had gone ahead without Clare and Mrs. Talbot.

The long dirt lane leading up to the Carlsons was rutted and potholed. Clare sometimes wondered if the Carlsons kept it that way to discourage visitors. Tony's rattletrap pickup truck couldn't be hurt by a little jouncing around, but nobody else would want to bring a car up this drive.

In contrast, the old farmhouse was well cared for and the huge vegetable gardens weed free and well mulched for winter, except where lettuce and broccoli and late corn still grew. Chickens scurried out of the way of the car. Phyllis came to the door at Clare's knock.

"Oh, hi. Come on in."

She was a tall thin woman with blond hair worn in a single braid down her back. Today she wore a T-shirt and faded jeans and was barefoot. Her face held enviable serenity; however primitive their life-style, she'd obviously found contentment.

Clare followed her in. "I came to apologize. I completely forgot about our plans today."

Phyllis said comfortably over her shoulder, "Don't be silly. I didn't expect you after the fire at Mrs. Talbot's. Tell me, how is she?"

"Fine, apparently." Clare sat at the well-scrubbed kitchen table. "It was scary, though."

"I went ahead, anyway. Tony gave me a hand." Phyllis indicated the rows of jars holding applesauce that filled the limited counter space in this old-fashioned kitchen. "I froze most of the apples. If you'd like, we can still get together someday and can some more. Please, take some of these home with you. And a few for Mrs. Talbot."

"Oh, Phyllis..." Absurdly Clare felt tears sting her eyes.

"Is there anything we can do?"

"I don't think so. Anne will be moving in with us for the time being. Her house was completely destroyed."

"We walked over to see it," Tony said from the kitchen doorway. "She was lucky to get out."

Clare had never felt very comfortable with him. Perhaps it was only because his bearded face was so unreadable. But he'd been a good neighbor, and she tried not to let the prejudices of other people color how she saw him.

"Very lucky," she agreed soberly. "If it hadn't been for Jake..."

"We haven't met him." The flat statement seemed tinged with suspicion, a little like the old-time islanders:

Jake was a newcomer, which automatically made him untrustworthy.

"Jake's an old friend of my husband's," Clare said.

Tony grunted. "You're being careful nights?"

Some caution made her lie. "My mother-in-law and I'll be taking turns sitting up." She couldn't imagine either of the Carlsons as the arsonist, but she didn't really know them that well. When she got right down to it, wasn't Tony as likely as Bart Petersen or Suzette Fowler? "I hope you're doing the same," she added.

"Son of a bitch'd run into a real surprise if he came here," Tony said brusquely. His blue eyes were cold. "I got a regular goddamned arsenal here, and I wouldn't mind using it."

How comforting. Shortly thereafter, Clare excused herself and hurried home with a few applesauce jars under her arm and a promise from Phyllis that she'd drop off more.

"Remember, if you want to get together someday, I have all those apples in the freezer," Phyllis called from the porch.

Clare waved her gratitude. But it was Tony she was thinking about as she picked her way down the rutted lane. Tony, with the arsenal he intended to use to protect himself and his woman when doomsday came. If Tony thought he had something to gain by burning out his neighbors now, would a little matter of a conscience stop him?

CLARE HEARD snippets of gossip from the minute she got to work on Monday. At lunchtime in the bakery she heard more, and in line at the grocery store on her way home.

"Somebody's got it in for that neighborhood," people said. "Mental illness," someone murmured. "Runs in families." And later, "He's always been angry."

He? Clare wondered, disturbed. There weren't all that many men—or boys—in her neighborhood. Tony Carlson, Bart Petersen, Jake, Mike. Bart had a two-year-old son. Which one was supposed to be angry? Or had they been talking about somebody else? Jake's father maybe? She'd wondered herself about him.

She got home right before Mike, who slammed in the door within minutes after school let out. Clare had been stripping her bed. Now she came to the top of the stairs. "Hi. How was your day?"

He blundered up the stairs and pushed past her. With shock, she saw he'd been crying. He went into his bedroom, dropped his book bag and flung himself facedown on the bed.

"Mike." Clare followed, sitting beside him. She gently stroked his hair. "What's wrong?"

He shook his head violently.

"You didn't get report cards yet."

No reaction.

"Didn't you talk about going home with Ian today?"

Even muffled, Mike's voice was acid with bitterness and hurt. "He's decided I'm shit. He asked somebody else, instead."

"That's what this is about? You had a fight?"

Mike turned his puffy tear-streaked face toward her. "It's not that."

"Then what?" The way puzzle pieces suddenly came together, words connected. "Crazy." "Runs in families." "Always been angry." *Mike.* Nausea swept over her. But she didn't want to jump to conclusions. Carefully she asked, "Was it just Ian?"

"Everybody was talking about the fire when I got to school today. At first people were really cool, since it was my grandma who got hurt." His voice became duller. "Then I heard whispers. You know, the kind where they quit talking when they see you? At lunchtime nobody sat with me. Nobody!"

She was so angry it was hard to speak normally. "Not even Geoff?"

"He had a play rehearsal. I don't know. I guess he hasn't dropped me."

"Did you actually hear what they were saying?"

He sniffed, and she handed him a tissue. "Yeah, eventually. It was Ian. Jeez, I thought he was my friend!" Mike squeezed his eyes shut. "I walked up behind him, and he was talking about how my dad was crazy, too, and how he liked fires. He liked 'em so much, he set himself on fire." Mike lifted himself on one elbow and looked at her with the hurt bewilderment of a young child. "He was *laughing*."

"Ian Mullin, huh?" Clare said grimly, "I know exactly where he got his opinion."

She should have picked up on it sooner. She remembered Roger Mullin telling Bart Petersen, "We have troubled kids all right. We could all name a few." Just as he'd been challenged to name them, he'd backed into her. At the time she didn't understand his discomfiture when he saw her. Now she did. He'd been going to name her son.

Mike frowned. "What d'ya mean?"

"His father. That SOB." She bit back the rest of what she felt like saying. "What did you do?"

"I punched him out."

Just the way to quell rumors about violence and insanity. On the other hand, right this minute she wouldn't mind slugging Roger Mullin. Not that she could let her son guess she sympathized with his violent impulse.

"Oh, Mike. That's just going to get you into trouble. And it won't shut them up."

"It shut *him* up," her son said. "And..."

"And?"

"I got suspended for two days."

"I see."

He rolled onto his back and stared at the ceiling. "I wouldn't have gone to school tomorrow, anyway!" he declared passionately. "I'll never go again."

Clare smoothed his hair back from his forehead. "Yes, you are," she told him. "In the first place, you have to. In the second place, if you're going to keep your pride, you can't let them know they've hurt you. There are times when holding on to your pride means convincing at least part of the world that you don't give a damn. I think this is one of those times."

"Can't we move?" he begged.

Not without making those jerks ashamed of themselves first, she vowed silently. And what about Jake? What she said was, "Even if it was the right thing to do, we couldn't afford to move. Anyway, we've been happy here." If "happy" could describe the bland state her life was before she'd found out what it was like in Jake's arms.

Mike was silent.

"I'll bet you'll find you have some real friends," she added bracingly, hoping she was right. "Like Geoff. And sooner or later, the arsonist will be caught."

"Yeah," he said despondently. "Sure."

"I'll tell you what." Clare ruffled his hair. "I was going to take the morning ferry to pick up your grandma from the hospital. Why don't we hustle and make it onto the evening one, instead? We can have a fancy dinner, do some early Christmas shopping and spend the night in Anacortes, then all catch the morning ferry back. What do you say?''

He sat up. "Anything to get out off this island."

"Then let's move!''

ALTHOUGH THEY PULLED into the terminal at the last minute, the ferry was half-empty. Up on the passenger deck, Mike slumped on the wide padded seat and became engrossed in a book. Too unsettled to do the same, Clare gazed out the window as they wended through narrow channels to call at Orcas, Shaw and Lopez islands before turning toward Anacortes.

Despite her instinctive reaction of anger at the people who whispered about Mike, Clare knew she had some thinking to do. If only she could prove he'd been home when one of the fires was set! In fact, the truth was that he could easily have slipped out and returned as furtively. They had gasoline in a can in their own garage. Mike used it to run the lawn mower. Means and opportunity. He had both.

She felt traitorous even considering the possibility that Mike might have committed a crime as terrible as setting his own grandmother's house on fire. But if everyone else was talking, she had to seriously think this through. He was angry and rebellious; could he have so much hate in his heart?

No. No and no and no! She wouldn't believe it. He was a good kid dealing with some complicated emotions. His mother had died, his father had killed himself, and he was dependent on a stepmother for a home. Of course he was angry and even rebellious! But he wasn't crazy, and he loved his grandmother. If Mike had been the arsonist, he'd have been more likely to burn Jake's house than Mrs. Talbot's. And fire scared him as much as it did Clare.

Except...she had a flash memory of the way he'd stared at the blaze consuming the Kirks' house. He'd looked hypnotized. And when their own house in Oregon had burned down, his first reaction hadn't been shock or fear, but fascination.

I mean, it's awful, but look at those colors. I wish I had my camera.

No! She wouldn't think it! Fires had a way of hypnotizing everybody. All she had to do was remember her neighbors, all staring, mesmerized. Mike was no different.

She'd heard footsteps going down the stairs last night. Had she ever heard them come back up? She'd assumed Mike was asleep in his room, but she hadn't actually seen him. He *was* in his room the night the Kirks' burned, but he could have slipped home before the smell of smoke awakened her. The bookstore fire would have been the hardest for a boy his age to set, but even it was within the realm of possibility. Town wasn't two miles away. He rode it on his mountain bike all the time.

Maybe that was why no gasoline was used. Carrying a can on his bike would've been tough, and a dead giveaway if he'd been seen.

But why the bookstore?

Clare sneaked a look at her stepson, reading across from her. In too-big jeans and a sacky T-shirt, he looked so normal. It was impossible to imagine him pouring gasoline all over the Kirks' front steps, flinging a match onto it, then running home to bed.

Her throat closed. And his grandmother's house...

But the bookstore, that made a twisted kind of sense. He resented Jake. The arsonist had used Jake's books to light the blaze.

Then why not burn down Jake's house? Why the two empty cottages? Why her mother-in-law's?

Could he be angry that his grandmother hadn't taken him in after his father died?

But he understood why she hadn't!

Did he? a small voice whispered in Clare's head. Or was she expecting too much understanding from a boy his age?

No. Mike *was* a normal boy. She wouldn't believe otherwise.

At the hospital, Anne sat propped against pillows, so frail that she didn't look like the same woman Clare was used to seeing wearing gardening gloves, pruning shears in hand. Her gray hair was matted, her brown eyes staring listlessly at the chattering faces on the television set. At the sight of Clare and Mike, she turned off the TV and struggled to sit up.

"I didn't expect to see you until tomorrow."

"We decided to spend the night over here." Clare took her hand. "We were anxious about you."

Awkwardly Mike asked, "Are you okay, Grandma?"

"I feel fine," she said, her voice quavering. "I'm sure all this fussing is unnecessary."

"It's best to be cautious," Clare said. "But we're looking forward to taking you home with us."

Mrs. Talbot's eyes filled with tears. "You don't have room for me. I think maybe the time has come for me to go into a retirement home. Don wanted me to, you know."

"He didn't," Clare protested. "He just thought you'd be better off without a yard to take of and the long ferry ride if you became ill. But what did he know? You love your garden. There's no reason on earth to give it up."

"Yeah, you can rebuild, Grandma," Mike seconded. "It'll be cool. You've been wanting new carpet and stuff, anyway."

"But it would take so long."

"So what? You can live with us."

"And my garden." She sounded as feeble as she looked. "Everything must have been killed. I'd be starting all over."

Clare started to assure her that she and Mike would help, but her stepson interrupted her.

"I went over there yesterday," he said. "Your roses and boxwood and stuff look okay. The ones right around the house were burned, but in most of the garden you can hardly tell there was a fire. You're the one who's always telling me how tough those roses are."

"My Zepherine Drouhin?"

"That's the one on the arch, right? That smells so good? It's fine," he said confidently.

"Oh, my." Mrs. Talbot was crying in earnest now. "And here I've been imagining... You're sure?"

Mike tried to look wounded. "Would I lie?"

Maybe, but Clare knew suddenly, with passionate certainty, that he wouldn't have set those fires. He'd cared enough to go over and check his grandmother's garden so that he could reassure her. He would never have burned the house down in the first place.

Eventually Clare suggested he go get a snack in the cafeteria and bring her back a soda. He departed happily, leaving silence in his wake. Clare was just having second thoughts about adding another worry to Mrs. Talbot's already full plate, when she asked quietly, "What is it?"

She'd have to know soon enough. And Clare's instinct told her it would be good for her mother-in-law to feel needed right now.

So she said, "There's been talk. About Mike." She repeated what she'd overheard and Mike's story of what he'd faced at school.

Mrs. Talbot reacted just as Clare had hoped she would. In outrage, she said, "People are actually suggesting that my grandson set *my* house on fire?"

"I'm afraid so, and since nobody has the guts to say it to my face, I can't even argue."

"But it's so ridiculous!" Mrs. Talbot looked stronger by the second. "He's been either home or at my house when those fires were set. How could he...?"

"I can't prove he was home. He says you two didn't even wake up the other night."

"Well, that's true, but..."

"The night before last, I didn't check his bedroom before I ran over to your place. I assumed he was home, but I don't know for a fact that he was."

Mrs. Talbot's brow furrowed. "Surely you don't think..."

"Not in a million years," Clare said strongly.

"Then what can we do?"

"As soon as you're home and well enough, we can take turns sitting up. The arsonist isn't going to stop now. Next time there's a fire, I want one of us to be able to vouch for Mike's whereabouts."

Her mother-in-law nodded firmly. "I feel well enough right now. Why, I can nap during the day."

Clare's anxiety eased a little. "Thank you," she said simply.

"He's my grandson, you know."

"I've never forgotten that for a minute."

Mrs. Talbot's voice was stiff. "Then why have you been so reluctant to accept any help from me?"

Clare rose from where she'd been sitting on the edge of the bed and went to the window. "We've taken so much! I'm not even your daughter."

"My son loved you. You're raising my grandson. Doesn't that make us family?"

Clare turned to face Mike's grandmother. "I've never felt as if we knew each other very well."

"Perhaps that's my fault," Mrs. Talbot said unhappily. "I don't know how I got so estranged from Don."

"Estranged?" On a rush of shock, Clare went swiftly back to the bed. "Oh, no! Is that how you felt? Don was trying to spare you! Your health—"

"I didn't want to be spared. He was my only child."

Clare felt as if her chest were being squeezed. "I'm sorry."

"Of course," Mrs. Talbot spoke stiffly again, "you managed fine without me..."

Clare's vision blurred as tears overflowed. "No," she whispered. "No, I didn't manage fine. I'd have given anything to have you there."

The two women's gazes, unguarded at last, met. "I would have come," Mrs. Talbot said. "It...hurt that you didn't want me."

Clare wiped at her tears. "Back when Don was first diagnosed, he understood that he'd deteriorate. He thought it would be too hard on you. That's why we went to Oregon."

"I thought..." Her mother-in-law hesitated. "I thought that for some reason you hadn't taken to me. I was afraid I'd given the impression I didn't like Don's remarrying or didn't approve of you."

"No. Never," Clare said, her voice stifled. "It wasn't that, I promise."

"I wish you had let me help."

"I'm sorry," Clare said again. "It was so hard, but I didn't want to go against his wishes. And I didn't know you."

"You do now," Mrs. Talbot pointed out, "and you still don't like to accept any help."

Clare had already been analyzing her own reluctance, and now she admitted, "It got so I felt helpless all the time." She looked away. "I couldn't even make Don take his medicine. If I'd gotten help sooner..." She squeezed her fingers together so tightly they hurt. "I hated feeling that way! I wanted to be...to be strong and competent. I wanted Mike to respect me. I guess..." This was hard to say. "I guess I thought if I didn't admit to needing help, that proved I was strong."

The look in Mrs. Talbot's eyes was so gentle it was like a salve for a burn Clare hadn't known she suffered.

"You *are* strong, dear. This is a dreadful thing to confess, but I suppose I would've liked it if you weren't quite so strong. Perhaps—" her smile was just a little wry "—single parents are so used to coping alone they never learn they don't have to be everything to their children. And for all practical purposes, you've been a single parent almost from the beginning."

Clare smiled back tremulously. "I think you're right. But the truth is, I really need you this time. I will not let Mike be railroaded," she said fiercely.

"You mean, *we* won't."

Their eyes met again, then Clare reached for her mother-in-law's hands. "We," she agreed.

CHAPTER NINE

CLARE WAITED apprehensively on Jake's front porch after ringing his doorbell. The cowardly part of her hoped he wasn't home.

No such luck. Jake opened the door. His hair was rumpled, his gray button-down shirt wrinkled and the sleeves rolled up. He looked tired and preoccupied, creases carved semipermanently between his dark brows. If he was surprised to see her, it didn't show on his face. "Clare," he said with no particular inflection.

She took a deep breath and held out her offering. "I brought you some homemade bread. I wanted to thank you for...for installing the garbage disposal. And to make sure you're recovered from the smoke."

"I'm fine." The grooves in his cheeks deepening, he hesitated, then stood back. "Do you have time to come in?"

How like him to give her an out, not to say, "Would you *like* to come in?"

"Thank you." Clutching the wrapped loaf of bread like a security blanket, Clare stepped into his living room. "It looks different in here," she said. "More like a real home."

"Not hard. Come into the kitchen. Would you like a cup of coffee?"

"Sure. Actually I was hoping to talk to you."

In the kitchen, he gave her a brief unreadable look before turning to open a cupboard. "So talk."

Once upon a time, he'd coaxed her, prodded her, even teased her. Now the best he could do was an abrupt "So talk"?

Her fault, she reminded herself.

She didn't remember this table, gleaming maple with wrought-iron legs and matching chairs. In the center a charming earthenware llama lazily contemplated the view out the tall windows.

Clare deposited the still-warm bread on the tile counter and then sat at the table. "It's the fires," she said. "They're making me nervous."

"Not nervous enough to keep you from being stupid." Jake put a mug of coffee in front of her. "Still take cream?"

"Exactly what is that supposed to mean?" she snapped.

"I indulge myself. Nonfat milk isn't the same."

She glared; he gazed blandly back. From between gritted teeth, Clare said, "You know that's not what I'm talking about."

A muscle twitched in his cheek. "It's dangerous to go trotting out your door in the middle of the night when you think an arsonist has just set a fire nearby. Doing it once is foolish. The second time is goddamned stupid!"

"You were running around out there, too!"

"I'm a man."

She suppressed her instinctive outrage. "Which makes you invincible?"

"Less vulnerable."

"This guy isn't a rapist," she pointed out tartly. "He sets fires, remember?"

Jake pulled out another chair and sat down, long legs angled out into the kitchen. "And he presumably doesn't want to get caught."

"Well, maybe not—but if he's burning houses in his own neighborhood, he's *going* to get caught."

He raised a brow. "This is a pretty small neighborhood. That would make it someone you know well."

Clare's anger suddenly deflated, and she reached out to cradle the coffee mug in her hands. "I don't like thinking that," she admitted. "But doesn't it seem funny the way the fires are concentrated in this neighborhood?" She resisted the impulse to jump to her feet and pace. "It's like we're being surrounded. The Kirks', the rental, Anne's..."

"And the bookstore."

"Where the arsonist burned *your* books."

His frown lines deepened, though his steady gaze didn't waver from her face. "What are you suggesting?"

"I don't know!" Now Clare did leap up, gripping the back of the chair so tightly her fingers whitened. "I just have this sense of events closing in. Can it be coincidence that Don died in a fire and now all these fires are being set right near us? Maybe you're the target. Maybe Mike is. Do you know there's talk about him? He was ostracized at school the other day. Everybody figures he must be 'crazy like his dad.'" She tasted the bitterness in her voice.

Jake swore and slapped a hand on the table. "Mike's a decent kid! How the hell can anybody suggest...?"

Clare didn't want to defend the indefensible, but fairness made her say, "Then who? Why this neighborhood?" She let out a breath. "Something terrible is going to happen if we don't figure out who hates one of us."

Jake's eyes narrowed. "You're making a big assumption."

"Then why are the fires all here?" she asked stubbornly.

"It's convenient."

"If that's so, the bookstore wasn't."

"A copycat crime."

Her chin came up. "Do you believe that?"

Their eyes held for a long glittering moment; then his mouth twisted. "No," he said abruptly. "I think you're right."

She should have felt triumph. Instead, overwhelming relief made her muscles so weak she had to grope her way back into the chair. "Really?"

The faintest trace of amusement colored his voice. "You sound surprised."

"Sometimes I wondered if I wasn't the one who was nutty."

"You? You're the one who's too literal to go crazy, remember?"

She wrinkled her nose. "What I think I said was that I'd be obsessive-compulsive, instead of hearing voices. I haven't been quite sure whether believing one of us is the target qualifies me as obsessive or paranoid."

"I'd put it in the bizarre but conceivable category." He looked away from her and pinched the bridge of his nose. The furrows between his brows hadn't gone away. "I assume you came by for more reason than to warn me."

"I did want to thank you," she murmured.

Without otherwise moving, Jake rolled his eyes toward her. She couldn't help noticing that they were a little bloodshot.

Clare picked up her coffee, more as a defense than because she wanted any. "Okay. I was hoping you'd...well, talk about these people. After all, you grew up with half of them. I just thought..." She fidgeted, then concluded in a rush, "I thought you might have some insight."

"You mean, you thought I'd gossip," he said dryly.

"Unfair." Clare looked down at the shining surface of the table. In a low voice she said, "I've never liked gossip. That's partly why I'm asking. I don't *know* much about my neighbors. Now I wish I did."

"You're right." Jake sounded weary. "I didn't really think that about you." Now he was massaging his temples. "My...youth is not a time I enjoy thinking about."

"Then maybe you shouldn't have moved back here."

He ignored her comment. "Who shall we start with? Bart Petersen? Hell, why not? Bart was a nonentity. Always a shrimp—I don't think he did his growing until after we were out of high school. He wasn't good at sports, wasn't one of the brains. Good God, I hardly remember him." Jake's grunt wasn't one of amusement. "Doesn't say much for me, does it? He was a nobody, so I ignored him."

Clare chose not to point out that few kids were confident enough and sensitive enough to go out of their way to befriend a nobody. Instead, she said thoughtfully, "Do you suppose that's why he became a volunteer fireman? Belated confirmation of his masculinity and all that?"

"God knows."

"He's a contractor now, you know. He probably wears a big leather tool belt and a hard hat and yells at people."

Jake raised an eyebrow. "Let's not get too carried away with the 'wimp transformed' idea."

"No, but it's interesting." And it gave Bart Petersen plenty of reason to harbor resentment against some of his peers and neighbors. Don and Jake wouldn't even have had to mock him; he could hate them just because they'd ignored him. Don's mother might even have earned his enmity with some overheard remark about why her son wasn't interested in being friends with the younger Petersen boy.

"What about Suzette?" Clare asked, frowning. "Her house is just beyond the rental that burned, you know. Not only did she have the fire at the bookstore, she lives in this neighborhood, too."

"The authorities are having a field day with that," Jake agreed. He took a swallow of coffee. "They've been giving Suzette hell."

Clare waited.

Jake slumped lower in his chair. She might have thought him completely relaxed had he not been rubbing his neck. "I always liked her," he said abruptly. "I may have been the only person. Suzette was . . . abrasive. She was always little and skinny and had these big brown eyes, but, damn, did she have a mouth on her. The truth was, she was probably smarter than the other girls, but then it just seemed like she fought conformity for the hell of it. We'd have an assembly to vote for cheerleaders, and she'd stand up and want to know why the school didn't have a girls' basketball team. I remember she went out with some buddy of Don's, and the next day he said he touched her breast and she told him she'd break his fingers if his hand wasn't off her in five seconds." Jake grinned crookedly. "Most people thought she was a bitch. I wished I had her confidence."

"Hard to imagine you so humble," Clare teased.

Her comment had the oddest effect. His expression went blank. Closed, as though he'd slammed down a shutter. His tone was remote. "Have you met my father?"

"Actually I haven't. I saw him—" She stopped. "Somebody pointed him out to me. I could see the resemblance."

The look in Jake's eyes was so cold she shrank back in her chair.

"I'd rather not be reminded of that," he said harshly.

She sat up indignantly. "But you're the one who mentioned him—"

Jake spoke right over her in that same remote voice. "I don't know how much more I can tell you. Old Mrs. Brewer was here in those days, but her son's ten years older than I am. He was long gone by the time I became friends with Don. I don't quite picture her out with a gas can and book of matches."

Clare got a grip on her temper. Right now she needed Jake. She couldn't afford to be hurt or angry because he shut her out. What had she expected? A slide show complete with reminiscences of his childhood?

Face it, Clare thought, her heart squeezing. *He may want you—and that is open to question at the moment—but he's not going to share any more of himself than he can help.* After seeing him with his father, she had to wonder if he was *capable* of really loving anyone.

And she certainly couldn't ask him how much his father hated him. What if the circle of these fires was closing in on Jake, not Clare or Mike or Mrs. Talbot? Had the possibility occurred to Jake once he'd seen his charred books at Suzette's store? His father was making it pretty obvious he didn't want Jake back on the island. The scene in the grocery store made it clear he wasn't exactly rational where his son was concerned. But was he crazy enough to try to *kill* Jake, or frame him as an arsonist?

No. She couldn't ask.

Clare tried to sound just as detached when she asked, "Did you know Linda Michaels, who owns the bed-and-breakfast?"

"She's a newcomer. She chatted while I checked in. Said she's been here seven or eight years."

A newcomer, Clare thought wryly.

Jake was watching her, although she couldn't make out what he was thinking. "Tell me about the Carlsons," he said. "I've heard talk."

She gave him a cool look. "Like the talk about Mike?"

"I didn't say I believed it."

"No. Sorry." She bit her lip and tried to collect her thoughts. "They're convinced the world as we know it is going to end. I don't know, a nuclear blast or something. Their goal is to be ready. I hear they have a bomb shelter. They're farming the old Dwyer place, marketing some produce to local restaurants. Phyllis makes jewelry and sells it at fairs, like the Edmonds Arts and Crafts Festival. I have a pair of her earrings—"

"Hippies."

"I suppose so. They're also nice people. Anne and I were supposed to help her pick apples from the Kirks' trees and make applesauce on Sunday. Of course we didn't show up, but Phyllis saved half-a-dozen jars of applesauce for us. She says she froze most of the crop, and if we want more applesauce, we can still get together to make some."

Jake's mouth took on a cynical slant. "You're saying she couldn't possibly have set the fire at Mrs. Talbot's because she wanted your help to make applesauce the next morning?"

Clare knew her annoyance was irrational, given that she had asked him to speculate in the same way about his old friends. And given her own uneasy thoughts about Tony. "No," she said shortly. "I'm saying the Carlsons are nice people who don't have a reason in the world to be doing this. We're friends. They wouldn't target Mike or me."

"What if one of them happens to enjoy setting fires?"

"Then you and I are wasting our time. He—or she—won't be caught until he does something dumb."

The silence, at least on her side, was a depressed one. She was surprised when Jake said, "You haven't asked me about Alison."

"We did talk about her once, and besides, her house isn't exactly in the neighborhood." The magnificent white Victorian Alison had inherited from her father was on the opposite side of the main road from the lane where Clare and Jake lived.

Jake stood and began rattling around in the kitchen behind her. "Close enough. It isn't a quarter of a mile as a crow flies. You noticed her at that first fire, didn't you? Besides, just because the target is somebody in this neighborhood doesn't mean the arsonist lives here."

"I suppose that's true," Clare agreed. She wouldn't let herself turn her head to watch him. The way he moved with such effortless grace had an instant intense effect on her. And now she had more memories to superimpose themselves over the present. She remembered being carried up the stairs, lowered to her feet. And oh, God, the way he'd moved above her, in her, muscles sliding so smoothly under his sweat-slick skin . . .

A shaft of near-agonizing pleasure pierced her, the point in her belly. Clare sat very still and closed her eyes. *Don't think about it,* she told herself fiercely. Sex, however good, wasn't enough. She couldn't settle for so little.

Even if she didn't have Mike to think about.

"She did have reason to hate Don." Remembering with a stir of uneasiness the way that very reserved woman had looked at Mike riding away on his bike that morning not so long ago, Clare asked, "How did she feel about you? Have you run into her yet?"

"Once at the grocery store. She professed to be pleased to see me. We inquired after each other's lives." He shrugged. "She never liked me, but the feeling was mutual. I suppose we were jealous of each other."

"Because of Don?" Troubled, Clare said, "But you must have had other friends."

"Not many." His tone didn't invite questions. There they went again. The oblique glimpse of his youth, the slammed door when she tried to step in.

Well, to hell with him. She'd gotten what she'd come for. Clare stood up. Stiffly she said, "Thank you for your help. I'm sorry to bring back unpleasant recollections."

He didn't move. "You don't have to go."

"Mike'll be wondering where I am."

"Isn't Mrs. Talbot at your house?"

"Well, yes, but—"

"Then why are you in such a hurry?"

"Did I say I was?" Oh, that was a mature comeback.

"Clare..." His voice had inexplicably roughened.

She took a step back and bumped into the chair. "No. Don't start that. I shouldn't have..."

"Why not?"

"You know all the reasons." She aimed for firm and sounded breathless.

"I know what I felt the other night."

He'd said the right thing to bring her down with a thump. "Good," she said acidly, "because you certainly didn't share it."

Jake stalked toward her. His brows had lowered, giving his face a grim cast. "You were damned close-mouthed yourself."

If she wouldn't have looked ridiculous, Clare might have retreated around the table. As it was, she stood her ground. "What was I supposed to say?"

"What do you feel?"

"I don't know!" she cried, her fingernails biting into her palms. "I don't *want* to know! I have to put Mike first. Don't you see that?"

"No," Jake said flatly. "He's a kid. He'll come around."

"Come around to what?"

Here was his chance, she thought. All he had to do was say, *To our relationship. To me as a stepfather. I love you. Will you marry me?* And she would say—what?

God help her, she was afraid she'd babble, *Yes, yes.*

But she didn't have to worry, because Jake didn't go down on bended knee. Instead, he searched her face with an odd intensity.

"When you ran into me the other night, you were scared of me. I've been wondering why."

So had she. "I... For a minute I didn't know who you were."

"You were scared even when you did."

Clare opened her mouth to protest. *What makes you think that?* she could ask. But the way he waited, shoulders held rigidly, as though in expectation of a blow, stopped her. They had very few things going for them, but one of them was honesty.

"I've had dreams. Nightmares." She pushed back her hair, shrugged. Tapped her fingers on the back of the chair. "You were all mixed up in them. There's always smoke and fire. The other night... For a minute I didn't know whether I was dreaming."

His gaze didn't waver. "You were afraid of Don, weren't you?"

"Toward the end. He...wasn't rational." She wouldn't apologize.

"But he changed during your marriage. Changed terribly."

Clare said incredulously, "What are you asking? Whether I think all men change like that? Whether I'm afraid of you because I think you're going to become some kind of monster?"

His rigid body relaxed and he backed up a step. "I give you more credit than that. I just thought you might have trouble trusting a man."

She let out a rusty laugh. "I trust you. Up to a point. If I knew you better, I might trust you more."

"Knew me better?" He gave a mirthless laugh. "We've been through a hell of a lot together. If you don't know me after all that..."

She tried to soften what had to be said. "I know you're loyal and courageous and protective. You've listened to me, held me—" she faltered "—always been there when I needed you."

"Not quite," he said grimly.

"Like I said before, close enough." Clare's smile failed before it was born. "But there's so much about yourself you never say. Think how long we knew each other, and I had no idea what you wrote! You never talk about your childhood, your friends, your writing..." She gestured helplessly. "I know more about Phyllis Carlson or Bart Petersen than I do about you! That doesn't say much for our relationship."

His mouth tightened. "Aren't actions supposed to speak louder than words?"

"I think," she said slowly, "that we aren't talking about whether I trust you. The real question is, do *you* trust *me?*"

"Oh, for God's sake!"

"Then why won't you talk to me?"

Impatiently he asked, "What have we been doing here tonight?"

"Let me amend that. Why won't you talk to me about yourself?"

He muttered a curse and paced the length of the kitchen and back. "What do you want to know?" he growled. "What I did today? Fine. I'll tell you. I stared at the goddamned computer screen for six hours and salvaged one page from it. The glamour of a writer's life! Oh, and I don't want to forget today's menu. Oatmeal with raisins for breakfast and a turkey sandwich for lunch. Have I disappointed you?"

Sadness formed a lump in her throat, and for a moment she couldn't trust her voice. "No," she finally said. "I got about what I expected."

"And what the hell's that supposed to mean?"

"You truly don't know what I'm talking about, do you?"

"No, I don't." His voice had thickened. "I've cut myself open and bared my guts for you, lady. I tell you I'm glad my best friend is dead because his death freed you. You think it was easy to admit that? What else do you want?"

She made one last try. "Tell me about your father."

His eyes glittered; the air vibrated with tension. Very softly he said, "To hell with you."

Clare felt brittle, as though she would shatter at the smallest touch. "Actually," she said, "I think I'll just go home."

His voice was low and silky. "Let me walk you to the door."

All the way there, her neck prickled with her awareness of him prowling behind her like a big angry cat, silent and controlled but dangerous. Had she really thought they could share information like friends, without reference to the other night?

She wasn't sure whether it was a reluctance to leave things like this after their long history or the hunger for something forbidden she'd suppressed that made her turn back at the door.

"Thank you for your help." How prissy she sounded!

"Kiss me." His voice was gritty, the expression on his face tortured. "Then tell me you don't feel everything I do."

"That's not the point."

"Kiss me."

"Jake..."

He cursed again and reached for her. She was already melting into his embrace before his mouth touched hers. Clare curled her fingers in a tight grip on his shirt and held on as he kissed her with shattering thoroughness. He was a man who thought he was losing a woman he wanted badly, but he knew better than to try to reclaim her with brute force. Instead, he used the passion she couldn't deny to remind her of what she was losing, too.

By the time he was through, her cheeks were wet with tears. Jake must have tasted the saltiness, because he lifted his head and a spasm twisted his face.

"I can learn," he said hoarsely.

Clare scrubbed at her cheeks and backed out the door. "Can you?"

"Give me a chance."

"I . . . I have to think."

His eyes, dark and turbulent, held hers. "Don't forget to feel."

She was still backing away, her arms crossed protectively. "No, I . . ." *How can I help it?*

"And Clare—be careful."

She'd managed to forget fire and smoke. Now she nodded shakily. "You, too."

"Call if you need me."

"I will." Her searching foot found the first step. She took one last hungry look at his face, lean and intense, then turned and fled.

THE NEXT EVENING, Clare marched across Roger Mullin's porch and rang his doorbell. She was glad he answered the door, not his wife or Ian.

"Clare!" He didn't quite hide his dismay.

"I'd like to talk to you," she said quietly.

"Uh, sure." He backed up. "Come on in."

From farther in the house came the sound of canned laughter from a television set. The living room just to the right of the front door was formal, the furniture cherry with Queen Anne legs and tapestry upholstery. Roger switched on a lamp and gestured toward the couch, but Clare didn't sit.

"Ian apparently thinks Mike is setting the fires. I'd like to know where he got that idea."

Roger didn't meet her eyes. "I'll talk to him. He isn't home right now—"

"Was it from you?"

"God, Clare, I never said…" He took a couple of steps away from her, swung back. Rubbing a hand over his balding head, he said in an agitated voice, "I may have repeated things I'd heard, but never as fact! If my boy misunderstood, I'm sorry."

"You *know* Mike," she said numbly.

"Yeah." His jaw worked. When at last he looked squarely at her, she saw no regret. "He's got a hot temper. I've thought for a long time that he was an accident waiting to happen. If I'm wrong, all I can say again is I'm sorry."

"He's a kid. You started that rumor and all you can say is 'I'm sorry'?"

"Goddamn it, I didn't start it!" Roger was still uncomfortable, but heading for the refuge of anger. "Somebody saw him running away from that rental right before it exploded into flames. And I know you don't want to hear this, Clare, but we'd be fools to ignore his family history. You're a nice lady. I'd hate to see you get hurt again. But maybe you'd better face facts."

"Who?" she demanded. "Who claims to have seen him?"

Her expression must have been blistering, because he backed up a step. "I, uh, don't know. I heard talk—"

"And you believe everything you hear."

"Damn it, your husband—"

"Was mentally ill." Her voice was as icy as the anger that crackled around her heart. "Mike is a normal kid who's had a rough couple of years. You and your son have just made them worse."

She'd have liked to think she had left him ashamed, but figured anybody who would jump to that kind of conclusion about a fourteen-year-old boy wasn't decent enough to be capable of shame.

The only good part of her evening was that she came home to find Geoff lounging on her living-room couch watching a basketball game on television with Mike as though nothing had changed. Maybe for him it hadn't. "Hey, Mrs. T," he said, starting to stand up.

She could have kissed him, but kept her voice casual. "Hi, Geoff. Hi, Mike. Grandma in the kitchen?"

"Yeah, I think so." Mike suddenly whooped. "That was the ugliest move I've seen in a long time! No wonder the ref called it blocking!"

She left the two boys arguing about whether a foul had been committed. In the kitchen, she told Mrs. Talbot what she'd learned.

Her lips thinned. "I never did like that man."

"Me, either," Clare admitted.

They sat in depressed silence for a moment. Finally Clare straightened her shoulders. "What we need to find out is who claims to have seen him that night. Assuming this isn't one of those rumors that appeared out of nowhere."

Mrs. Talbot gave a crisp nod. "I'll call everybody I know."

CLARE'S FIRST ATTEMPTS to find out who'd started the rumors about Mike were futile. Sally Petersen promised to ask around for her, but shook her head when she reported back to Clare.

"Nobody remembers. They all just heard..." Her blue eyes were compassionate. "Is there someplace you could send Mike for a while? Do you have family he could live with for the school year?"

Clare tried to smile. "I can't do that. If we have to, I'll move, but I won't send him away. He's lost too much already."

Mrs. Talbot tried, but her friends hadn't heard the talk and weren't any help.

When Clare made the neighborhood rounds, Linda Michaels claimed not to have heard anything about Mike. Phyllis didn't answer Clare's knock at the kitchen door, but she tracked down Tony, who was splitting wood behind the old farmhouse. Hair tied back with a leather thong, he shook his head. "We didn't see anything that night. Sirens woke us. Sorry." His expression of regret sounded perfunctory.

Clare's friend Sharon volunteered to talk to kids at school and see if she couldn't find out something specific, but by the next day she'd reported failure.

"Not everybody agrees with the Mullin boy. I hope Mike knows that. Some of the kids don't think it's fair that Mike should be blamed just because of the way his dad died. The girls especially are reserving judgment. Mostly the gossip was just gossip."

"Geoff has stuck by him."

"I'm glad. As far as who started the whole thing, I think it was Ian. Nobody really *knows* anything."

Suzette hadn't been home when Clare stopped by, so she made a special trip back to town after talking to Sharon. Clare stuck her head in her own office to collect messages, although the real-estate business had slowed to a trickle, thanks to the time of year. The string of arson fires weren't helping, either. Right now, who in their right mind would buy a beachfront cottage and leave it sitting empty for the rest of the fall and winter?

There was no message from the lawyer who'd looked at the marina. Clare tried calling him, only to be told by his secretary he wasn't available. Clare left her home phone number, then went next door.

Already the bookstore looked like a bookstore again. There was new carpeting, and the bookshelves were restocked, if a bit more thinly than before. When Clare walked in, Suzette was working on a window display of home-improvement manuals.

"What do you think?" she asked, sinking back on her heels.

Lavishly illustrated books on decorating, architecture, plumbing and maintenance were arranged against a backdrop of blue-green and rose kitchen tiles, half unrolled wallpaper and a few tools, casually laid out.

"It's gorgeous!" Clare exclaimed. "You make me want to tackle my house."

"That's the general idea." Suzette moved a book a few inches, tilted her head, then nodded in satisfaction. "What can I do for you?"

By chance, Clare's gaze fell on Jake's new book, face out on the new-fiction shelf. She reached for it. "I haven't read this one yet."

"Surely he'd give you one," Suzette said in surprise.

"Oh, I'd rather just buy it."

Suzette didn't comment, although she looked as if she wanted to. As she rang up the book, Clare said, "I've been wanting to ask you something, anyway. There are rumors floating around that Mike started these fires. I'm trying to find out where they started."

"Alison."

"What?" To the best of Clare's knowledge, Don's old girlfriend had seen Mike only once. How could she possibly claim to have recognized him fleeing in the dark?

"I've been debating whether to call you." The bookstore owner handed Clare the receipt, her gaze as direct as always. "Alison came in to talk to me about it. She happened to be passing the rental that night it burned, saw someone running away from the fire. She thought it was Mike, but wasn't sure. She didn't want to get him in trouble without being more positive."

"Has she gone to the fire marshal?"

"I don't know," Suzette admitted. "I told her she should. I don't mean that as some kind of indictment of your son. I see him around the neighborhood, but I really don't know him. I just figured you'd rather have any accusations out in the open."

"Damn right I would!"

Uncomfortably Suzette said, "I don't know how the word's gotten around. I wouldn't have said Alison was a gossip. But maybe she asked advice from a couple of other people, too, and one of them has a big mouth. I'm sorry. I owe you one. I should've called you."

"Don't worry about it."

Maybe some of Jake's cynicism was rubbing off on her, because on the way home it occurred to Clare how convenient it was for Suzette Fowler to have the finger pointed away from her. Was there any chance that she'd made the whole thing up, assuming Clare wouldn't confront Alison and find out the truth? Or, if Alison really *had* come to Suzette, that Suzette had then turned around and deftly spread the story in the most damaging places just to ease the pressure on herself?

Clare was so busy brooding she didn't see the police car parked in front of her house until she turned into the driveway.

CHAPTER TEN

MIKE SAT STIFFLY in an armchair. His grandmother hovered over him looking shaky and frightened. Two policemen, one with a notebook flipped open on his lap, faced him from the couch.

When the front door slammed behind Clare, all four heads turned.

"Thank heavens!" Mrs. Talbot exclaimed in relief, pressing a hand to her chest. "I didn't know where you were. Clare, these officers want to talk to Mike about the fires."

Taking up a stance beside her son, Clare gave the policemen a long cool stare. "You were planning to talk to him without a parent present?"

They flicked a glance at each other. "His grandmother is here," said the one with the notebook.

"As you no doubt know, she is two days out of the hospital," Clare said icily. She made her voice gentler. "Mom, you'd better sit down."

Not until Mrs. Talbot gave her a startled look did Clare realize what she'd called her. Mom. Where had that come from? Why had it felt so natural?

But she couldn't let herself be distracted and think about it, not right now. She knew one of the policemen. Where from? Clare flipped through her mental files until she came up with the right picture. High-school parent group. His wife had served as vice president last year, and he'd cooked at the annual pancake breakfast. Lieutenant . . .

"Lieutenant Russell."

"That's right, Mrs. Talbot." He looked somewhere between relieved that she recognized him and discomfited. "This is Officer Karolevitz."

She didn't lie and say that it was nice to meet him. She was too scared.

"What's this all about?" Clare asked instead.

Lieutenant Russell, a lean balding man in his late forties, straightened the notebook on his knees. To his credit, his eyes met Clare's when he said, "A witness tentatively places Mike at the scene of one of the fires."

"That rental."

He didn't ask her how she knew. "Yes."

Clare laid a hand on her son's rigid shoulder. "Mike?"

"I wasn't there!" he burst out. "I spent the night at Grandma's! Remember? I didn't even wake up."

Officer Karolevitz raised his eyebrows. "All those sirens and you didn't even wake up."

"That's right." Mike returned the policeman's interested gaze belligerently.

His grandmother spoke up, almost timidly. "I didn't, either."

"Mike was home with me when the other places burned." Clare looked from one officer to the other, her voice confident, admitting no doubt. "I woke him myself when I smelled smoke from the Kirks'."

"You're sure he was asleep."

"Yes."

Lieutenant Russell stood up. "Then we'll leave it at that for the moment."

She accompanied them out to the porch, knowing full well that she'd be seeing them again. His "for the moment" made that clear.

"Can you tell me who accused Mike?" she asked.

"There was no accusation, Mrs. Talbot. A concerned citizen saw a figure dressed in dark clothes running away from the fire. Apparently something about the figure struck the person who came to us as familiar, but not until this person saw Mike in passing the other day. The identification was far from positive. If Mike wasn't there, you have nothing to worry about."

If. There it was again, the vague threat, the implication that she, as well as her son, might not be telling the truth.

What if she had to admit to having lied? But how could she have done any differently?

Clare waited until the police car pulled away before she went back into the house. Mike hadn't moved.

"They don't believe me, do they?"

"I think this was just another tip they had to check out."

"Yeah, right!" He leapt to his feet, glaring at her. "The only reason they didn't arrest me was because *you* said I was home all those times!"

He spat it out as though he hated her. Vaguely aware of his grandmother watching in shock, Clare sank onto the couch. "Weren't you?"

He saw only her. "You lied to them."

"About what?" How calm she sounded!

"The night of the Kirks' fire. I was already awake when you came into my room. Maybe I never was asleep."

"Are you saying you could have set the fire without my knowing?"

"Yeah, that's what I'm saying!" Mike kicked the ottoman, sending it rolling across the room to crash into the coffee table. His voice rose to a shout. "I'm saying you told those cops I was home every night and you don't know for sure that I was, do you?"

He had never needed her faith more than he did right now. A great stillness descended on Clare, and she held out a hand to him. "Yes. Yes, I do. I trust you."

"How can you?" he burst out. "I'm in trouble all the time! You had to go see the principal. And I've been grounded, and—"

"Mike." Clare stood up. "You wouldn't be a normal kid if you didn't get in trouble sometimes. But you've never done anything to hurt anyone. I know you wouldn't."

He stood there in front of her, the anger dropping away to leave him looking very young and vulnerable. His voice cracked. "You're sure?"

She smiled. "I'm sure."

Mike's face crumpled and he stumbled into her embrace. She held him as he cried. Blinking away tears, his grandmother held a finger to her lips and tiptoed out of the room.

It was a while before Mike dragged in a ragged breath and lifted his head. Grabbing the hem of his T-shirt, he wiped his wet cheeks. With a sniff, he said, "I've been so scared."

"Scared?" Staring at him, Clare sat down again. "Why?"

"I, um . . ." His face worked. "I got to wondering if maybe I wasn't . . . I don't know, blacking out or something. And maybe setting the fires. You know what I mean?"

"Blacking out?" Clare echoed. "What on earth would make you think . . . ?"

"Dad was crazy." Her stepson sounded like he had a huge lump in his throat. "Maybe I will be, too."

"Oh, no," she whispered. "Oh, Mike, I had no idea you were worrying. Come here." She patted the couch next to her. "Sit down."

He sat.

She took both his hands. "I've done lots of reading on the subject. It's true that schizophrenia can run in families. But your dad was the only schizophrenic on either side of your family. With one parent who was ill, your chance of developing the disease isn't that much higher than anyone else's. And you don't have a single symptom of mental illness."

Beseeching, his eyes searched hers. "But I could get it, couldn't I?"

She wouldn't lie. "Sure you could. But from what I read, at most your chances are one in ten of developing schizophrenia. That means, chances are *nine* out of ten that you won't. And you can't live your life afraid of what might be. There are lots of awful diseases any of us could get. But right now we're healthy. Let's rejoice in that and not worry about the future. Okay?"

"You're sure I couldn't have blacked out or something?"

"That isn't a symptom of schizophrenia." She took a deep breath. "Do you remember when your dad got sick?"

He frowned. "You mean, at first? I guess not really."

"Well, his thinking became bizarre. He'd pop out with the weirdest comments or ideas. Completely nonsensical. At first I'd tease him, but then I realized he didn't *see* that what he'd said was unreasonable. He got paranoid, thought people were talking about him, plotting against him. I'd wake up at night and find him peering through the blinds out the window. Sometimes he'd say somebody was out there. He was, uh..."

"Crazy."

"Ill."

"And you're saying I'm not."

"Yeah. You're a normal teenage boy. Sometimes irresponsible—"

He stiffened.

"—sometimes a pain in the butt. But you're also thoughtful, good company, funny..." Clare felt her smile tremble, but it was a real smile nonetheless. "You're a neat kid."

"Yeah?"

It almost broke her heart to hear the hope and doubt in his voice.

"Yeah."

Mike thought about it for a minute, squared his shoulders and nodded. "Okay. So I guess it was dumb to think the fires had anything to do with me."

"Not dumb. After the way your father died, this is all pretty creepy." She stopped, gave a shrug. "But if they have anything to do with us, it's because some very sick person has a point to make. It's *not* because there's anything wrong with you or me."

Her son gave a mock salute. "Yes, ma'am!"

Gratified by his cheekiness, Clare said, "Hey, that's what I want to hear. Now, if you were just as obedient *all* the time..."

"In your dreams."

Normal.

HE DIDN'T KNOW if he should be doing this, but Jake knocked on Clare's front door, anyway. After the way he'd acted the other day, she sure as hell wouldn't be knocking on his anytime soon. He probably wouldn't catch her alone, not with Mrs. Talbot living here, but at least Mike would be in school.

It was Clare who opened the door, her eyes going wide when she saw him. "Jake."

"Yeah, in person." He rubbed damp palms over denim-clad thighs. "Uh, may I come in?"

Clare only hesitated for a second before she stood back. "Of course," she said, sounding about as thrilled as she'd be at inviting a stray dog inside.

She didn't suggest they go back to the kitchen as she had other times. Instead, she waved a hand at the couch and sat herself in an overstuffed armchair, a safe distance away.

"The bread was good."

"I'm glad."

Oh, hell. He might as well get to it. "I wanted to apologize for the other day. I was rude when you got there, and things didn't improve. I had no business kissing you just to put pressure on you."

Her clear eyes met his. "No, you didn't."

Trust Clare to be straightforward. Which was one reason her waffling about him was such a puzzle.

"On the other hand," she said, "I know I must be frustrating you. I'm not usually so... indecisive." She wrinkled her nose. "Or maybe I am."

"You were never—" he began automatically.

She interrupted. "Yes, I was. In fact, maybe I *am* indecisive when it comes to the big things, and I just never realized it before."

He knew he was going to be sorry he'd asked, but he did anyway, gruffly. "When you met Don, did you have trouble making up your mind?"

"No." Clare looked apologetic. "But you have to understand, in those days life was simpler. He was handsome and charismatic and we had fun together. That was enough then. I didn't have to think about other people."

"Mike."

"Children change you."

Jake had never thought much about having his own children, but in a sudden sharp moment of longing, he did. He imagined Clare pregnant, belly swollen, breasts fuller, an inner gaze softening a face that was more intelligent than pretty. And the baby, a little girl, maybe, with Clare's eyes and laugh and graceful, fine-boned body...

He sucked in a breath. "I imagine they do."

They stared at one another as Jake wondered what the hell kind of parent he'd be, considering the example his own had set. Not the time to think about it. Jake cleared his throat. "Mrs. Talbot's fire. Have the police discovered anything?"

"Not that they're telling us." Clare's bangs ruffled when she let out a breath. "Oh, that's not entirely true. Gasoline was used to start the fire. It was squirted all over the downstairs hall and into the kitchen. Remember how fast it raced in there? Then I guess the arsonist quietly stepped out the front door, tossed a match back in and strolled away."

"How'd he get in?"

"They don't know. Too much was destroyed."

Jake grunted. "The son of a bitch was trying to kill her."

"At the very least, he didn't care if he did."

Jake gave a growl and rose to his feet. "Why? God-damn it, *why?*"

Her head bowed and her heavy chestnut hair fell forward over her shoulder. The line of cheek and slender neck the action revealed moved him unbearably, to a kind of anguish.

What she said in a stifled voice hurt even worse. "Mike was afraid he was blacking out and setting the fires."

"Oh, no."

Clare lifted her head and he saw that her eyes sparkled with tears. "Oh, yeah. It turns out he's been afraid he'll have schizophrenia like Don. I . . . didn't realize he was worrying."

Jake grimaced. "And I had to show up, reminding him of his father."

Never less than generous, she rose swiftly and came to him. "He had problems even before you came. Maybe it's good that we all had to take another look at the past. I just . . . I don't know what the fires have to do with it. I wish they'd stop."

The last was a cry in the dark, a child's wish before sleep. He wanted to take her into his arms and promise that she would be safe, that he would take care of her forever. He was afraid she didn't want his promises. And he couldn't forget the fear on her face even after she'd recognized him outside her mother-in-law's. She hadn't stumbled into his arms then; she'd recoiled. After seeing that reaction, he couldn't force himself on her.

He also couldn't forget his own fear: that the fires were an attack on him, not her. If he was right, the closer he stuck to her, the more he'd be putting her in danger. The familiar sick feeling rose in his throat. Okay, his father had beat him, but this was a step further. This was nuts. Was his *father* nuts? Would the man who'd said, "Why don't you go back wherever the hell you came from?'' burn out everybody Jake had ever cared about, not to mention a few incidental strangers, just to make sure he did?

In a perverted sort of way, it made sense; the Kirks' fire was a warning, a warm-up. Then the one in Suzette's bookstore—she was an old friend and his books were used to fuel the destruction. Another empty house—a sadist toying with his fearful victims. And finally Mrs. Talbot's—the home of the woman who had given Jake refuge.

What made his gut clench in terror was wondering whether his father had any idea how Jake felt about Clare and Mike. If he did, Jake's house wouldn't be next. Clare's would be.

"Are the police doing anything to protect you?" he demanded in frustration.

She made a soft despairing sound. "I don't think it's occurred to them that we *need* protection. And...I'm not sure I want to point it out. They've already been out here to talk to Mike."

"For God's sake, why?"

"Somebody claims to have seen him running away from that fire at the rental."

"They didn't say who?"

"No." She bit off the one word, pressing her lips together afterward. "Suzette Fowler says it was Alison."

"Alison?" he repeated incredulously. "Does she even *know* Mike?"

"She's seen him a time or two. I can't imagine how she could claim to have recognized him."

"But why the hell would she make it up?" he asked in bafflement. "If she hardly knows him..."

"He *is* Don's son."

"Ancient history." It just didn't make sense. God knows he'd never liked Alison, but he suspected that had more to do with his own youthful insecurities than it did with her personality.

His searching gaze took in the blue shadows beneath Clare's eyes. "You don't look like you've been sleeping much."

"Anne and I have been taking turns sitting up. Next time I want to be able to swear to where Mike was."

Jake pictured her alone in the dark, hour after hour, listening for the shatter of glass or the creak of a porch stair, straining to smell smoke, catch the first wail of a distant siren. What the hell would she *do* if somebody broke the pane of glass on the front door and unlocked it? What would an old lady do?

The thought moved him to impotent rage, and his hands curled into fists at his sides. "Let me help."

One moment he was drowning in her deep blue eyes, the next she'd ducked her head. "I... You know how Mike feels..."

Jake swore and turned away. "I'll sit on the porch!" And advertise to the world that he loved this woman. Smart. But if the wrong person already knew...

"Then you couldn't swear to the police that Mike was in his bed," Clare pointed out reasonably. "What good would that do?"

"Damn it, Clare, let me in! Let me do *something!*"

"We're okay, Jake. Really. We nap days..."

Only his formidable self-control kept him from punching a hole in the wall. He couldn't remember the last time he'd felt this urge to release intense frustration in violence.

Back off, he told himself.

"Is that where Mrs. Talbot is now?" He nodded toward the ceiling, proud that his voice was no more than gravelly. "Asleep?"

"No, she and a friend took the ferry to Anacortes. She needs to replenish her wardrobe. She's feeling fine, and I think getting away will be good for her."

So, they were alone in the house, he and Clare. The realization tightened more than his anxiety. Which meant it was time he got out of here. If there was any hope for him, he had to give her space.

"If you don't have to work, you should go have a nap," he said roughly. "You ought to be safe in the daytime."

"I'm off today, since I covered the office this weekend. I guess I will lie down for an hour or two."

He wondered what her bedroom looked like, her bed. Flowered sheets or plain, heaps of pillows or a single firm one? Did she sleep sprawled on her back or curled up like a kitten? Jake imagined her hair spread over the pillow, her thick lashes forming crescents against her pale cheeks, her mouth soft as she murmured in her sleep.

His name.

Hell.

She was gazing up at him, her expression holding surprise, and something else. Something that made his pulse speed even as it made him wonder what his own face showed.

"Clare..." Gravel had ground down into fine grit.

She tried to smile. "I know. Call if I need you."

"Yeah." The simple casual word came out sounding raw. Who needed whom?

Her eyes were huge and shadowed as she studied him. He braced himself for her insincere *I will.*

But maybe weariness had lowered her defenses, because very softly she said, "Sometimes I do."

He deliberately misunderstood. "Call?"

Her teeth closed on her lower lip to still its tremble. Suddenly she was fidgeting, poking at her bangs, evading his gaze. Chickening out. But being Clare, not entirely. Her voice was just audible. "Need you."

Exultation, fierce and hot, competed with emotions more bittersweet. He closed his eyes for a moment, then opened them. Carefully he asked, "Is this one of those times?"

She gave a tiny nod.

Jake pulled her into his arms before she could draw another breath. Or have second thoughts.

If he'd had any doubts about what kind of need she was expressing, the way her body melted against his answered them. Her arms wrapped around his neck as though she never meant to let go. Even as he tasted her sweetness, met the demand of her lips and tongue with rising passion, he felt her fragility, the faint tremor running through her.

A gentleman would consider this taking advantage of her. He couldn't afford gentlemanly qualms.

"Where's your bedroom?" he asked.

She started to push back in alarm. "You're not planning to carry me again, are you?"

"Hell, yes." He grinned rakishly. "It's good for my masculine ego."

"Because you can heft me that far?"

She might have been tired, must have been desperate to have surrendered to her confused feelings for him, but still she could tease him. God, he loved her.

His muscles tensed and he froze in the act of swinging her up into his arms. Love? He'd never used the word before, not for her or anyone else. Not even to himself.

But that was what he'd felt for her all along, however many other selfish words he'd used to disguise it. Want. Need. Obsession. Love was bigger and more frightening, implying as it did that he would put her first.

Ahead of his best friend.

The knowledge that he had done so, would do so again, had lost the power to sting, Jake discovered somewhat to his surprise. Maybe because he was suddenly quite sure that the man he'd known, the best friend who'd shielded him from the cruelty of others, would have wanted him to shield Clare in turn. That friend had been lost long before Jake had held Clare for the first time.

He felt like a damned fool to have an understanding so simple assume the force of a revelation. Nonetheless, he also felt lightened, powerful. Clare was a featherweight in his arms as he joyfully mounted the stairs.

"That door," she whispered.

Her bedroom was downright austere: cream-colored blinds, pale yellow walls, a white-painted dresser and a twin bed, covered with a white eyelet comforter. As Jake slowly set Clare on her feet, he saw the photos arranged on the dresser. In miscellaneous antique frames were school pictures of Mike, a teenaged Don, a wedding picture of him and Clare. Memory jabbed at Jake.

He hadn't met her until the wedding. He'd flown in late and missed the rehearsal. Waiting at the altar with his best friend, Jake had turned to see the bride coming down the aisle in a traditional white gown with pearls sewn around the high neck. Even before she'd pushed back the veil, Jake had felt an odd twisting sensation inside, which he was surprised to identify as envy of Don. Not for this particular woman, but for everything this ceremony symbolized. Everything he hadn't known he wanted. Or so he told himself.

Then he'd seen her face—soft mouth, high cheekbones, strong brows and those eyes: huge, deep blue and gently glowing. She hadn't even glanced at him, but his gut had finished twisting into a knot so painful he'd had to concentrate on his breathing to keep from groaning aloud.

He'd done his duty at the reception. Toasted the newly wedded couple, danced once with the bride, congratulated Don. Then he'd gone back to his solitary home on the Oregon coast and tried to forget the longings awakened by Don's new wife.

And now here they were in her bedroom, Jake's hands wrapped around her waist, Don's picture on her bureau.

"Yours is there, too," she said quietly.

Jake gave a start. Yes, he *was*. there, in a snapshot taken while he played basketball with a much younger Mike. He was grinning at the boy, who was in the act of lunging for the ball. Strangely, Jake remembered the moment—turning to see Clare taking the picture, his sudden self-consciousness. His parents hadn't even owned a camera, didn't seem to regret not having one to record his childhood. He wasn't used to having someone want to take his picture, even if it was only because he was with Mike.

"Weren't all your photo albums burned?" he asked.

"That was probably the saddest thing I lost." Clare reached out and began playing with one of his shirt buttons, her gaze unfocused, as though she wasn't noticing what she was doing. "When I got here, one of the first things I did was go through Anne's pictures and have some of them copied. Luckily I'd always sent her ones of Mike and Don and places we lived. Anything I thought would interest her. So I was able to replace some of the best ones. But I had a few of you—'' She stopped.

Right this second, he didn't want to think too much about the past. If it wasn't over and done with, they wouldn't have a future. So he offered a light, ''Afraid you'd forget my face?''

Her eyes cleared. ''Never,'' she said simply.

''You know one of the things I like best about you?''

''Mmm?'' Her fingers were undoing the buttons now; she sounded dreamy.

His voice had become husky. ''You're never coy.''

''I'm not a good liar.''

He framed her face with his hands. ''Thank God.''

Her own slipped inside his shirt and splayed on his chest. Under her touch, his heartbeat picked up time.

''That, uh, feels good.'' *Brilliant*, he thought. *Famous writer in action.*

Clare's eyes widened in mock surprise, and a smile trembled at the corners of her mouth. ''The man speaks!''

He was dead serious. ''I told you I could learn.''

''So you did. Well, then, it was a good start.'' Maybe she couldn't be coy, but she could flirt. Despite his rocketing hunger for her, a reluctant grin touched his mouth when she leaned forward to press a butterfly kiss to his chest while her hands eased around him to gently knead the taut muscles in his back. Her breath tickled when she whispered, ''How about this? Does it feel good?''

''Oh, yeah.'' Drawing a ragged breath, he just stood there, letting her take control. She was a gutsy woman in more ways than one. On some level he'd been confident she was attracted to him, but he was also still astonished to know that she was. Why him?

Her fingers had moved to his zipper, and he groaned. "Unfair, lady."

She gave him a teasing smile, though her cheeks were pink and her eyes glowed as blue and soft and accepting as they had when she'd married Don.

It was the accepting that undid Jake. His shaking hands gripped her shoulders and he bent his head to capture her mouth. From then on *he* was in charge.

But he didn't forget to use words. Maybe these particular ones weren't what she had in mind, not if what she really wanted was to plumb his soul, but he had a feeling both kinds were required.

He wasn't used to speaking what he felt, but it became easier as he undressed her, as she uttered little whimpers and cries of pleasure.

"Do you know how I love to touch you?" he asked huskily. "Your skin is like silk, and so pale. And your breasts are perfect." He kissed the pink tip of one, then drew it into his mouth. Moving lower, over her flat stomach, he murmured, "Have you any idea how many times I've dreamed of exploring your body like this? Of kissing you here, and here, and here?"

At the last "here," she gasped, "Jake!"

He kept talking until he was hoarse, until he'd entered her tight passage in a convulsive thrust that made him feel so intensely it robbed him of coherence. By that time she was whispering, too.

"Oh, yes. Oh, please. Like that. Jake!"

There it was again, his name cried with such astonishment, such wonder, such artlessness. Such love, he wanted to think.

Assuming he could have thought. What man could when the woman he loved had her legs wrapped around him, her arms holding him, her body rising and falling in perfect rhythm with his? What man could think when his woman called his name like that, as though only he could summon feelings so sharp and sweet?

Afterward he rolled onto his side, drawing Clare with him. She nestled in the curve of his arm, her head on his shoulder and her thick hair spread across his arm and chest. He kissed the top of her head, inhaling her scent, and his gaze went back to her bureau.

Set in the silver frame, Don—his expression fixed for all time—was in his wedding getup, grinning at the camera, his arm laid almost casually over his bride's shoulders. But the woman beside Jake, though still young, had tiny crinkles beside her eyes now, and she carried herself differently, with a confidence and poise and reserve missing from that pretty girl in the picture. It recorded a moment long past.

Jake realized he was smiling, if painfully. Somehow he'd never quite said goodbye to Don, and this was an ironic moment to do it, when he had just made passionate love to Don's wife. But it was a goodbye that should have been said long ago.

Jake mouthed, *I miss you,* and *I'll take good care of her.* And then his gaze drifted back to the woman in his arms. He could just see the pale sweep of her temple and the curve of her cheek and the way short tendrils of hair clung damply to her high forehead. Shifting slightly to see more of her face, he felt how limply her body went with his.

"Clare," he whispered.

No response. Her lashes were fanned on her cheeks, her lips parted.

She was sound asleep, draped all over him.

Damn it, Clare, let me in! But wasn't that what she'd just done?

Closing his eyes, he smiled and wrapped his arms more securely around her. By God, at least for this short time she was safe, and she was his.

CHAPTER ELEVEN

CLARE AWOKE to the heavy sweet scent of old roses and the warmth of sunlight on her face. Groggily she opened her eyes and turned her head to see by her clock that it was late afternoon. She'd fallen asleep...

In Jake's arms. Clare sat up, the sheet sliding to her waist. With it tumbled a single rose, semidouble and deep pink. Cut, presumably, in her mother-in-law's garden. Clare smiled and held the thornless bloom to her nose to breathe in the fragrance.

Jake was gone, although he must have left fairly recently, or the rose petals would be falling. Mike would be home soon, and Mrs. Talbot not too long afterward. Clare figured she'd better shower and be dressed at least before her son arrived. He didn't know about their nocturnal watch; if he found out, he'd want to share it, and she had no intention of explaining why he couldn't.

In the shower, holding her face up to the warm spray, she thought about Jake—his whispered words of passion, his tenderness, his involuntary reactions to her touch. She'd once thought his iron control never cracked. Now she knew better.

I can learn, he'd said. Maybe he could. If she gave him a chance. If *Mike* gave him a chance.

She'd been making too many assumptions about Mike's attitude. It was time—past time—she confronted him about his feelings, found out what they really were, instead of guessing. She owed Jake that much.

When Mike thundered in the front door ten minutes later, she let him have his snack and listened as he told her about an algebra test.

"I didn't ace it," he concluded, "but I guess I did okay."

"Thank heavens." Clare wrinkled her nose. "*I* couldn't help you if you were having trouble."

"Why not?" He shoved a whole cookie in his mouth.

"Math wasn't my strong suit. Geometry stopped me in my tracks."

"Well," he said condescendingly, "girls usually aren't as good at it, you know."

Clare let out a distinct growl.

He grinned. "Got ya."

She stuck out her tongue.

"So what'd you do today?"

She hoped she didn't flush. "Oh, lazed around. I even took a nap, believe it or not."

Mike shoved back his chair. "Well, hey, I'm going to shoot some baskets with Geoff. I don't have much homework," he added hastily.

"Umm . . . could I talk to you about something first?"

Her son sank back into the chair, his expression wary. "I guess so."

"It's Jake," Clare said quietly. "I think the way you've rejected him has hurt his feelings."

Mike shot to his feet. "*His* feelings? Who cares?"

She held his gaze. "I do. Jake was good to us."

"You mean, he was good to *you*," Mike said rudely.

"No, that's not what I mean. You can't have forgotten the time he spent with you, the games he took you to, the hours he spent shooting basketball with you, catching while you practiced your pitching, helping you with that science project. Don't you remember?''

"All he wanted was to impress you."

Okay, to the crux of it. "Why do you think that?" she asked.

"Because it's what Dad said—" He stopped; they stared at each other. "Well, it was true!" Mike cried. "Maybe the other stuff wasn't, but I saw the way he looked at you." No mistaking which "he" Mike meant.

Her throat constricted, Clare said, "I never noticed. Jake never said a word. He never...never touched me that way. I swear."

Mike's face contorted. "That's not true! I saw you! You were hugging, and..."

"And what?" Clare pushed herself to her feet, holding her chin high, voice level. "Jake held me like a friend does. No more and no less."

Mike was crying. "Dad thought you were going to leave us."

"And you?"

"I..." He ducked his head. "I was afraid. Dad was scary sometimes..."

"Oh, sweetheart." She came around the table in such a rush she bumped her hip painfully against a chair. "I would never have left you! Never. *Or* your dad. I promised him for better or worse, and I meant it. He was ill. He needed me. No matter how awful he got, I wouldn't have deserted him. And most of all, I wouldn't have deserted you."

Mike stood stiff when she wrapped her arms around him. "Then how come you spent so much time with *him?*" The hatred and longing and fear in the way he said the one word, in the way he avoided speaking Jake's name, terrified Clare.

She swallowed and stepped back. Her own eyes were dry and burning. "Because I needed to talk to another adult. Sometimes I had to lean on someone else, just for a few minutes."

He sneered, "Yeah, well, if Dad hadn't died—"

"I would not have left you!" Eyes dry no longer, she dashed away the first tear. "What do I have to say to convince you?"

"You could quit seeing him."

Her stepson's voice was so cold a chill gripped her heart. This was as bad—worse—than she'd imagined. But she had to try.

"Even if I had a relationship with Jake, it doesn't mean I wouldn't still be your mother. Other mothers remarry."

"But I'm not really your kid." Oh, Lord, he was trying hard to sound offhand, as though he didn't care. "You're not stuck with me like they are."

"I *am* stuck." She threw up her hands. "I don't have you only out of some legal obligation. Mike, I *love* you. You're my son. If I was to marry Jake or anyone else, you'd still be my son. You'd just have a stepfather."

He wiped angrily at fresh tears. "Yeah, well, I'm not going to live with *him*. Dad would roll over in his grave or something. I mean, he loved me. I owe him *something*."

They both heard the creak of floorboards at the same time and swung around, Clare's hands still lifted imploringly, Mike's cheeks wet with tears of longing and anger.

Jake filled the kitchen doorway. His clear penetrating gaze moved swiftly from Mike's face to Clare's. "I'm sorry. I heard crying, but I shouldn't have walked in."

"It's okay." What else could she say?

But her son pulled violently back. "I can go live with Grandma. As soon as her house gets built—"

"Mike," Jake said.

The boy turned to glare at the dark contained man who hadn't moved from the doorway.

Jake's voice had a rough uneven timbre. "I loved your father. For his sake, I'd never do anything to hurt you."

Mike stood close enough to her that Clare felt the way his body jerked, as though it had absorbed a blow. For a long moment he remained frozen. Then his face contorted with emotions he couldn't possibly express, and he rushed toward the kitchen door.

Jake didn't move out of his way quite fast enough, but Mike didn't even slow down, shouldering past him. His feet thundered on the stairs, and his bedroom door slammed above.

Clare's legs gave way, and she sank into a kitchen chair, still staring dumbly after her son.

In a couple of strides, Jake reached her. He leaned forward and gripped her arms, his face intense. "Don't let him make you feel guilty for something that never happened," he said tautly.

Clare drew a ragged breath. "I...don't know that I feel guilty," she began.

Jake wasn't listening. "I won't say this again. You gave Don everything that was humanly possible. Damn it, Mike, too!" He uttered a harsh laugh. "Do you know what hell that year was for me? I wanted you so badly..." His fingers flexed. More quietly he corrected himself. "Loved you. But I couldn't tell you, couldn't help you. I could hold you when you cried, but not the way I wanted to." He abruptly straightened, releasing her as he backed away. His gray eyes held remembered torment, his voice had become raw. "I loved you and I hated you, for your loyalty and courage. Mike's a young fool not to see how lucky he is.''

And then he was gone, leaving Clare paralyzed.

She was torn by such powerful emotions it took her a moment to analyze them. Her sense of loss was so profound she felt as though her heart had just been ripped out of her chest. Here Jake had confessed to loving her in a way every woman dreamed of being loved, yet she would have to turn him away. She knew it and he knew it. Mike had to come first.

And yet she also had an odd sensation of freedom, of weightlessness. It was true she no longer felt guilty. She had done her best, would never have betrayed Don. She was human; she'd occasionally had unworthy thoughts, felt her body reacting to a handsome man. So what?

Perhaps what she'd had trouble accepting was that her love for Don had died long before he had. Even now she felt a queer wrench of pity at the thought of his pathetic dependence. It, more than his anger and paranoia, had killed her romantic love. He'd become a child; as such, she would never have deserted him. But in one way, she'd been widowed much longer than the fourteen months since Don's death.

For an instant she wished she'd let Jake see that she wasn't bound by the past. But sitting in the silent kitchen, she knew how irrelevant her self-revelation was.

Mike's fears and his need to believe in his father might be too deeply buried to excise. Of course he would grow up and leave home someday, but Jake had waited for her so long now. She could hardly expect him to wait years. She wasn't sure she could bear it if he did.

Suddenly restless, desperate to get away from the emptiness that yawned before her, Clare jumped to her feet. She'd go confront Alison Pierce, find out whether she was really the one who'd fingered Mike, and if so, why.

Clare posted a message for Mike on the refrigerator and grabbed her purse and, after a brief search, car keys. She carefully didn't look toward the blackened remains of her mother-in-law's house. Mrs. Talbot had lined up a construction firm to level what was left, but they wouldn't be able to start for a couple of weeks.

Clare knew that Alison didn't work; gossip had it that the inheritance from her father was so generous she needn't ever hold a job again. He'd been smart enough to buy up huge chunks of land, including waterfront, on several of the islands back in the 1950s, and had developed much of it himself. He'd died only four months earlier; probably Alison hadn't decided yet what to do about the house or her future.

What Clare didn't know was what Alison *did* all day, and therefore the likelihood of her being home. But a dark green sports car sat in front of the wide porch of the magnificent Victorian house she'd grown up in and inherited. Standing on a hilltop, so that it commanded a view of the bay, the old house was startlingly tall. Windows in the dark granite foundation indicated a full basement, and three stories rose above that. The contrast to Clare's own shabby little rental was almost ludicrous.

Clare didn't have to knock on the front door; before she started up the steps to the wide porch, Alison came around the side of the house.

"Clare." Her voice was as cool and unruffled as her appearance, despite the fact that she was dressed for some kind of rough work in leather gloves and overalls.

Clare felt a prickling sense of wariness. What was it about this woman?

"Hello, Alison. Am I interrupting?"

The auburn-haired woman glanced down at her gloved hands. "Oh, I was stacking firewood. I just bought a few cords. Green, and it weighs a ton, but it'll be seasoned by next winter. What can I do for you?"

Beat around the bush or be direct? Both Clare's instincts and personality demanded the second.

"I've heard that you're the one who claims to have seen Mike running away from the fire at that rental."

Alison's beautiful face displayed not the slightest hint of discomfort. "That's right," she said calmly. "I almost came to you, but we don't really know each other... Well, it would've been awkward. In the end I decided I couldn't in good conscience not go to the police. I hope you understand that I wouldn't for worlds hurt Don's son. But if it really was him, if he's been setting the fires, then it's better if he gets help now."

"You don't know Mike. How could you be so sure it was him you saw?"

The delicate eyebrows rose. "I'm not positive. I told the police I couldn't be sure."

Rage slowly rose in Clare's gorge. "Didn't you realize what that kind of rumor would do to him?"

"Perhaps we should sit down."

"No, thank you," Clare said coldly.

"Well . . ." Alison stripped off her gloves, for the first time seeming to hesitate over her next words. Then, in a fluid motion, she lifted her head and met Clare's gaze again. "You know how Don died, but there's something about him you probably *don't* know."

"And what is that?" Clare asked, her voice still cold.

"He loved fire. When we were in school, he set small ones just for fun. Everyone knew he was doing it."

Clare's eyes narrowed. "Everyone knew. Isn't that a little vague?"

Alison's expression became distressed. "I saw him set one. Don just laughed. It was a prank, he said. After that janitor was hurt, I didn't think so, but..." She gestured affectingly. "I wasn't very old, and imagined myself in love with him. Of course I couldn't bring myself to turn him in. I always hoped that fire scared him. There weren't any more around here. After he left...well, I hoped." She pressed her lips together. "Then I heard how he died."

Clare was momentarily silenced. Was it possible? But she didn't believe it—couldn't. Not Don! Despite his masculine arrogance, he was basically a kind man. He wouldn't have hurt someone for fun. And surely if he'd been addicted to setting fires, he wouldn't have been able to stop. Not for all of those years.

Until the day he died, choosing so horrible and inexplicable a method.

Still... Clare shook her head. "I don't believe it," she said. "Even if it was true, what does it have to do with Mike?"

Alison looked at her with pity. "How could I help thinking of him as soon as the fires began? I understand your reluctance, but surely you, too—"

"No." Clare backed away. "No. Not Mike. He was home."

"Are you certain?"

No. Dear God, she wasn't certain. But she wouldn't believe it.

"You're wrong," she said.

"I hope so." Alison's mouth twisted. "I mean that, Clare. For Don's sake."

Don, whom she'd *imagined* she loved? Nodding curtly, Clare got into her car. Slamming the door was eminently satisfying.

The drive home was too short. When she got there, she sat in her car, thinking.

Truth or lies? But why would Alison lie?

Because she *hadn't* seen Mike running away from that fire and needed to bolster her claim that she had? But then, why claim to have seen him in the first place?

Clare's thoughts jumped back. *Everyone knew he was doing it.* Another lie? Or had Jake and Suzette not wanted to tell her?

Don had set his own house on fire and burned himself to death. She realized she couldn't deny the possibility that he had indeed been a petty arsonist when he was a teenager.

But not Mike! Schizophrenia might be hereditary, but not pyromania. Unless—oh, God!—unless Mike was horribly attracted to fire *because* of the way his father had died, not despite it. Did he imagine his father as some kind of martyr who had sacrificed himself on a burning altar? Was he fascinated by fire because Don had died in it?

Gaze resting on the blackened hulk of her mother-in-law's house, Clare felt sick to her stomach. She breathed slowly, combating the nausea. Damn it, she was jumping to conclusions again! She'd talk to Jake, maybe to Suzette. Force the issue.

What she didn't want was for Mike to hear this story about his father.

She entered the house quietly, with a glance at the stairs. Mike's bedroom door was closed, although that didn't mean he was still sulking in there. Whatever his emotional state, he was undoubtedly still hungry. She'd put dinner on and worry about mending fences later.

What she'd forgotten was that her mother-in-law would be home by now. She was already peeling the top off a frozen entrée.

"Anne! I'll make dinner."

"Nonsense. I picked up a few groceries while I was on the mainland, and I figured we'd go instant tonight. Norma says this brand of lasagna is decent."

"Mike won't care, as long as there's enough of it."

The two women exchanged smiles. Clare noticed how pink her mother-in-law's cheeks were, how lightly she moved compared to the past few days.

"Did you have a good time?" Clare asked.

"I have to admit there's something cheering about spending a fortune. Even if I now owe the same fortune to my credit-card company. Let's hope the insurance comes through quickly." She popped the lasagna into the oven. "Would you like to see my new wardrobe?"

"Are you kidding? Lead on."

In the living room, Clare helped her cut the tags off the elegant dresses and blouses in Mrs. Talbot's favorite shades of rust and coral and hang the garments in the hall closet. Everything else they stacked neatly in some plastic cubes Clare had bought as a temporary furnishing. Misty materialized as cats are wont to do at such moments and helped, pouncing on the tags as they were cut off and diving into empty bags.

"You'll be the envy of every woman on the island," Clare told her mother-in-law, folding a handsome Laurel Burch sweatshirt and simultaneously shooing the cat off a dress lying on the couch.

"But won't I look silly out digging in the garden in brand-new slacks and sweatshirt?"

"There's always the thrift store," Clare suggested, only half-facetiously.

"That's not a bad idea." Mrs. Talbot looked thoughtful. "I would so hate to snag something new." Then her face cleared and she reached for the last bag. "I bought a present for you."

Clare gave an "ooh" of pleasure when Mrs. Talbot handed her a silk blouse in a luscious shade of turquoise. "It's gorgeous! How sweet of you! You didn't need to—"

"I wanted to," Mrs. Talbot said firmly. "I hope it fits. And this is for Mike." She held up a No Fear T-shirt. "Do you think he'll like it?"

"He'll love it!" Clare glanced involuntarily toward the hall. "Is he up in his room?"

"No, I peeked in there when I got home. I assumed he was over at Geoff's or someplace." Her brow crinkled. "Didn't he tell you where he was going?"

"No. We...had a scene earlier." She almost added that it was no big deal, but something in her mother-in-law's steady gaze stopped her. They were supposed to be allies, weren't they? Why hide the worst from her?

She looked down at her lap, where she stroked the turquoise silk. "It was about Jake. He's been...well, courting me, I suppose. Mike hates him. I wanted to find out why."

Mrs. Talbot sat next to her on the couch. "Did you?" she asked gently.

Clare let out a sigh. "Yes. That last year, Don got suspicious of everyone. He was convinced Jake and I were..." This was unexpectedly hard to say.

"Having an affair."

She looked up. "How did you know?"

Her mother-in-law's smile was sad and a little crooked. "Remember, I talked to Don regularly. He told me."

Clare stared at her in shock.

"I didn't take his accusation seriously, of course. After all, he also thought you were trying to poison him. Besides—" she hesitated only a moment "—I knew Jake wouldn't do that to him."

After a brief silence, Clare said, "I wish you and I had known each other better."

Mrs. Talbot had no trouble understanding this seeming non sequitur. "I do, too. It wasn't that I thought badly of you. It's just that I didn't know you well enough to be sure."

"No. I understand."

"But Mike believed his father?"

"Apparently. I didn't realize it until Jake showed up here and Mike was so hostile."

Mrs. Talbot patted her hand. "Let me talk to him. Perhaps he'll listen to me."

A month ago, Clare would have wanted to handle it herself. Now she felt a rush of relief. "I don't know if it'll do any good, but . . . bless you."

"Were you off looking for him?"

"Off? Oh. No." She hesitated again, but confiding was getting easier. "I went to see Alison Pierce."

Her mother-in-law looked surprised and perturbed. "Why?"

Clare told her.

In outrage, Mrs. Talbot exclaimed, "She claims to have seen Mike?"

"That's not the worst of it." Clare hoped this wasn't a mistake. Don had been Mrs. Talbot's son, after all. If she had a heart attack because of the stress and upset, Clare would blame herself. But she was also increasingly convinced that Don had been wrong in believing his mother should be protected. In the ways that counted, she was strong. Clare continued, "Did you know that when Don and Jake were in high school, there was a series of small deliberately set fires?"

"This last month I could hardly help but remember," Mrs. Talbot said tartly. "But the police never figured out who was setting them."

"Alison claims it was Don."

Her mouth literally dropped open. "Don?"

"She says everyone knew."

"But that's absurd! Don was upset by them!"

"Suzette Fowler mentioned the fires, too. She told me that the last one was more serious, that a janitor was hurt."

The pink bloom in the older woman's cheeks had turned to a hectic flush, and her spine was ramrod straight. "That's right. He was badly burned. There were no more fires after that."

"Alison says she saw Don set one of them."

"Don?" her mother-in-law echoed. Her voice rose in agitation. "Why, he couldn't possibly have been responsible. He missed part of the year after he broke his leg and was in traction for several weeks. I remember Jake stopping by after school to tell us about that last fire, the one where the fellow was hurt."

They stared at each other. "But then, why..." Clare faltered.

"That's the question, isn't it?" Mrs. Talbot sounded grim.

Conscious of her growing fear, Clare tried to think. "Alison might lie if she'd set the fires herself, but wouldn't Don have known?"

"You'd think so. She clung to him so, it'd be a wonder if she was by herself long enough to crumple up the paper!"

Interested in the astringent tone, Clare said, "You didn't like her."

"Oh, well, I wouldn't say..." She grimaced. "Yes, I would. No, I wasn't crazy about her. But I was never quite sure why. She was always polite, just...chilly. I never warmed to her. Or felt she did to me."

Clare sank onto the couch. "Thank goodness I'm not the only one! She's so attractive and...*pleasant*. And I can't stand her."

Mrs. Talbot looked at Clare thoughtfully. "Is it because of Don?"

"That's what I keep telling myself, but..." Clare hesitated. "I can't put my finger on it. There's just something about her eyes that repels me. I wonder sometimes if she feels anything. But she must!"

"She did for Don. She called incessantly, got mad if he forgot to call back or made plans to do something with another friend. I tried to tell myself she was just immature, but it seemed more than that to me. She was strange."

"Then I'm not imagining it," Clare said slowly.

"Or else we both are."

Still thinking aloud, Clare asked, "If Don knew she was the pyromaniac, would he have kept quiet to protect her, do you think?"

"After that janitor was hurt, I wouldn't have thought so. But I can't be sure. He was loyal to those he loved."

They sat in silence again, Clare gazing distractedly out the window. At last she said, "Could Alison be lying to protect someone else? Didn't I hear she's engaged to Tom Petersen?"

"Yes, but he'd already graduated that year. Surely he'd have been noticeable hanging around the high school."

"Bart?"

Mrs. Talbot looked dissatisfied. "Her fiancé's brother? Isn't that stretching it?"

"What I don't understand," Clare said, troubled, "is why, if it's not true, she told me the story at all. She claims to have seen Mike running away from the fire. Fine. Why not leave it at that?"

"The only thing it accomplishes," her mother-in-law said slowly, "is to make Mike look like a better suspect."

"I suppose she told the fire marshal. I wonder why we haven't seen him."

"He sent the police officers."

Clare jumped up. "I'm going to call him. I refuse to let that woman tar Don with her lies."

Of course the fire marshal wasn't in his office; he'd gone home for the day. The anonymous voice assured Clare she would have him call.

Clare was about to start phoning around in search of her son when he came home, sulky but not as withdrawn as she'd feared. The T-shirt cheered him up, and after dinner when he and Clare were briefly alone he said, "Uh, Clare?"

"Yes?"

He hung his head. "I, uh, guess I never really thought you and Jake were...you know. I mean, I don't think you would. But I know he wanted to, and...jeez, he was Dad's best friend!"

"He may have wanted to," Clare said, "but he never once even suggested it. I know you're having trouble believing that, but Jake cared too much for your father to try to steal his wife."

On a new burst of sullenness, Mike said, "Isn't that what he's trying to do now?"

Clare touched his arm. "Your father is dead. He'd be the last one to want us to spend the rest of our lives mourning him."

"A year's not very long." Mike looked over his shoulder. "Here comes Grandma. Let's just forget it, okay?"

"I love you," Clare said.

Any normal fourteen-year-old boy would've had trouble forcing the words out. Mike didn't do any worse than any other boy that age. "I, uh...I guess...I mean..." He lowered his voice to just above a whisper and said hurriedly, "I love you, too."

Warmed by his awkward admission, Clare waited until he'd gone up to his room before she volunteered to take the first shift.

"But, Clare," Mrs. Talbot protested, "you never woke me last night! You must be exhausted."

"I slept all day," Clare confessed. "And you must be dead on your feet after that day of shopping."

Honesty warred with pride before her mother-in-law said, "Promise to wake me up when you get sleepy."

"Cross my heart."

The night was quiet and tedious. With Mrs. Talbot asleep in the living room, Clare couldn't even turn on a radio. As much as she loved to read, five or six unrelieved hours were more than enough, especially since she'd started with Jake's newest novel. It was powerful and disturbing. She found herself hunting for Jake in it—and for herself. She found neither.

She finished it in record time and then tried to concentrate on another book. Eventually she found herself rereading passages three and four times and realized she must be dozing in between. She awakened her mother-in-law with a gentle shake and stumbled to bed herself, falling into a deep and dreamless sleep.

"Nothing," Mrs. Talbot reported the next morning. Seeing Clare's inquiring glance, she added, "Mike's already left for school. I told him you had trouble dropping off last night. He thudded up and down the stairs rather heavily a few times, but otherwise cooperated in letting you sleep."

"Good Lord, it's ten o'clock!" Clare exclaimed. "I suppose I should stick my head in at the office, although I don't know why. Between interest rates and the mad arsonist, nobody's buying anything."

Real estate was seasonal work at best, so she'd been socking away money for the slow winter months. Thanks to Jake's purchase of the Mueller house, she thought she could scrape through the winter. It would have been nice to do better than scrape. Chili and macaroni and cheese got old, day after day.

The phone rang before she finished her first cup of coffee. The fire marshal conceded that he'd heard the rumor that Don had set the fires at the high school twenty years before. He listened to her—or, more accurately, Mrs. Talbot's—story noncommittally.

"It's possible," he said, clearing his throat, "that Don didn't set all of them. Fire often draws copycats unfortunately. It might be that he was particularly careful, but whoever imitated him wasn't, which explains the one more serious blaze. Or perhaps *he* was the copycat. He might have thought the first fire was an amusing prank and set another one just for fun. So you see, I'm afraid his absence from school for a few weeks doesn't eliminate the possibility that he did indeed set at least one of the fires."

Logically he was right. Irrationally Clare was furious. She slammed the phone down a little too hard.

"What did he say?" Mrs. Talbot asked anxiously.

Clare told her.

"I suppose it's conceivable," her mother-in-law admitted. "He pulled his share of pranks. But fire!"

"No, I don't believe it, either," Clare agreed. "But maybe Alison does. Maybe she misinterpreted something she saw and..." Hearing how thin that sounded, she gave up.

"Maybe," Mrs. Talbot said, sounding equally doubtful. How did you misinterpret the sight of someone tossing a lighted match into a wastebasket full of paper?

Clare took the first shift again that night. Twice she slipped upstairs to check on Mike. Both times he was a silent dark lump in bed.

Making herself yet another cup of coffee after one of her trips upstairs, Clare wondered how long they could go on this way if the arsonist didn't make a move soon.

At the moment, she had only a small lamp on, which gave her enough light to read in the corner of the kitchen where she'd pulled the rocking chair. The floor beneath it creaked slightly as she rocked, but the book lay unopened on her lap.

After so many nights sitting up, the darkness beyond the circle of light was familiar. If she stepped quietly down the hall, she'd hear her mother-in-law's rhythmic breathing; if she opened the back door, it would be the equally soft shush of the water washing up on the beach.

She sighed and let the rocking chair drift to a stop. In the ensuing silence, she heard a creak, from either farther away in the house or outside. Tensing, Clare rose to her feet as soundlessly as possible. Probably Mike was just getting up to go to the bathroom, but until she knew for sure she couldn't lower her guard.

In the kitchen doorway she stood and listened. No sounds came to her from upstairs; Mrs. Talbot's breathing didn't alter. Clare was on the verge of relaxing—after all, old houses did make unexplainable noises—when the glass pane in the front door suddenly shattered. The faint illumination from the kitchen was enough to let her see the dark hand that reached in to unfasten the dead bolt.

CHAPTER TWELVE

IN THE CLOSE DARKNESS of the hall, Clare stood paralyzed by shock and indecision. If she raced for the phone and called 911, she'd leave Mrs. Talbot vulnerable. All it would take was a few squirts of gasoline and a tossed match, and her mother-in-law would be cut off in the living room. But Clare had nothing she could use as a weapon.

Well, then, find something! she told herself sharply. The hand had already unfastened the dead bolt and was turning the doorknob.

Silently Clare crept backward into the kitchen. She looked wildly around in the muted glow of the small lamp. The broom was too flimsy. If only she had a cast-iron pan. Then her eye fell on the nearly full wine bottle sitting on the counter. She'd used a splash of the burgundy when she'd made spaghetti sauce earlier.

She snatched it by the neck and edged up to the doorway. Dear God. Enough faint illumination fell into the hall for her to see that the dark figure was pouring liquid from a gas can. He—she?—wore a mask and bulky black clothing. Clare strained her eyes. Was it a man or woman? But the lighting was too poor to penetrate the disguise. In the darkness the figure had an air of menace. He was coming toward the kitchen, head down, but the moment Clare moved she'd be seen. But no, the intruder paused and turned toward the stairs. The gasoline gurgled as it gushed out onto the wood steps. He was making sure no one escaped from this house tonight.

Fury blotted out some of Clare's terror. She rushed out of hiding, counting on surprise. She swung the bottle like some ancient warrior might have a battle-ax, feeling a bloodlust alien to her modern upbringing. Distantly she heard herself screaming, too.

But just as she swung, aiming for the head, the figure straightened and turned, deflecting her blow. The bottle struck, but with a soft thud. On a shoulder, maybe, or upraised forearm. Nonetheless, she'd used enough force that the arsonist staggered and half fell onto the stairs. Clare, yelling for Mike and Anne, wound up for another shot, but the intruder reared off the step and swung first, with the gas can. It was metal, not plastic like the new ones. The sharp edge hit Clare on her shoulder and knocked her against the wall.

"Clare!" She heard the gasp from behind her, and, using her moment of distraction, the arsonist barreled forward, sending her crashing to her knees. She turned her head to see Mrs. Talbot knocked aside. Then the dark figure was gone, out the front door.

Though she slipped on the wet floor, Clare ran for the door, switching on the porch light as she went. Too late. She stood on the top step and heard the thud of footsteps, but she wasn't certain which way they'd gone.

"Damn, damn, damn!" She'd had him cornered!

The smell of gasoline struck her like another blow when she reentered the house.

"Anne! Are you all right?"

The thunder of feet on the stairs preceded Mike's anxious call. "Mom! What's going on?"

"Be careful," she called. She snapped on the hall light, the movement sending a painful jab through her shoulder. Mrs. Talbot stood in the living-room doorway, clutching the frame. Her eyes were huge and shocked, and she was more obviously fragile than ever, but her voice was surprisingly calm.

"We'd better call the police," she said.

Tempting as it was to have hysterics, Clare settled for a moderate "Yes." She cradled her arm to avoid moving her shoulder. "At least we're one step ahead."

Her mother-in-law glanced, as Clare did, at Mike, and nodded. Standing there in nothing but his pajama bottoms, he stared back at them.

"What are you talking about?"

"You," Clare said briskly. "You accused me of lying to the police that day. I don't have to anymore. No one can claim you're the arsonist now."

"Oh." Mike pushed out his lower lip as he thought about it. At last, in a voice that sounded years younger and more lighthearted, he said, "Yeah, that's cool. Only . . . how are we going to clean this up?"

"God knows."

In the end, Clare tracked back through the gasoline and called the police from the kitchen, while Mrs. Talbot and Mike flung open all the living-room and kitchen windows. Then they waited.

It was Clare who suddenly remembered poor Misty. Mike found her hiding under his bed. When he went to drag her out, Clare stopped him.

"She won't like all the company that's coming," she said ruefully.

Of course the police and fire departments arrived with sirens wailing. On their heels came half the neighbors. Clare never even saw Jake arrive; he was just *there*. Among the professions of shock and suggestions for soaking up the gasoline, he stood in stony silence.

Clare's unnatural state of ferocity deserted her quite abruptly. One minute she was on her feet, pacing, her fingers clenching as she muttered, "If I'd just hit him harder." The next minute her hands were shaking and her legs were wobbling and she absolutely had to sit down. Lieutenant Russell scooted a kitchen chair under her in the nick of time. Out of the corner of her eye she saw Jake, in the kitchen doorway, make a sharp motion forward, then stop himself.

Blackness swirled. Clare leaned forward and put her head between her knees until her vision cleared. "I'm sorry," she murmured, straightening. "I don't know what's wrong with me."

"Shock," the lieutenant said. "Here. Drink this tea."

It helped. Or perhaps she'd just gotten a grip on herself. "I suppose you want to ask questions."

With admirable restraint, he said, "I'd certainly like to know what happened."

She wasn't sure he was aware that Jake stood behind him in the kitchen doorway, listening.

"My mother-in-law and I have been sitting up nights," she began. "Taking turns."

A muscle in Jake's jaw spasmed.

The police officer shook his head. "Lucky it was your turn," he said.

Clare recited events in the order they'd occurred. Something about Jake's cold expression made her conclude with a mixture of misery and defiance, "I should've been better prepared, but I didn't expect this. That's not why we were sitting up. I thought... We wanted to be able to swear to Mike's presence at home the next time there was a fire."

"If you hadn't been awake..." The lieutenant had the sense not to finish his sentence. "Okay, back to the intruder. Do you think you injured him?"

Everything had happened so fast. Clare frowned. "Probably no worse than he got me. There might be a bruise."

The policeman nodded. "Let's go over your description again. You didn't see the face?"

"No. He—she—wore a mask. One of those knit ones for skiing, with holes for the eyes and mouth."

"He didn't speak?"

"Maybe a grunt." She drew a steadying breath. "Nothing that would help me be sure of gender, or recognize it."

"Any sense of height?"

"Taller than I am, I think," Clare said, trying to picture those frightening few moments. "But not huge. Maybe..." Involuntarily her gaze went to Jake, whose eyes narrowed.

Lieutenant Russell swung around in his chair. His mouth tightened. "Mr. Radovich. Did you have something to contribute?"

"No."

"Then why are you here?"

"We're old friends." The grimness of his tone kept Clare from feeling warmed by his protective presence.

The policeman's eyebrows went up. "Well, I'm through with Ms. Talbot, anyway." He glanced back at her. "The aid car is still here if you'd like to go to the clinic and have that shoulder checked."

"Heavens, no!" She moved it gingerly. "I'd rather soak in a hot bath."

"It's up to you," he said.

Most of the neighbors had left, Clare discovered. Fire fighters were in the process of ripping up the shabby hall carpet and rolling it toward the front door.

"Make sure you take it well away from the house," Jake said from behind Clare.

"Back-seat driver," she muttered, and the fire fighters gave him irritated glances. But in all fairness Clare realized that Jake wasn't just being bossy. He was making sure the gasoline-soaked carpet wasn't left conveniently near enough to the house to be used in a second attempt.

With buckets and hoses, the fire fighters washed out the hall, diluting any gasoline that might have soaked into the wood. They were so thorough water sloshed around on the floor as they tromped out in their big boots, leaving silence in their wake.

"I'll mop," Clare said. When she turned toward the kitchen, she almost walked right into the solid wall formed by Jake's body.

"You had to play heroine on your own." His eyes glittered with anger and, she dimly realized, fear. For her, for Mike, for the woman who'd mothered him.

"You know why," she tried.

"You didn't trust me, did you?" His voice was flat, dead. "Maybe you should've thought about the fact that you weren't endangering only yourself. With your lack of trust, you risked Mike's life, too, and Mrs. Talbot's."

The night had been stressful to put it mildly. Clare was in no mood to be reproached, even if she understood that fear for her was behind his anger. "Don't talk to me about trust!" she snapped. "You trust me even less than I do you! You're a stranger to me, Jacob Stanek." She put extra bite into his nom de plume.

In his eyes she suddenly saw naked pain, and he leaned toward her, his body vibrating with tension. "What is it you want to know?" he asked in a low furious voice. "Do you want to hear all about my father? Well, I'll tell you. He was a violent son of a bitch who beat the shit out of my mother until she was too cowed to fight back. Then he started on me. You want to hear about what it felt like to hide my bruises every day so the other kids wouldn't feel sorry for me? Or would you rather know what it feels like to have anger wound so tight I thought I'd explode from it? Maybe I should give you a rundown on how many times I slugged some kid, wishing it was my own father. Imagining *his* blood spurting from his nose, him crumpling to his knees, hiding his head in his arms, begging for mercy."

Sweat had broken out on Jake's forehead, and he was breathing hard. "Or would you rather hear more about my friendship with Don? The friendship I betrayed every time I looked at you?" His expression held something close to contempt for her. "And you think *you* have ghosts that need laying to rest." He turned and blundered toward the door with none of his usual grace.

When Mrs. Talbot stepped forward and laid a hand on his arm, he paused, head bowed, back rigid. "Jake..." she began.

"Forget it," he said in an unrecognizable voice. Then he kept going, letting the screen door slam behind him.

Paralyzed for the second time tonight, Clare could only watch him go. Shame gripped her in sharp talons. He was right. Why had she thought it so important that he share his painful childhood with her? She'd turned it into some sort of test, a proof of his devotion. As if she needed it! Jake had demonstrated his love in the ways that really mattered countless times. But that hadn't been enough for her. Oh, no. She'd wanted to possess him utterly, every waking moment; she'd wanted him to bare every tormented corner of his soul. She'd wanted him to crawl for her.

She tried to swallow and realized she was crying in huge silent sobs. Through the blur, she imagined she saw contempt on her mother-in-law's face, too, and felt she deserved it.

What she'd forgotten was her stepson.

The boy's voice cracked. "It's my fault, isn't it?"

She turned to face him, unable to answer.

He saw her face and his own twisted as he tried not to cry. "I was afraid I'd lose you," he whispered.

"I know." Clare squeezed the words past the lump in her throat. "Come here."

He came, and she took him into her arms, a little boy who happened to be a head taller than she was. They cried together, for new losses and old.

Clare didn't ask whether he was still afraid. She had a feeling that it didn't matter anymore, that Jake had walked out her door for the last time.

WHILE MIKE WAS at school the next morning, Clare and her mother-in-law scrubbed the floor and walls again and made a trip to town to choose new carpet.

Clare called Jake half-a-dozen times, but all she got was his answering machine. She left two messages, the first a tremulous "Jake, this is Clare. I'm sorry. Please call me." An hour later she waited for the beep, then said, "Please, Jake." The call after that she hung up when she heard the mechanical reproduction of his voice. What was the use? She could feel the emptiness through the telephone wires. He wasn't ignoring her calls; he was gone. And she couldn't blame him.

Clare picked up Mike at school, using the excuse that she had to go to the grocery store. Her worries were too vague and unfounded to be shared. The fire might have killed him, too, but she had no reason to think it had been aimed at him in particular. There were better grounds for believing her mother-in-law was the target. And yet...

If last night's attempt to burn down their house hadn't failed, Mike might have been blamed. Would have been blamed, if that fire was the last. Between the rumors about Don and Alison's claim to have seen Mike running away from the one blaze, too much of the community already believed he was guilty.

Cruel gossip, Clare wondered, or a deliberate attempt to frame him?

Her appetite had completely vanished, but she made spaghetti, using the sauce she'd made the night before, and set the table with extra care. Taking the garlic bread out of the oven, she had a rueful remembrance that this was the same menu she'd had the night she'd told Mike that Jake was moving to Dorset. It felt like an eternity ago, but couldn't have been more than six weeks.

They'd come so far, she thought, smiling at her stepson as she put the bread on the table.

"This looks good," Mrs. Talbot said with pleasure. "I feel guilty letting you make such an effort!"

"Don't be silly," Clare said. "We shouldn't let some creep disrupt our lives too much."

"Can I take a turn sitting up tonight?" Mike asked eagerly.

Clare's parental instinct was to say no. On the other hand, she was very tired, and her mother-in-law wasn't strong enough to take over. Mike could raise an alarm as well as she could.

Only weeks ago he'd have gotten sullen at her hesitation. Instead, he said persuasively, "It's not like I'm some little kid or something. I mean, I'm bigger than you are."

"Okay," she said. "As long as you promise to start yelling the second you hear anything at all. No investigating. Okay?"

"*You* investigated."

"Yeah, and it was dumb."

"But you almost caught the guy..."

She leveled a look at Mike, and he rolled his eyes.

"All right, all right, I'll wake you up if I hear anything." He stuffed a nauseatingly huge bite into his mouth. Around it, he mumbled, "Hey, Grandma, would you pass the broccoli?"

Her eyes met Clare's, and neither mother nor grandmother commented on his table manners. He could eat with his toes, as far as Clare was concerned, so long as he did it cheerfully. Obviously Mrs. Talbot felt the same.

Clare just wished she could rejoice in the strides Mike was making and shake her vague uneasiness.

Deciding to tackle it head-on, she said as matter-of-factly as possible, "Listen. We all need to be careful for a while. Mike, that goes for you, too. No bike riding alone, don't get in a car with anybody but Grandma or me, don't answer the door when you're by yourself without knowing who's there first. No, I take that back. Don't answer it at all unless it's Jake or Geoff."

"Why should we be careful?" he asked in the middle of twirling spaghetti onto his fork. "I mean, I can see why at night, but why the rest of the time?"

"I don't know," she admitted. "No, that's not true. The thing is, the other fires were all set in empty buildings—first the Kirks', then the bookstore, then the rental.

But your Grandma's was different, and so was last night. It was like..."

"Like he was trying to kill us," Mike finished solemnly.

She gave a small nod.

With the innocence of youth, he hadn't looked at it that way before. She hated making him face such an ugly possibility, especially when he was walking out from under the shadow of his father's death and his own fears. But it was better to be safe than sorry, wasn't it?

"Mike, do you know Jake's father?" she asked.

He'd been brooding—although that, of course, didn't stop him from eating at the same time. "Uh...yeah, I guess. He's the guy with the auto-body shop, right?"

She was conscious of Mrs. Talbot stirring. "Right," Clare said.

Mike just looked blankly at her. "So? What about him?"

"Have you ever seen him around here?"

"Here?" His expression changed to surprise. "You mean, our neighborhood? Of course not!"

"How about Alison Pierce?" she asked.

"Who?"

"Alison Pierce," Clare repeated. "She owns that big Victorian at the corner of Cross Island Road. I was talking to her and Sharon one day when you rode your bike into town."

His lip curled. "Why would I pay attention to some women you happened to be talking to?"

He might have if he'd seen Alison's peculiar reaction upon finding out who he was. But how to describe or explain that? "She was your dad's girlfriend in high school," Clare offered.

That got through, but he still shook his head. "I remember Dad talking about her once, but I don't know who she is. Does it matter? What about her?"

"Oh, nothing. No, it doesn't matter." Clare gave up. It seemed odd to her, given the size of the community, that her stepson had no idea who Alison was, but then it was also true that teenage boys weren't very interested in their mother's peers. And she herself only occasionally saw Alison around town. Maybe she did most of her shopping on the mainland.

Clare didn't know what else to ask—or say—about Jake's father. In a way, her suspicion seemed farfetched. But hate was a rare emotion, and the man definitely felt it. Still, did it make sense that he'd go after Mrs. Talbot, instead of the son who'd—in his eyes—earned his enmity?

So Clare let it go. How could she warn Mike about some woman he didn't even know or a man he barely did when her own disquiet was so amorphous? It wasn't as if she could claim to have seen a resemblance between the dark figure in her hall and either Alison or Jake's father. Alison was tall enough to have been the intruder, but that was hardly an identification. And the attacker could have been a man just as well. If only Clare had gotten a better look! No matter how often she squeezed her eyes shut and tried to picture details—the gloved hands or the height or the thickness of a thigh or forearm—she couldn't reach any conclusions.

She let Mike take the first two hours that night, after which he shook her awake. "I can stay up longer if you want," he offered, bright-eyed.

Clare groaned, resisting the urge to bury her head under the pillow. "No, you have to go to school tomorrow. I'll get up. You go to bed."

"It was actually kind of cool. It was so quiet. I read half of *A Separate Peace*. For English, you know. Mr. Holland won't believe it."

It had been quiet only because Mike hadn't had somebody to talk to. She'd like it to be quiet again.

"Go to bed," she repeated more firmly.

He went reluctantly. Clare huddled in the kitchen pretending to read, but really listening to night creaks, her muscles jerking and her hand jumping for the phone every time the Hide-A-Bed in the living room squeaked when Mrs. Talbot rolled over.

At 4 a.m. she woke her mother-in-law and stumbled off to bed herself. By the time Clare showered in the morning and made her way downstairs, Mike had already left for school.

"Shoot," Clare said, pouring coffee. "I meant to tell him I'd pick him up after school again. Did he take the bus?"

"No, his bike." Mrs. Talbot, looking old and weary this morning, had been pouring milk on her cereal, but she stopped with the carton suspended above the bowl. Her brow crinkled worriedly. "I didn't think... You really believe he's in danger?"

Clare hoped her smile was reassuring. "I don't know why he would be. I'm sure I'm being overly cautious. I'll just feel better when this whole thing is over."

"Won't we all." Mrs. Talbot finished pouring her milk and set down the carton. She sat with a very straight back, which lent her dignity but not the illusion of sturdiness she was probably striving for. "Which reminds me, a crew is coming tomorrow to start demolishing my house. The foundation is all that can be salvaged."

"I'm sorry," Clare said gently. "I've been trying not to look over there. As many years as you spent in that house, you must feel a terrible sense of loss."

Her mother-in-law's eyes filled with tears. "Oh, dear. It's so ridiculous. The house was shabby, anyway. Mike's right. I have been wishing I could remodel."

"Which is not quite the same thing as having to start all over."

Mrs. Talbot reached a hand across the table. "And of all people, you know what that feels like."

Absurdly Clare was crying, too, as she met the clasp. "It was the little things that bothered me. The photographs and, oh, a favorite shirt, my books. And that was nothing compared to what you've lost. Don's baby pictures, and that beautiful old quilt on your bed, and furniture that belonged to your parents..."

"But this time nobody died." Her mother-in-law blinked away the tears and gave a small sniff. "I still have you and Mike."

"More to the point, we still have *you.*" They smiled at each other somewhat foolishly, and Clare knew they'd gained something from the horrors of this past month. On impulse she asked, "How do you feel about being called Mom? Since it keeps slipping out, anyway?"

Her own mother had died of cancer when Clare was a teenager. Maybe she'd resisted the idea of replacing her. But now it felt right.

The delicate papery fingers tightened on her hand. Very formally Anne Talbot said, "I'd be honored."

"Good. Now I'd better scoot, or I'm going to be late for work."

"Wait." Mrs. Talbot took a deep breath. "Last night...were you implying that Jake's *father* might be the arsonist?"

Clare grimaced. "It's occurred to me, that's all. I saw him and Jake have a confrontation one day. He seemed to really hate Jake."

"But it's *us* he's gone after." She stopped. "No, you're suggesting it's me, aren't you? That he's angry because I helped Jake and defended him when he was a boy."

"Either that," Clare said, "or he doesn't care about you, but he knows Jake does."

"You mean, he's trying to hurt Jake by hurting me. Oh, God." She grasped the back of a chair. "It makes a horrible kind of sense."

"But only if he's really sick."

Her mother-in-law's eyes met hers. "Somebody is."

Clare could only nod.

"JAKE, THIS IS CLARE. I'm sorry. Please call me."

Jake's hand reached for the phone, then stopped short, curling into a fist. His knuckles showed white. The silence quivered as though she were waiting, and then came the click of her hanging up. His machine beeped and the red light began to flash.

What was she sorry about? That she'd hurt his feelings? He didn't want to hear stumbling apologies, didn't want to assure her it didn't matter.

Why hadn't he kept his goddamned mouth shut? What had been the point of trying to make her feel guilty? Guilty. Hell. She'd suffered too much from that particular emotion already. All he'd been doing was lashing out from his own frustration, his own hurt. *Love me,* he'd been crying.

And she'd chosen to love Mike, instead.

Blindly Jake stared at the screen of his computer. He was trying to work. The deadline for his latest book was looming, and a month ago he'd thrown out his half-completed manuscript and started all over. Ironic that this might be the best thing he'd ever written. His other books were cynical, detached, written from the viewpoint of a narrator coolly observing the foibles and perversities of others. This time the narrator had inexplicably become involved, might even turn out to be the murderer. Jake was leaning that way right now. He'd shock his editor, but what the hell. He had to channel his own occasionally murderous impulses somehow, didn't he? Writing had always been his outlet; all that had changed was that his emotions had become more turbulent, less easily squelched. He didn't want to observe anymore; he wanted to *live*.

His vision cleared and he read over the paragraphs on the screen. He didn't like the sound of that first sentence. The rhythm was a little off. He fiddled with it, moved on to the next. Within a few minutes he was immersed, unconscious of the silent house around him.

Until the phone rang again. "Please, Jake." Her voice broke on his name, just a quiver, but it was enough to make his muscles go rigid. If he were a better man, he'd talk to her. Would it kill him to say, "I was scared for you. I was letting off steam?" Answer: Yes, it might kill him. Because it also meant admitting that he understood her choice, even thought it was the right one. Mike should come first.

Jake closed his eyes and massaged the bridge of his nose. He'd do for Don's son what he should have done for Don: walk away. Jake had spent a lifetime paying the price for a childhood in which no one had really loved him, not enough to put him first. Even if it was within his power, he couldn't rob Mike of the gift of a kind of love only a few were fortunate enough to receive.

He'd walk away—but not until he knew Clare and Mike were safe. Until then, he'd do his damnedest to make sure they were, even if it meant guarding their house like a German shepherd tied out on a chain. Even—especially—if it meant bringing down his own father.

IT WOULDN'T HAVE MATTERED if she *had* been late for work, Clare thought ruefully. For lack of anything better to do, she made some random phone calls hoping to gain a listing—for what good that did at this time of year.

She was about ready to cut out early for the day when Joanne said over the intercom, "Line two for you, Clare. It's Mr. Sheehan."

The Seattle lawyer interested in the marina. She'd almost given up on him after her several phone calls had gone unanswered and time had passed.

Heart pounding, she picked up the phone. "Mr. Sheehan," she said in a good imitation of a warm unconcerned tone. "How are you?"

He was fine. He wanted to make an offer.

Yes! she breathed, pumping a fist into the air. Joanne, peeking around the office door, grinned.

"Are you free Saturday so that I can present a written offer?" Mr. Sheehan asked.

"You bet," Clare said, amazed that she sounded no more than pleasantly professional. "What kind of figure did you have in mind?"

It was definitely within the negotiating range. They discussed it briefly, then set up an appointment for Saturday morning.

She immediately called the marina owner. "Marty, I have an offer for you. He's coming up Saturday to present it officially, but here's what he quoted me."

"I can't go that low," Marty said, "but I don't suppose he expected I would."

She agreed. "Have you figured out what the bottom dollar is you could take?"

He had, and the difference wasn't that great. Clare hung up the phone, convinced the sale was in the bag, and wandered into her boss's office to talk about it.

Half an hour later she glanced at the clock and leapt from the chair. "Three-forty-five! Oh, no! I was supposed to pick up Mike at school. I've got to run."

She didn't even give Alan time to remark. She darted out, snatched her purse from her office, called, "I'm going home!" to Joanne and raced to her car.

The high-school grounds were nearly deserted. A few cars were sprinkled throughout the big parking lot; half-a-dozen bikes remained chained to the racks. Mike's wasn't among them.

Feeling foolish but unaccountably anxious, she carefully followed his usual route home without catching up with him. She didn't see his bike propped against the garage, which meant either that he hadn't come home or that he'd actually put it away, a rare occurrence. Instead of looking, Clare hurried into the house.

"Mike? Mom? Anybody home?"

Mrs. Talbot appeared from the kitchen. She wore an apron and her hands were floury. "I was just baking cookies," she said in explanation. Then her expression changed. "Weren't you picking Mike up at school?"

"I was late." She made herself think rationally, despite the panic that ricocheted around in her chest. "He hasn't called?"

"No. He isn't that late yet."

"I know." Clare made a face. "I'm being silly, aren't I?"

"No," Mrs. Talbot said slowly. "If nothing else, after we warned him to be careful, he should know better than to stop somewhere on the way home without letting us know."

"Geoff's." Clare grasped for a simple explanation. "I'll call Geoff."

Mike's friend answered the phone. "Hi, Mrs. T. No, Mike's not here. He said he'd call me later."

Trying to disguise her urgency, Clare asked, "Was he heading straight home?"

"I think so. Is something wrong?"

"It's just that he isn't here yet," she said, unable to keep the worry from her voice.

"Well...maybe he went to shoot baskets at the elementary school." Geoff stopped. "No, he didn't have his ball with him."

Oh, God. Her heart was racing and her mouth felt dry and her palms were sweating. *Please come home, Mike. Please, please, please.*

She was amazed to hear herself say calmly, "Well, it's a little premature to get too anxious, Geoff. Have him call if you hear from him."

"Sure," he said.

She hung up and faced her mother-in-law, who was wringing her hands. "Where else might he have gone?" Clare asked.

"Ryan's?"

Clare tried. No answer.

"I don't know," Mrs. Talbot said in a voice that cracked. "Ian Mullin's... But he's mad at him. Who else?"

They stared at each other. "He doesn't have that many friends," Clare said. She had to think. He was just a kid. Kids did dumb things. But what? *What?*

"I'll call everyone he knows," she said, reaching for the phone again.

It didn't take long. Ten minutes later she'd exhausted Mike's list of acquaintances. Some weren't home. Those who were hadn't seen Mike since fifth period, or lunch, or...

Clare hung up the receiver and looked at the clock. He was an hour late now. Her anxiety had become full-blown terror.

"I'm going to call Jake."

While she dialed, Mrs. Talbot hovered. Clare gave a cry of frustration when after four rings Jake's brusque message played. "Jake Radovich. Leave a message and I'll return your call as soon as possible."

Let him be there, she prayed. *Let him be listening.*

"Jake," she said, her voice suddenly tremulous, "Mike is missing. He didn't come home from school. I don't know what to do. Please, if you're there..." Silence. "Please, we need you," she finished, and then carefully returned the receiver to its cradle.

"The police?" Mrs. Talbot suggested.

"Are they going to listen?" Clare pushed her hair back from her face. "A teenage boy who's late home from school? Don't they have to be missing for twenty-four hours or something before the police will do anything?"

"I don't know." Her mother-in-law lowered herself carefully onto a kitchen chair. She appeared to have shrunk. "But the average teenage boy wasn't in a house someone tried to set on fire two nights ago."

For Clare, a driving sense of urgency made sitting here impossible. Mike had his flaws, but worrying her unnecessarily wasn't one of them. Even those times when he'd been deliberately late home, she'd always known where he was. No, something was terribly wrong, and she couldn't wait for the police. Mike might not have that much time.

"I'm going looking for him," she said, the words coming before she'd even realized she'd made up her mind. "You call the police."

CHAPTER THIRTEEN

ALISON'S CAR was parked in front of the Victorian mansion. The house sat quietly, the windows blank eyes. Like other houses of the era, it had varying rooflines, bay windows poking out here and there, and half-a-dozen brick chimneys. With the first floor starting a good eight feet from the ground atop a granite-block foundation, it was enormous, made taller by its position on a hill. Gingerbread, painted gray-blue, decorated the gables above the narrow attic windows. Beautiful as the place was, Clare couldn't imagine living alone in a house this size.

Mike's mountain bike was nowhere to be seen. Which proved nothing. It could be around the other side of the house or in the barn. Or not here at all. This was probably a wild-goose chase; instinct had brought Clare here first, but even if Alison had kidnapped Mike, she might just as likely have dragged him off into the woods somewhere. Or the kidnapper/arsonist might be someone Clare didn't even know or hadn't suspected. But she didn't think so.

She'd come to terms with her memories of Don, and she didn't think her reaction to Alison stemmed from jealousy or even an awkward awareness of having shared the same man. Alison gave her the creeps, plain and simple. And Clare couldn't help wondering if she'd recognized the strangeness in the other woman because she knew mental illness in a way most people didn't. She'd lived with it. Don's had been different; he'd been angry and frightened. But she'd seen it steal the man he once was, had seen something alien look at her from his eyes. She had that same feeling when her gaze met Alison Pierce's.

Stomach fluttering, her heartbeat nearly as jumpy, Clare got out of her car and resolutely climbed the ten steps to the front porch. She hadn't even thought of what to say. She could hardly demand her stepson back. What if she was wrong?

Make an excuse that would mean Alison had to invite her in, she decided. But what?

She rang the bell and heard the muffled sound of chimes inside the house. Through the wavery leaded glass of the oval inset in the handsome oak door, she saw Alison coming.

Mike, Clare thought. *Talk about Mike. Alison wouldn't believe anything else. Say you're worried about the rumors. Won't she squelch them for the sake of Don's son?*

"I'm sorry to bother you," Clare began as the door swung open. "But I wonder if I could talk to you..." Her words trailed off. They seemed pointless, given that Alison held a handgun pointed at her chest.

Through a constricted throat, Clare said, "Then Mike *is* here."

"Oh, yes," Alison agreed pleasantly. "Why don't you come in?"

"What if I say no?"

"I must insist," the other woman said in a mockery of social grace. "Upstairs," she added, stepping back.

Clare should have been more frightened than she was. She couldn't seem to fight her way free of a dizzying sense of unreality. Alison looked so much her usual self—

her beautiful auburn hair stylishly twisted into a French knot, a cream-colored silk shirt accented by polished wooden beads, her dark brown wool slacks impeccably fitted. The whole idea of her as an arsonist had always seemed a little crazy, however cold she appeared. But here she was, holding the dull black gun in a steady hand.

Clare climbed the long gracious staircase to the second floor, then followed Alison's directions up another narrower set of steps to what must be the attic. Servants' quarters, perhaps, when the house had been built by some lumber or shipping baron. It was hot up there, the air close.

"End of the hall," Alison said from behind her.

What if she tried to take the gun right now? Clare thought. Could she surprise Alison, wrestle it away from her? A glance over her shoulder told her the other woman was prepared. She was hanging a good ten feet back, and she waved the gun peremptorily when Clare hesitated.

"In that room," Alison snapped.

The door was narrow but solid; Clare noted with apprehension that it locked. An old-fashioned key was in the keyhole.

Inside was a bedroom with a sloping roof and yellowing wallpaper. A massive canopied bed and matching walnut dresser were the only furnishings. Mike was crouched on the floor at the foot of the bed, his face pale and eyes dark as he faced the door. Blood trickled down his forehead.

"Mike!" Clare exclaimed. With a sick rush of fury, she saw that his hands and feet were tied to the bed frame with blue nylon rope. She swung around. "You're insane!"

Alison's sculpted brows rose. "Perhaps, but also quite efficient, if I do say so myself. No, no." She leveled the gun at Clare's chest. "Don't come any closer. I'd rather not kill you this way, but I will if I have to. If I leave the gun, the police will think you came after Mike and he shot you."

"The police are on their way right now."

Alison laughed. "Oh, I seriously doubt that. And *I'll* be on my way in just a minute."

Clare's feeling of unreality was being replaced by active fear. She should have rushed Alison sooner, even at the front door. Now she'd be dead by the time she reached the woman. And then she'd be no use to Mike at all.

"Of course, my house will be the unfortunate target of the arsonist today." Alison smiled at Mike. "You. Only this time you'll have made a mistake and gotten caught by the fire. Perhaps because your stepmother arrived and tried to stop you. It will be such a tragedy." She shook her head in mock pity, but her eyes were bright with malice and something even more disturbing, which replaced their usual emptiness. "You'll die just the way Don did. The way I killed him."

Mike sucked in an audible breath. Clare was suddenly so light-headed she swayed. Alison's words rang in her mind. *The way I killed him.* So Don hadn't chosen his death, after all, neither the time nor the way of it.

Breathing slowly, she made an effort to steady herself. She was careful not to look at Mike. "Why us?" she asked. "Isn't Don the one you hated?"

"But, you see, Mike is dangerous to me." Alison's tone was one of complete reason. "He *saw* me that day. We passed on the beach, even spoke to each other. He didn't pay a great deal of attention, but eventually he would have noticed me and remembered. Once he realized I'd known his father, common sense would have told him I had something to do with that fire. I prefer not to take that chance.''

''But you could have moved somewhere else!'' With incredulity, Clare for a moment forgot her main objective: catch Alison off guard, then rush her. ''You'd never have had to cross Mike's path!''

Simply and coldly Alison said, ''But I didn't want to move. Why should I?''

In the face of such monstrous egoism, Clare was momentarily speechless. Her expression must have shown her revulsion, however, because a muscle jerked in Alison's cheek.

''Don killed my unborn baby. It's only just, don't you think, that I should kill his son?''

Clare sensed the quiver that ran through Mike, still crouched on the floor beside her. She seemed to have passed beyond shock herself. ''Don killed . . . ?''

''I was pregnant that summer.'' Alison lifted her chin. Her voice was tight with pain and bitterness. ''I hadn't had a chance to tell him. I never got a chance. He wrote— Can you imagine that? We loved each other, we were engaged, and he didn't even tell me face-to-face. Oh, no, he wrote to say he was *married.*'' She spit the word out.

''What did you do?'' Clare whispered.

''What could I do? I got an abortion, of course. I could hardly bless Don with a baby at that point, could I?'' Her brooding gaze rested on Mike, the son who'd taken the place of her child, the son of the woman she must have hated almost as much as Don.

''If you'd told him—''

''He'd have done what?'' Alison's lip curled. ''Paid child support, I suppose. What kind of life would I have had?''

Probably not a pleasant one. Clare couldn't deny that. Even these days, an unmarried unskilled eighteen-year-old mother had few prospects. From what Jake had said, Clare guessed that Alison's parents hadn't been warm, accepting people. And Don had treated her cruelly.

But he hadn't known about the baby.

"I'm sorry," she said. Under the circumstances, the sentiment should have been false; expressing it was probably inappropriate. But she meant it all the same.

Alison's face twitched with conflicting emotions, but she was unlikely to let herself be confused from her objective at this point. Nor did she. Her hand had dropped a little. Now she lifted it, braced it with the other one. "So am I," she said, but with little visible regret. "If you'd just stayed home, you wouldn't have had to be involved."

Of course, the other night, when she'd come to their house, Alison had apparently considered Clare and Anne expendable. Clare didn't bother reminding her. Instead, she said simply, "Mike is my son. I couldn't stay home."

A ghost of envy, or something more bitter, crossed Alison's classical features. "Ah, well. I'll be on my way. I ought to tell you that I'll be starting the fire just on the other side of this door, so I wouldn't try to break it down if I were you. And of course, the window is so high from the ground." She backed into the hall. "I believe I'll take the ferry to Anacortes. Have a nice dinner, do a little shopping. What a shock when I return!"

"Nobody will believe you. Not after the other night. They *know* Mike isn't the arsonist."

Alison smiled. "Haven't you heard the fire marshal talk about copycat crimes? They'll believe it."

Clare lunged forward; the door slammed in her face and she heard the key turn.

JAKE HADN'T LIKED IT when Clare arrived home that afternoon early without Mike. Damn it, she was smart enough to take precautions where the boy was concerned, wasn't she? She'd turned into the driveway without noticing his Porsche tucked into a wide shoulder and hurried into the house. He sat up straighter, frowning. Was something wrong?

But nothing happened. Mike didn't appear, and the cops didn't pull up at the house with their sirens wailing. With Mrs. Talbot's house leveled, Jake could see Clare's back door, as well as her front, from here, which was why he'd chosen this parking spot. Question was, what did he expect to see? What the hell good was he doing sitting out here like a modern-day Sir Lancelot?

He hadn't intended to make this a twenty-four-hour-a-day vigil, but he had an uneasy feeling. Events were accelerating. By two-thirty he'd flicked off his computer and decided to come over here. At least he'd know if something happened—if the flicker of orange flame appeared in an upstairs window, if someone screamed. The alternative was to go home, and he was damned if he'd do that.

He leaned his head back against the padded seat and waited. Half an hour passed, forty-five minutes. Haydn's Surprise Symphony washed over him almost unnoticed. He'd feel better if Mike would show up.

Instead, Clare came out of the house and headed straight for her car. He was too far away to decide whether the expression on her face was worry or just preoccupation. Hell, maybe she'd started dinner and discovered she didn't have any tomato sauce or sour cream. As she backed out of the driveway, he waged an inner war: follow her, or continue to keep an eye on the house?

The house won. He knew Mrs. Talbot was there, and she could be the target just as well as Mike or Clare. The arsonist hadn't yet taken to hijacking cars on the island roads. He or she was more likely to show up here with the intention of torching the place once and for all. And, damn it, Clare couldn't get in too much trouble, could she?

He settled back, unable to relax altogether. The minutes seemed to crawl; the music rose to a crescendo and impatiently he turned off the CD player. Where the hell was Mike? Where was Clare going?

Up the road a car appeared, slowed, hesitated. Tensing, he was watching it turn into the bed-and-breakfast when out of the corner of his eye he saw movement at Clare's. It was Mrs. Talbot, who'd come out onto the porch and was looking up the road. Her odd stillness had Jake out of his car and heading down the driveway before he even registered alarm.

So intently was the old woman watching—or listening—that she didn't see him until he'd almost reached the house. When she did, a look of such relief crossed her face his anxiety increased tenfold.

"Jake!" she cried. "Thank God. I didn't know what to do."

He was at her side in seconds. "What's wrong?"

The words rushed out. "Mike never came home from school. Clare went looking for him and I called the police, but they didn't sound very interested." She was wringing her hands. "I keep listening for sirens, but there's nothing. And I haven't heard from Clare and..."

Damn Clare! he thought furiously. She had to go rushing off alone. When he got his hands on her— He broke off. His anger was too obviously a cover for more chilling thoughts.

"Where did she go?" he asked in a voice that sounded one hell of a lot calmer than he felt.

"She intended to try Alison Pierce's first." Mrs. Talbot pressed her lips together. "We think..."

What they thought fell into place easily. Too easily, like words his subconscious had already arranged before his fingers touched the keyboard. Of course he'd considered Alison, but he'd let himself be distracted by his private fear that his own father might be lashing out.

"I know what you think." Alison had better reason to hate Don Talbot than anyone else. How that could have become an obsession with Don's family Jake didn't know, but it made as much sense as thinking an abusive man might start torching houses just to punish his grown son. "I'll go after her," he said. "Try the police again. Talk to that Lieutenant Russell."

"Yes, all right." She turned toward the house.

"Where would she go next?"

Mrs. Talbot stopped without looking back. "I hate to tell you, but it's occurred to us—"

"That my father would make a likely suspect?"

"Yes. I'm sorry."

"Don't be." Jake didn't wait for a response. He ran up the driveway, threw himself into his car and gunned the engine. *Damn her,* he thought in anguish. Half an hour had passed since Clare had left. Too much could happen in that time. If Alison was the arsonist, he might be too late. And if Clare had gone on to his father's and Jake followed her, that might be just what the SOB wanted.

"BREAK THE DOOR DOWN," Mike cried. His face was pale, his eyes big and dark. "Hurry!"

"She'd just shoot me," Clare said numbly. She dropped to her knees beside him and hugged him, as much to comfort herself as him. He couldn't hug back, but he burrowed into her body like a toddler trying to hide from the world.

Outside the door came a few thuds and then a familiar gurgle. Gasoline. Alison was soaking the hall. When she set a match to it, the fire would explode. There was no way on earth they could escape that way, even once she'd left.

Clare reluctantly let Mike go. "Here. I've got to get you untied," she said frantically.

He ducked his head and tried to wipe wet cheeks on the shoulder of his shirt. She pretended not to see his tears.

She went for his hands first. This rope looped through the solid rail at the foot of the bed. Without an ax, she had no hope of breaking the bed apart. She had to untie the knots! The rope was nylon, too thick to cut with anything in her purse, but thin enough that the knots defied her fingers. Mike had probably yanked at the ropes, tightening them further.

Oh, God, what if she couldn't get this rope undone? She couldn't leave Mike, wouldn't. Outside the door came a whoosh and a roar that jerked Clare's head around. Fire. Smoke would be the first danger. How could she buy some time?

"The bedspread," she said aloud. Snatching it, she stuffed it along the crack at the bottom of the door. Then she grabbed her purse and dug in it for her keys. The point of one proved a better pry than her fingernail. Mike held still as she worked, but his breath whistled in and out.

At last the first knot loosened, and Clare gave a sob of relief. Still, seconds passed, a minute, before the rope fell to the floor and his hands were free.

He went for the knots at his ankles, but after an instant his own sob echoed hers. "They're too tight!"

"Let me." She glanced at the door. Smoke was seeping in all the way around it. "Just a minute."

Closer to the door, she heard the dragon's roar, the crackle of its breath. She laid a tentative palm against the wood and had to yank her hand back. Roasting hot. The door could start to burn any minute. She might not have time to finish untying Mike.

The rope went from one ankle, looped around the massive leg of the bed, then to his other ankle. Testing the weight of the bed, she tried lifting. The heavy wood groaned, but the bed barely shifted. She shot a panicky look at the door. Flames licked around the edge of it.

"We've got to get out of here," she said. "Mike, when I lift, you pull the rope out."

"Let *me* lift," he said practically. "I'm stronger than you are."

Not a child.

"Hurry!"

He heaved until veins stood out on his forehead and muscles bulged in his arms. Reluctantly, with whimpers and groans, the huge canopied bed lifted from the floor. Clare yanked, and the rope slipped out. His ankles were still tied together, but he was free.

Breathing was getting difficult. "Come on. Out the window."

"But it's too high."

"We have no choice."

They crawled, so thick was the smoke becoming. The tall sash window had been painted shut probably years before. Clare took a drawer from the bureau and smashed the glass. Behind them the flames took a hungry leap forward, but greedily Clare sucked in a breath of the fresh air.

One look out, and what little hope she'd nourished almost vanished. On this side of the house, the ground dropped away below the foundation. A retaining wall created a narrow terrace above a plunge of another ten feet. They would never survive a jump.

Think, she told herself. "We can get to that roof," she said. "It'll be a few minutes before the fire gets that far."

The small, steeply pitched offshoot of roof topped first- and second-story bay windows that jutted out from the house.

"What good does a few minutes do us?"

"Your grandma knew where I was going. She was supposed to call the police. Pray God they listened."

"Go, Mom." Mike coughed. "Hurry."

She wanted to argue and couldn't. He was right. She would have to be the one to step first onto the window ledge and then jump sideways and down. Without her ankles tied, she'd have a better chance of finding purchase. Once she was safely straddling the roof, she could grab Mike when his turn came.

"Okay, okay," she agreed. Her blood thundered in her ears. Vertigo made her head swim as she inched out the window and crouched on the ledge, trying not to look down. She didn't let herself hesitate, just . . . leapt.

She hit the roof hard, spread-eagled, and slid a frightening few inches before her arms, hooked over the peak, stopped her descent. Half sobbing, Clare struggled to pull herself up.

Don't look down, don't look down, played like a mantra in her head, a needle stuck on an old scratched record. Her eyes were squeezed shut until she heaved herself onto the peak of the roof and swung her right leg over so that her back was to the drop.

"Your turn. Come on!"

Mike was already out on the ledge. She saw him take a deep breath, steel himself and jump. He thudded next to her, his feet scrabbling for a nonexistent toehold on the dry shakes. He was sliding, but he'd thrown his arms over the ridge of the roof and caught himself. Clare grabbed his upper arms and hauled upward. They were both gasping for breath and shaking by the time he sat upright on the sharp peak, awkwardly perched with his knees bent.

"Now what?" he asked.

"We wait."

"Do you think we could swing down into the window below us?"

Right. She and Arnold Schwarzenegger. "No," she said. "Besides, it probably wouldn't do us any good. If I were Alison, I'd have poured gasoline all the way down the stairs to the front door. It would have been safer that way for her to start the fire."

"I guess so," Mike admitted after a moment.

Clare forced herself to look around, even though it made her heart leap into her throat. No place to go. "Her car's gone," she said.

"She killed Dad."

"Yeah. I'm sorry."

"I'm not," he said, surprising her. "It's really awful, but I didn't like thinking he did it himself. You know?"

Clare knew. It was as though a burden had been removed from her. She could let go of the anger and guilt, and feel regret alone.

The first flames whooshed out of the window they'd emerged from. So quickly. The crackle was a roar as the old house, dried by the passing century to tinder, was eaten alive. How long did they have?

"Maybe we should jump." Mike was trying to sound nonchalant—Jean-Claude Van Damme in a tight spot—but his voice squeaked.

Clare closed her eyes and took long slow breaths. Trying not to reveal how much the idea terrified her, she said, "If we hang from our fingers, we won't fall quite so far."

The roaring had intensified; the heat blasted them. Smoke rose in a thick black column. Somebody would see it and call the fire department, but too late.

Too late. Suddenly the past was superimposed on the present, and she was no longer clinging to the roof but running toward the inferno that had been her home, screaming, "Don! Mike! Please..." She felt her feet sinking into the sand, giving her the illusion of moving in slow motion. A wall crashed inward, and the incandescent colors leapt higher against the oily black smoke, day turned to night. *Oh, God! Don! Mike!* All the while she'd known she was too late, that her husband was dead and perhaps her stepson, as well.

Well, Mike hadn't died that day, but he might now. Even if he survived the fall, he could end up in a wheelchair. On welling anguish, jolted back to the present, Clare faced the reality. Alison Pierce could win. Clare, too, might die. She might never see Jake again, never be able to tell him she loved him. In that instant it seemed terribly important that he know how she felt, even if she couldn't marry him, even if she had to choose Mike. *Let me tell him,* she prayed. *Give me that chance.*

Anger crashed over her in a strengthening tide. *I'll come back from the grave to haunt her,* she swore. *I'll find some way to pay her back.*

The heat was nearly unbearable now. She was hunching away from it. But oh, Lord, did she have the courage to hang out over space and let herself fall?

"A car's coming!" Mike shifted to see better. He started to slip and had to grab her. His voice shook. "It's Jake! Jake!" he yelled.

Clare twisted to look toward the front of the house. The black Porsche hadn't stopped moving, and still Mike screamed, "Jake! Jake!" She was calling his name, too, waving despite her precarious perch, hope magically restored. As he leapt out of the car and looked around, she screamed louder.

His head lifted and he saw them. As though in a mime show, exaggerated alarm twisted his face. "I'll be right back!" he yelled, and ran for the barn.

A ladder. *Please, please, please, let Alison have a ladder.*

"Mom. I don't know if we can wait."

She turned and had to duck her head at the blast of heat. Fire had eaten through the walls of the house and would be licking at their corner of the roof in minutes. Seconds.

But Jake was back, and thank God he had a ladder. He propped it against the house and climbed, moving with incautious speed. It wasn't long enough; he reached the top and was six or eight feet below them and to one side of what was the second-story bay window.

"Clare," he said. That was all—her name and a look—and her insides turned to mush. But there was no time for that. He snapped, "You'll have to slide down and let me catch you. Mike, you first—you're in back. Clare can help you turn around."

"You go first, Mom—"

"No. He's right. Here. Take my hands."

He inched around and got his feet on the right side of the roof, rolled onto his stomach and slid down. At the last minute, his fingers gripped the peak, slowed his descent—and then he let go.

Mike thudded into Jake, who'd wrapped his legs around the rung of the ladder and waited with arms outstretched. The ladder rocked, slid sideways. And crashed to a stop against the main wall of the house.

How Jake held the boy, still tied at the ankles, and got him down, Clare never knew. She couldn't watch. Instead, she rolled herself onto her stomach and clung to the rough-textured, cedar shakes. Sparks rained down. She flinched when they stung exposed skin. Some danced down the steep slope, while others charred blackened circles. The roof would ignite any second.

"Your turn," Jake called.

She snatched one panicky glance over her shoulder. She could see only the top of his head where he waited on the ladder as he had for Mike. He was so far away, the drop if he couldn't catch her appalling.

And I thought I needed him before, she thought half-hysterically as she let herself begin the slide. Her fingernails gouged the soft wood; her cheek scraped it. She hung, suspended by her fingertips, eyes squeezed shut, terror gripping her.

"Now!" Jake commanded, and she let go.

CHAPTER FOURTEEN

CLARE'S STOMACH gave a sickening lurch as she slid.
Despite her resolve to let go, her fingers scrabbled desperately, unsuccessfully, for some hold on the grooved
cedar shakes. Her knee banged a sharp edge—the gut-
ter, which then scraped her stomach—and then she was
free-falling.

The next instant she slammed into something solid.
Arms wrapped around her; the ladder teetered. Jake was
swearing, his voice hoarse. Then the ladder stabilized,
and he crushed her against him.

"Oh, my God, Clare..." he whispered against her hair.
His arms trembled, from the strain or relief, and some
distant part of her knew that her teeth chattered.

"I hate heights," she mumbled.

He laughed, a raw sound of relief. "Then what do you
say we get down?"

"Good idea."

With her foot she groped for a rung, found one, eased
herself a step lower, still clinging to Jake, who stayed put.
Another step, and another. She clutched at his legs, his
ankles, then the ladder. She didn't look up, concentrated on placing her feet, carefully moving each hand,
emptying her mind.

The next thing she knew, Mike grabbed her ankle.
"Don't kick me, Mom."

She scrambled the last few feet, swaying when she hit the ground. Mike continued to brace the ladder. Jake was just above, descending almost as hastily as he'd climbed. Sparks showered them, and Clare shook her head when she smelled hair burning. So intense was the heat they might have been standing in the open door of an oven.

"Let's get the hell out of here!" Jake said when he jumped to the ground. Gripping her elbow, he lifted Mike like a sack of potatoes and carried him as they ran.

Not until they'd reached Jake's car did he set Mike down. They turned as one to see the handsome old house burn. Flames leapt from every window. Over the roar of the blaze, the roof groaned as it collapsed inward. Clare's car was too close; the paint had blistered and blackened, and she wondered if the poor thing would be salvageable.

"Sirens," Mike said. "I hear sirens."

"A bit late." Cheeks wet, Clare looked at Jake. "If it wasn't for you . . ."

His arms closed around her with bruising force. Vaguely she knew that he'd reached for Mike, too. Past and present became one again. Jake had held them another time, as another house burned. He had held them then, as he did now, out of love.

By the time the first fire truck pulled in, the bay windows were gone. The flesh of the house had melted, leaving its bones, the heavy old timbers, to glow red hot in the midst of the conflagration. The fire fighters attached their hoses to the tanker truck, but the pitifully small streams of water were aimed at Clare's car, the barn and the open fields of dry grass.

Lieutenant Russell approached them unseen. "Where's Ms. Pierce?" he asked sharply.

Clare turned. "Catching the ferry," she said. "She thought she might go shopping, have a nice dinner. Fortify herself for the shock awaiting her when she returns."

She expected surprise or even doubt, was met, instead, with a matter-of-fact nod. "Ah. I'll have her detained on the other side." The police officer looked at his watch. "No, by God! The ferry hasn't left yet. Don't go anywhere."

He raced to his cruiser, where he talked on his radio for a few minutes. When he came back, he said, "Are you ready to tell me what happened?"

Mike's chin came up. "Are you going to think I did this?"

Their gazes held. "That's what I was meant to think, isn't it?"

"She killed my dad."

The lieutenant lifted his brows. "She told you that?" he said incredulously.

"It's a long story." Clare was suddenly so weary she could hardly stand. "Do you want to hear it now?"

He wanted. First, however, he took a look at the lump on Mike's head and agreed not to send him rushing off in the ambulance.

They sat on a rock retaining wall down the driveway. Mike started the recitation. He'd been on his way home from school. Alison had been waiting at the foot of her driveway. She'd claimed to need help moving a piece of furniture. He was just the strong back she wanted, she said.

"She was going to pay me five bucks."

"But I warned you to be careful," Clare said.

"I know I was dumb." He grimaced. "The thing is, she was just some lady. You know? I mean, I'm bigger than she is! I never thought a woman..." His gaze shied away from his stepmother's. "I didn't know her name or anything. She was wearing these big sunglasses, and all I could tell was that she looked kind of familiar. I just never thought... And she asked me like she assumed I'd help. She said it would just take a minute. It didn't seem like a big deal."

"It's my fault," Clare admitted. "I didn't want to scare you, so my warnings were too vague. I'm sorry. I should've given you more credit."

"You mean, you expected something like this?" he asked unbelievingly.

Clare glanced at Jake, who'd stayed silent. "I don't know what I expected."

"Jeez, Mom, she was crazy!" Mike looked at Clare like she was, too. "How were you supposed to know something so weird was going to happen?"

Lieutenant Russell cleared his throat. "Can we get back to the story?"

Mike continued. He'd preceded Alison up the stairs. When he stepped into the small attic bedroom, she knocked him over the head from behind.

"I'm not sure I was even unconscious. Just dazed, like. It all happened so fast. Next thing I knew, I was tied up."

"Well," Clare took up the story, "I've been wondering about Alison for quite a while. She was the only person I knew of who had a grudge against one of us." Thank God she didn't have to mention her other suspect—Jake's father. "It was Don she hated, but by extension Mike and his grandmother and maybe me, I don't know. And it all started to seem as though it was aimed at us. It couldn't be coincidence that we were at the center."

been investigating Ms. Pierce ever since she ... row suspicion on Mike, here," Lieutenant Russell said. "Until recently, she lived in a suburb of Portland, Oregon. They've had a rash of arson fires. A family-planning clinic that does abortions had two fires, which made the authorities think pro-life. But then a couple of churches were targets, both the same denomination, as well as some houses. No real pattern—"

"She had an abortion," Clare interrupted. She told them Alison's history. "Maybe she went to a pastor who somehow didn't meet her needs, and she resented it. Who knows?"

"Interesting." The lieutenant was taking notes. "They might want to find out if she knew the residents of those homes. She seems to be a woman who holds grudges."

"I wonder," Clare said slowly, "if she hasn't always been a little crazy. There were those fires in high school. And I think that in the end she scared Don off by being too needy. I suspect that no matter what happened, she wasn't going to react normally to it."

The policeman listened, pretty much in silence, as she told the rest of the story. Then he went off to his cruiser again, coming back to say abruptly, "She's in custody. I don't know if we can nail her for your husband's murder—"

"I did see her that day," Mike said, his voice strained. "I was down the beach and I saw the smoke, so I came home. This woman was standing there looking in that direction. I don't think she saw me until I was almost to her. She...she looked funny, like I'd startled her, and said real quick, 'I'd better go make sure someone's called the fire department,' and headed up toward—" he frowned "—the Lowells' house. Yeah, I remember kind of wondering, because they were away, but I guess I thought she

was staying there or something. And then I saw our hou
and I forgot.''

"Would you have recognized her?" Clare asked.

"Yeah." He was silent for a moment. "Yeah, if she
hadn't had the sunglasses on today, I would have. Because I *noticed* her that day, you know?''

"Then maybe we can get her for murder one," Lieutenant Russell said. "I'll be talking to the police down
there.''

Jake's hand had rested unobtrusively on Clare's
shoulder. Now he stood up. "I'd like to take Mike to the
doctor and then both of them home.''

"Sure." The policeman held out a hand to Mike. "I'm
sorry you fell under suspicion. Considering the way your
father died, it must have felt rotten.''

"It's okay," Mike said, shrugging awkwardly. "I
mean, you did have to check me out.''

The lieutenant looked at them all. "I'm even sorrier it
took us so long to respond today. I wasn't in the office,
and the dispatcher wasted time hunting for me to con-
firm Mrs. Talbot's story.''

"Which," Clare admitted, "is understandable, considering that our suspicions were based more on intui-
tion than facts.''

They left it at that.

Mike wedged himself into the back seat of Jake's
Porsche. "This is a really cool car," he said. "I wish I
could drive it.''

"Do you have your beginner's permit?''

"Not till next year.''

"Try me then," Jake said.

Talk about unreality. Feeling oddly numb, Clare listened to them. Was this Mike's way of trying to make

peace? Jake's way of saying, *I'll still be around if you want me?* What was *she* supposed to contribute?

At the clinic the doctor checked Mike's eyes and reactions. Clare took the chance to go to the front desk and call her mother-in-law, who snatched up the phone on the first ring. She listened stoically to the story, including the news that her only son had been murdered.

"Then it's all over now," she said at the end.

"I guess so. Except for the trial." Clare saw the doctor step out of the examining room. "Listen, I've got to go. I'll see you in a bit, okay?"

The doctor set down the file on the counter and smiled. "Your son may have one heck of a headache come morning, but I don't think you need to worry." She grinned at the boy, who'd appeared behind her. "He has a hard head."

Then it *was* all over, Clare thought numbly on the way back out to Jake's car. His gaze rested on her face; she felt it, but refused to meet it. Her own would give too much away.

Well, why not? She'd prayed for her chance, and now she had it. At home she'd let Mike go in and then she'd tell Jake. *I love you, but we can't do anything about it. Please understand.*

If she was going to break her heart, she might as well get it over with.

JAKE STOPPED the car in Clare's gravel driveway. Still without looking at him, she got out and released the catch to pop the front seat forward. Mike started to unfold himself from the back, but stopped halfway.

"I, uh, want to say something."

The boy wasn't looking his way, but Jake assumed the remark was intended for him.

"Yeah?"

Head ducked, Mike said clumsily, "I guess I always knew you were okay. I know I've been a jerk, and it was stupid of me, but Dad..." He stumbled to a stop, taking a deep breath before he concluded, "Anyway, I'm sorry, okay?"

He tried to leap out, but Jake shot a hand back to prevent him. At the grip on his arm, the boy lifted his head, a flush mantling his cheeks. Their eyes met, and Jake smiled, slowly and with warmth. Then he released Mike's arm and cuffed him lightly on the shoulder.

"It's okay," he said, echoing Mike's earlier response to the cop.

Not articulate, but enough. The kid blushed some more, mumbled, "I'm sorry," again, and managed to get out of the car without falling flat on his face.

From behind the wheel, Jake heard him say to Clare, "You don't have to come in. I'll explain to Grandma, if you want to... like, go with Jake."

"With Jake?" Clare's astonishment was plain in her voice. "Are you *sure?*"

"Yeah." Amazingly he sounded as if he meant it. At heart, he was a good kid.

"I do want to talk to him," she admitted.

To say a final goodbye? Jake wondered. It scared him, the way she'd been avoiding his gaze. She hadn't really looked at him since the cop had gotten there. She'd clutched him tightly enough up on that ladder, but cold reality had apparently set in since, he thought cynically—and with pain he didn't even try to disguise from himself. But why? Damn it, *why?* If Mike had been her excuse, what was she going to use now?

"I'll see you later, then." Mike bounded down the driveway, yelling over his shoulder, "If anybody wants you, I won't tell them where you are. I'll hold 'em off at the pass."

Laying his arm on the back of her seat, Jake leaned over so he could see Clare's stunned expression as she watched her stepson retreat.

He kept his tone light. "Have I just been given permission to ravish you?"

"He kind of gave that impression, didn't he?" She sounded dazed.

"He'll get over it."

Clare gave a choked laugh. "It's true I have something I want to say. I guess this is a day for confessions."

He didn't know if he wanted to hear this one, but he nodded at the seat. "Get in."

Wordlessly she complied. He drove through the tunnel of trees to his house, where he parked. Neither moved when Jake turned off the ignition.

She was staring straight ahead when she said in a small voice, "I love you."

His heart cramped in exultation and pain. "What?"

Now he really had to strain to hear her. "I love you. I think . . . I've loved you all along. When Don was alive, I couldn't let myself know that I did. And this past year. . . I tried to forget you. I worked hard at not thinking about you. Instead, I dreamed. And then when you showed up again, it was Mike. I couldn't hurt him." She fell silent.

"So why—" the words scraped his throat "—if you love me so much, didn't you come to me today? Why did you go over there by yourself?"

She turned to stare at him. "But. . . isn't that how you found us?"

"What are you talking about?"

"I called you." Her eyes were huge and blue, bottomless. "I did come to you today. Let's go inside. I'll show you."

He let them into the quiet house. She went straight to the kitchen, where his answering machine sat on the desk that was a convenient extension to the cabinets. The red light blinked three times, paused, blinked again.

Without a word, Clare pushed the play button. Her voice, thin and a little shaky, broke the silence.

"Jake, Mike is missing. He didn't come home from school. I don't know what to do. Please, if you're there—" her voice paused "—we need you." Click.

And where the hell had he been? Despising himself, he answered his own question: playing Sir Lancelot.

Her voice came again, floating disembodied in the room. "Jake, are you there? Oh, God, have you left?" There was a sound suspiciously like a sob. "Never mind." Click.

Jake reached out and took her hand. She squeezed back, almost as tightly as he gripped her.

Clare again, her voice steadier. "Just . . . just so you know, in case you come home, I'm going to Alison's to look for Mike. I don't know where I'll go after that, but I'm starting there. Mom—Mrs. Talbot—is calling the police, but I kind of doubt if they'll pay attention to our vague suspicions. Mike hasn't been gone that long. But I have a bad feeling. Anyway, I, uh . . . Lord, this is turning into a habit, isn't it? Me, begging for help. But it's your fault for always giving it. Thank God. I don't know what I'd do without you, Jake." Click.

Another moment of silence as they stood, fingers entwined, both facing the machine. At last Clare whispered, "Where were you?"

He drew her to face him, his mouth flattening. "I came so close to being too late."

"But you weren't. Thanks to you, we're all right."

"I was guarding you." Jake uttered a harsh laugh. "Incompetently, as it turned out, but I was there. If I'd just stayed home and answered my telephone, instead—"

Her hand covered his mouth. "You got there in time. But how...?"

He kissed her palm, then cradled it against his lean cheek. Letting out a breath, he said, "I saw you come home and then leave again. I almost followed you, but I was more worried about the arsonist going for your house a second time. What do I know? Anyway, eventually Mrs. Talbot came out on the porch to listen for sirens. She told me where you'd gone, and I got there as quickly as I could. If she hadn't come out on the porch..." The thought was unendurable. His hand tightened and he must have come close to crushing her fingers, because she gave a little gasp.

But instead of pulling away, she said softly, "I do love you. I mean it."

He groaned deep in his throat and kissed her. There was still so much that should be said. If she wanted to hear about every ugly moment of his childhood, he'd give her that. He'd give her anything, if only she'd have him.

But this didn't feel like the moment for words. He'd been driven by urgency ever since he realized she'd gone hunting for Mike. He had a flash of nightmarish memory: seeing that roiling column of smoke, pulling into the driveway to find flames shooting from the windows. And oh, God, the relief and terror when he saw Clare and Mike perched so frighteningly high off the ground. If there hadn't been a ladder in that barn...

Suddenly desperate to possess her, to know in the most basic way possible that she was safe, he backed her against the cabinet and deepened the kiss. Clare must have felt it, too, this primal urge to couple. Already she was whimpering, her hips moving helplessly against his, her hands kneading his shoulder muscles. She fueled his hunger, which exploded into a blaze of primitive need. He lifted his mouth from hers so that he could yank off her sweater. He caught a glimpse of her eyes, heavy-lidded and smoky, before her lashes veiled them and her lips softly touched his rough-shaven jaw.

She tugged at his shirt, and he shrugged it off heedlessly even as he worked on the catch of her bra. He made a raw sound of pleasure when the bra slipped down her shoulders. God, she was exquisite: small-boned, with a long graceful neck and tiny waist. Her breasts were ivory white, small but perfect, the swell enough to fill his hands.

He captured her mouth again while he struggled with the zipper of her jeans. It didn't help that she was peeling his T-shirt off at the same time.

"Oh, hell," he muttered, and let her go just long enough to shuck his clothes. Most times he'd have felt like a goddamned idiot stripping naked in the kitchen. Right now all he knew was that he wanted in her.

She'd gotten rid of her own jeans and stood there before him, the stark need in her eyes belied by the way she nibbled uncertainly on her lower lip.

"Am I scaring you?" he asked hoarsely.

"No." Her smile didn't quite make it. "I scare myself, I think."

He scared himself, too. His blood seemed to roar through his veins, and the ache in his groin was driving him as mercilessly as the belt his father used to wield.

Jake didn't know if he could stop; didn't want to stop. But if she wasn't ready, he had to.

He closed his eyes briefly, gritted his teeth and took a step back. "I'm doing it again, aren't I?"

"Pushing me?" The vulnerability disappeared in a smile of pure sexual teasing. "Not hard enough."

"I want you," he said.

She could have teased some more; instead, she visibly swallowed. The smile faded to leave aching vulnerability on her face. "You can have me. Anytime."

Jake snatched her up. Her legs came around his waist as naturally as though they'd been created for no other purpose. Her arms wound around his neck, and her mouth met his in a kiss of no subterfuge and even less art.

The desk at the end of the kitchen counter was the right height. He set her down there and, unable to wait, pressed slowly and inexorably into her. Muscles clenched around him, holding him as tightly as her arms did, accepting him and refusing to let him go. He'd never been loved with such generosity, so unconditionally. He felt like an animal, slamming into her, but she didn't let him feel shame even for this. Little sounds told him she wanted him as badly as he wanted her; she clutched at him with desperate hands and cries of need and satisfaction.

As much as his own physical release, he wanted to hear his name the way only she said it, with joy and surprise and wonder. A gift. When the end came and she cried out, "Jake!", her name came to his lips, and damned if it didn't sound as jubilant.

CLARE HAD NEVER FELT so wonderful. Which didn't make much sense, since her position was both undignified and uncomfortable. The wood was cold under her rear end; her head leaned against a cupboard, and her back was unsupported.

But Jake's mouth was moving tenderly from her forehead over her temple and down to her earlobe. His hands caressed her hips even as he withdrew from her. And oh, his body was so beautiful, lean and male, solid and powerful. Clare happily stroked her hands down his chest and felt the quiver of muscles responding, the shiver of sleek damp skin. Murmuring under her breath, she turned her mouth to meet his in a kiss of exquisite tenderness.

"We should probably put something on," she suggested without urgency. She'd used that all up. "In case the police or the fire marshal come."

Jake's chest vibrated under her hand when he reminded her, "Mike was going to head 'em off at the pass—or the driveway, as the case may be. We can depend on him."

Mike. The reminder of her stepson was enough to dampen her euphoria. "If he could see us now . . ."

"I don't think he'd be surprised."

Remembering the way he'd grinned as he dashed down the driveway, Clare made a face. "I'm afraid you're right. Although maybe he's innocent enough to imagine us doing nothing but having a heart-to-heart talk."

"Innocent?" Jake backed up, his smile slow and rakish. "A fourteen-year-old boy? Come on. Even you don't believe that."

"Are you suggesting that when he's late home it's because he's having wild sex with some girl?" she asked with acerbity.

Jake's tone was amused. "Is that what we had?"

She blushed. "I think so. Or am I the innocent one?"

"Probably, but yeah, that was wild sex. In fact, I didn't intend... Intend, hell. That was all hormones and no brains."

"I have a feeling I should be insulted."

"No," he said gruffly. "You were magnificent. You *are* magnificent. Every teenage boy's wet dream."

Clare was unreasonably flattered, despite the unromantic nature of the compliment. "But you're not a teenager."

"Where his hormones are concerned, every man is a teenager." Jake kissed her with such tenderness her heart skipped a few beats. When he lifted his head, he smiled. "And no, I wasn't suggesting Mike is having wild sex after school. Just that he wishes he was."

Remembering the *Penthouse* magazine she'd found under Mike's mattress when she was changing his sheets, Clare could hardly argue. And right this minute she was considerably more interested in her own hormones than in her stepson's.

But Jake backed away from her, leaving her feeling chilled. Creases had formed between his dark brows.

"Maybe we should get dressed," he said flatly. "We need to talk."

The chill penetrated her skin, went bone deep. Of course there were things that had to be said, but why did he suddenly look so remote?

In her apprehension, she was clumsy as she pulled on her jeans and sweater. Jake was dressed before she finished. "Shall we sit down in the living room?" he asked.

She gave a small nod. Squeezing her hands together, she took a seat on the leather sofa, and Jake settled right beside her, though he didn't touch her. The lines on his forehead and between nose and mouth were deeper than usual, giving his face a forbidding aspect.

His voice was clipped. "I should make a few confessions of my own."

"What do you mean?" she asked anxiously.

"You're right that I tried to shut you out. I don't even like to think about my childhood, much less talk about it." He sounded dispassionate, despite the topic. "I haven't in more years than I can remember. If I were a woman, I might not have gotten away with it. But men don't ask about things like that. Even Don..." Jake shrugged. "He never asked. He'd see some new bruises and say, 'Son of a bitch.' Subject closed."

Pity cramped her heart—pity and profound relief. He wouldn't be talking like this if he wasn't trying to please her. If he didn't love her enough to do that. "Jake—"

"No, let me finish. The irony was, I wanted to know all about you. I suppose—" he moved his shoulders uneasily "—the truth is, I wasn't sure what you'd see if I really let you in. Hell, any kid treated like I was has to wonder if it isn't his fault. You tell yourself you've gotten over that, but maybe you never do. I don't know."

"Jake," she said gently, "this isn't necessary. You're the one who was right. I was wrong. I *do* know you. You've showed me. I was, I don't know, making excuses, I guess. I wanted to be strong enough to stand alone." She told him the same thing she'd told her mother-in-law that day in the hospital, about how ingrained her sense of helplessness had become during those years of Don's illness. "You were the one person I let myself need, and I resented what I saw as a weakness. I think—" this was hard to say "—I turned that resentment on you."

Jake met her eyes grimly. "I don't suppose it helped that I was your husband's best friend."

"He's gone." With an astonishing sense of freedom, she could say it and mean it. "If Don had lived, I don't think I ever would have fully understood what I felt for you. Another example of my cowardice, I suppose."

"The kind of cowardice you showed today?"

"Physical and emotional courage are two different things."

"You have both."

"And you're prejudiced."

A light smoldered in his dark gray eyes. "You might say that." Still he didn't touch her, and the grim note remained in his voice. "I don't know if I can live with Don's ghost."

"I've exorcised him," Clare said with complete certainty. "In an odd way, it helps to know—" She stopped.

"That Alison murdered him?" At last Jake took her hand. "I feel like I should be surprised, but I'm not. The pieces didn't fit before."

"She was... triumphant." Remembering, Clare shuddered. "She'd hate to know that Mike and I were both relieved to find out that Don didn't kill himself. Horrible as that sounds."

Jake's fingers bit into hers. "Horrible? What's horrible is wondering whether you drove your best friend to commit suicide. I tried to tell myself he wouldn't have conceded the field that way, but hell, who knows? What if on some level the old Don could see what he'd become and deliberately decided to get out of our way? After everything he'd given me..."

"You didn't want to think he'd given me to you, too," she said slowly, understanding at last.

Jake grunted. "That's the stuff of nightmares."

Letting herself remember the man she'd married, Clare looked into Jake's eyes. "Would it be so bad if Don *had* willed me to you? I don't think I'd mind knowing that he ... approved.''

The twist of Jake's mouth was rueful. ''I have a suspicion he would.''

Her pulse picked up speed, but she tried to keep her tone light. ''Well, then?''

''There's someone else we have to think about.''

She didn't pretend to misunderstand. ''Mike gave you permission to ravish me, remember?''

''What if it was just impulse? Kids that age don't think ahead. He was grateful. That doesn't mean he wants me in his life.''

''Actually I think he was telling you that he did. But if not—'' Clare hesitated, then took the plunge, feeling *right* for the first time in longer than she could remember ''—well, then, he can darn well *learn* to accept you.''

The opaque gray of Jake's eyes heated to a color closer to molten silver. But the carefully guarded impassivity of his expression didn't crack. ''Why the turnaround?''

''I guess I'm just a little slow,'' she said, making a face that was somewhere between a smile and tears. ''I've been so busy thinking about my own fears I didn't look at things from Mike's point of view. But lately... Oh, I've been remembering all the time he spent with you and the way his face used to light up when you'd raise an eyebrow and say, 'So, you want to kick my butt on the basketball court?' Or, 'How about we dig up some clams for dinner?' Do you remember?''

Jake turned his face sharply away from her. But the muscles in his jaw clenched, and when, after a long pause, he answered, his voice was hoarse. ''Yeah. I remember.''

''I don't think Mike *wanted* to reject you. But he was afraid of losing his dad, too, and—'' she had to swallow the lump in her throat "—it's taken him a while to realize he can depend on us for the long haul."

"On *you* for the long haul."

"Today you're the one we depended on. And you came through. Mike's not stupid."

Jake sounded harsh. "Gratitude—"

"Isn't love," she interrupted, reaching for his hand. "I know. But you have something going for you. Mike already loved you. Why do you think he hated you so bitterly?"

At last he looked at her. In his eyes was such naked pain and vulnerability her heart splintered. "I don't know," Jake said. "I don't know why *you* love me."

In a voice thick with tears, she whispered, "Is there a *why* for love?"

"I think," he said rawly, "you're the first person ever to say those words to me. Or at least to mean them."

Clare leaned forward and kissed him, her lips soft. "Maybe," she murmured, "that's because you never let anybody before."

His fingers bit into hers as he searched her face with such intensity time seemed to hesitate and take a breath. The breath she wasn't taking, had no room for in her lungs.

She hardly recognized Jake's voice. "You mean it, don't you?"

"That I love you?"

"Yeah."

"I mean it."

"What if I don't talk to you? What if I don't know how?"

It was as though a heel had ground the splinters of her heart into even smaller shards. Tenderly, somehow smiling as she blinked back tears, Clare said, "You can learn. You said so yourself."

"How will you teach me?"

"I'll be persuasive. Maybe wild sex would do the trick."

One corner of his mouth turned up. The look in his eyes softened. "Then we're already off to a good start."

"Mmm." Her heart was magically intact again, thudding so hard in her chest she could hardly hear herself speak. "So, what do you say?"

"Will you marry me?"

Of course this was where they'd been heading, but somehow she was still stunned. She felt as though she'd been waiting for this moment her entire life. Or perhaps it was only since the first time he'd held her, the first time she'd needed him, this man who'd always been both a stranger and her best friend.

What she'd never guessed was that he'd needed her as badly.

"Yes." She tasted the salt of her tears. "With joy and all my heart."

Jake's mouth was a hairbreadth from hers as he made a wry addition, "And your teenage son."

"And Mike," Clare agreed shakily. "He'll love you, too. I know he will."

Just before he kissed her, Jake said, "Don was a lucky man. I'm even luckier."

Maybe, but Clare had a feeling she was the lucky one. Out of fire and madness had come love greater than she'd ever imagined. The Don she'd married, lost so long ago, would be happy for her.

BRIDE'S BAY RESORT

UNLOCK THE DOOR TO GREAT ROMANCE AT BRIDE'S BAY RESORT

Join Harlequin's new across-the-lines series, set in an exclusive hotel on an island off the coast of South Carolina.

Seven of your favorite authors will bring you exciting stories about fascinating heroes and heroines discovering love at Bride's Bay Resort.

Look for these fabulous stories coming to a store near you beginning in January 1996.

Visit Bride's Bay Resort each month wherever Harlequin books are sold.

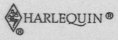

HARLEQUIN ®

BBAYG

Emergency!

Dr. Stephanie Sheldon counseled pregnant teens. Now she was pregnant herself after a poignant one-night stand with Dr. Talbot Robichaux. How was she going to explain *that* one to her class?

Well, maybe it would be easier than she thought. Talbot proposed a marriage of convenience, and right now marriage would be very convenient indeed—if it wasn't for his resentful teenage daughter.

There were other complications too: her missing twin's daughter showed up at Stephanie's New Orleans clinic one day. How could she not offer *her* a home? Suddenly this makeshift family was growing faster every day—as were her feelings for Tal!

Look for this heartwarming story from Karen Young in February 1996 wherever Harlequin books are sold.

NML-5

HARLEQUIN SUPERROMANCE®

a heartwarming trilogy by *Peg Sutherland*

Meet old friends and new ones on a trip to Sweetbranch, Alabama—where the most unexpected things can happen....

Queen of the Dixie Drive-In (Book 3)

Carson Delaney hasn't paid any particular attention to romance in years—not since she met Tony de Fuentes in California. Now she's back home in Sweetbranch to build a new life for herself and her sister. And the last person she expects to see there is Tony!

Look for *Queen of the Dixie Drive-In* this February wherever Harlequin Superromance novels are sold. And if you missed *Double Wedding Ring* (Book 1) and *Addy's Angels* (Book 2), it's still not too late to order them.

HARLEQUIN SUPERROMANCE®

From the bestselling author of
THE TAGGARTS OF TEXAS!

comes

THE CAMERONS
OF COLORADO

Cupid, Colorado...

This is ranch country, cowboy country—a land of high mountains and swift, cold rivers, of deer, elk and bear. The land is important here—family and neighbors are, too. 'Course, you have the chance to really get to know your neighbors in Cupid. Take the Camerons, for instance. The first Cameron came to Cupid more than a hundred years ago, and Camerons have owned and worked the Straight Arrow Ranch—the largest spread in these parts—ever since.

For kids and kisses, tears and laughter, wild horses and wilder men—come to the Straight Arrow Ranch, near Cupid, Colorado. Come meet the Camerons.

THE CAMERONS OF COLORADO
by Ruth Jean Dale

Kids, Critters and Cupid (Superromance#678)
available in February 1996

The Cupid Conspiracy (Temptation #579)
available in March 1996

The Cupid Chronicles (Superromance #687)
available in April 1996

Let

 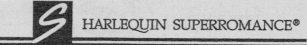
HARLEQUIN SUPERROMANCE®

welcome you home

Welcome to West Texas—and the Parker Ranch!

Long before the War Between the States, Parker sons and daughters ranched Parker land. Eighty-one-year-old Mae Parker aims to keep things that way. And as far as Mae—and almost everyone else on the ranch—is concerned, her word is law. Except to Rafe. And Rafe, thirty-five years old, iron-willed and *unmarried,* is Mae's favorite great-nephew. But he has no plans to buckle under to her by changing his marital status.

That's why Mae invites Shannon Bradley to the ranch. Something about Shannon—the only person other than Rafe who has ever stood up to Mae—gets under Rafe's skin. Still, after years of watching his great-aunt manipulate the rest of his family, he's damned if he'll fall in love to order!

Watch for *A Match Made In Texas* by Ginger Chambers
Available in February 1996
wherever Harlequin books are sold.

INTRODUCING...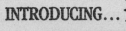

A collection of award-winning books by award-winning
authors! From Harlequin and Silhouette.

VALENTINE'S NIGHT
by Penny Jordan

VOTED BESTSELLING
HARLEQUIN PRESENTS!

Let award-winning Penny Jordan bring you a Valentine you
won't forget. *Valentine's Night* is full of sparks as our heroine
finds herself snowed in, stranded and sharing a bed with an
attractive stranger who makes thoughts of her fiancé fly
out the window.

"Women everywhere will find pieces of themselves in Jordan's
characters." —*Publishers Weekly*

Available this February wherever Harlequin books are sold.

What do women really want to know?

Only the world's largest publisher of romance
fiction could possibly attempt an answer.

HARLEQUIN ULTIMATE GUIDES™

How to Talk to a Naked Man,

Make the Most of Your Love Life, and Live Happily Ever After

The editors of Harlequin and Silhouette are
definitely experts on love, men and relationships.
And now they're ready to share that expertise with
women everywhere.

Jam-packed with vital, indispensable, lighthearted
tips to improve every area of your romantic life—even
how to get one! So don't just sit around and wonder
why, how or where—run to your nearest bookstore
for your copy now!

Available this February, at your favorite retail outlet.

This February, watch how
three tough guys handle the

Lieutenant Jake Cameron, Detective Cole Bennett and
Agent Seth Norris fight crime and put their lives on the
line every day. Now they're changing diapers, talking
baby talk and wheeling strollers.

Nobody told them there'd be days like this....

Three complete novels by some of your favorite
authors—in one special collection!

TIGERS BY NIGHT by Sandra Canfield
SOMEONE'S BABY by Sandra Kitt
COME HOME TO ME by Marisa Carroll

Available wherever Harlequin and Silhouette books are sold.